Music of the Winds

Ronald Yates

Copyright © 2012 Ronald M. Yates
All rights reserved.

ISBN: 0-6156-0462-5
ISBN-13: 9780615604626

Dedication

I dedicate this book to all the people of the world who do whatever they can to ensure a wonderful future for the children.

To my brother David, whose hearty laugh brought joy and guaranteed smiles to everyone that knew him.

ACKNOWLEDGMENT

I wish to acknowledge Bebe Spinner for her wonderful support and patience so that the messages of this book could be made available to readers. I am truly lucky to have such an amazing wife.

CHAPTERS

PRESENT

Chapter 1
Central Park

Powerful beings lined the path on both sides standing at equal distances holding large umbrellas that provided shade for Emily's important walk. Each morning this walk could lead to a cure for cancer. Emily circled the fountain and arrived at the entrance to the Mertz Library where she would follow-up on her recent studies of rare plants. Next, she would head to the research laboratory to keep track of her experiments.

Emily had her favorite classical radio station playing and felt the movement of "Pini di Roma" coursing through her. She thought the Italian composer Respighi perhaps felt an occurrence building in strength, an advancing power arriving to the new day. Emily loved to guess what each of the classical composers had in mind during the creation of a piece.

She monitored her experiments and took some notes on the unusual effects of a miniature orchid's leaves on a particular blood sample. It was time to leave the lab at the New York Botanical Gardens and board the 10:39 AM Metro North to Grand Central Station. Always thinking of the environment, Emily would use public transportation. Preferring not to take the subway, she took the Madison Avenue bus from Grand Central to East 77th Street. While walking the cobblestone sidewalks along the beautiful boulevard lined with trees that was Fifth Avenue, her thoughts went to Matthew and how much fun he had with the children from the orphanage in Westchester.

The buds had opened on the trees and spring had kept all its promises. The brightness of this beautiful day easily revealed the shine of life within the new green of spring. A beauty and freshness of scents marked the season's beginnings. A continual breeze brought a light applause as maple leaves moved back and forth against each other as if acknowledging the day's beauty. Upon sighting Matthew in the distance, Emily could not help smiling while taking in a deep breath of the morning air. Looking out at the great green, waves formed with ease as the spring breezes passed over the field of grass like a virtuoso. The sparkle of the dew seemed to dot the lawn with diamonds. Each blade of grass, aided by dew and connected by light, became one of the sun's oceans.

It was easy for Emily to spot him on the Great Lawn of Central Park. Matthew Monroe was a mighty man. At six feet two inches, with powerful broad shoulders, he was a very lean and ruggedly handsome man. There were beams of light bouncing brightly everywhere in the park on this beautiful spring Wednesday and this only enhanced his presence. His blond hair took on an extra-terrestrial sort of illumination. The glow around him looked like it could be touched. Walking with his smooth gait, he stood out; his good looks were impressive and his charisma could be felt from a distance.

Emily stepped onto the Great Lawn and began to run towards Matthew, waving and calling out, "Over here." Matthew barely heard her as there wasn't much power in her voice, though it didn't matter, he would recognize that running style anywhere. A balanced and elegant walk revealing her beauty with each step would become transformed. He smiled as she appeared to have the gait of a small duck running towards him, especially against the powerful 59th Street hotel skyline. He lifted and hugged her as she found his shoulders almost out of reach. There was always an excitement, for as each time they met it was like the first. They both knew that they were meant to be, yet Emily knew how difficult it has been for Matthew. Looking out at the Great

Lawn, she thought of how April brought a lush bright green to the grass with an abundance of rain this past year.

"Where are we meeting the children?" Matthew asked.

"On the Great Lawn near the Arthur Ross Pinetum area."

The sweet spring breezes brought the scents of Pinetum and the evergreens were glistening. The pine needles formed sturdy bundles on the conifer branches. Chocolate colored sparrows could be heard in busy conversation within the branches. Emily opened her blue blanket and spread it very carefully on the grass and sat down lightly. Matthew smiled as she radiated kindness and was so fine and enchanting.

"You won't hurt the grass," he said.

"Look Matthew, the children have arrived," exclaimed Emily. The age of the children of the orphanage ranged between three and twelve years old. Going to Central Park was a merry adventure for the orphans. Matthew turned and spotted the children running toward him, well ahead of their supervisors, with the exception of David who seldom left Allison's side. She was an assistant staff member that worked at the orphanage with whom David seemed to be most comfortable with. Emily loved the look on their faces; excited, shy, happy and amazed.

Across the large circular field, a tiny girl came into view. She had a wobbly run, flirting with the fun of the open green. Emily recognized this wobble, it had to be Valentina. Occasionally, she would topple and land on her seat with the lawn happy to cushion her fall. The children charged toward Matthew, circling around him and leaning towards him in a posture driven by awe. From the blanket, Emily was happy about the joy they felt living in that moment; only children seemed to be able to express a pure, bewildered excitement. A great dream was about to come true for them. They were about to play ball with one of the greatest and most popular Yankee of all time.

5

David, who was the oldest child approaching twelve, was a very mysterious boy. He would never speak unless into a mirror to the image of the person trying to communicate with him. His phobia had perplexed not only the doctors at the orphanage, but various specialists including neurologists as well as psychiatrists. Yet, for a boy of eleven years old, Matthew saw a special balance and coordination in his movements. He threw a ball harder and faster than many fifteen year olds with more experience in sports. For some reason, David was staring at Matthew with an upset expression. He seemed puzzled. Emily, aware of the situation, walked up to Matthew and said, "It appears that David is looking for some sort of explanation."

"An explanation for what?"

"I don't know, I thought perhaps that you might have an idea."

Allison, who always tried to be close by for David overheard their conversation. "David at times will become very sensitive to something and often the staff at the orphanage is left puzzled. Eventually, we hope that he will talk about what's concerning him."

Valentina, the youngest of the group who had just turned three, and who preferred staying with Emily had an unfortunate history. When she was only a year old, her family's home had suddenly burst into flames. Valentina's father saw that the fire had quickly surrounded them. The only path without flames led to the stairs of their basement. He sent his wife, carrying Valentina down the stairs to the basement for safety, as he decided to stay to fight off the flames.

Smacks of heat and ember to her face and eyes caused a momentary stop of her movement. Valentina's mother, finding strength unknown to her, lifted up the small basement window just enough to push her year-old daughter through the opening. "Go darling, go!" Valentina started crying and her mother screamed, "Please God, help us." An unknown young teenage girl with blond pigtails wearing a pink dress with white polka dots somehow lifted the baby girl into her arms. The last thing her mother saw was Valentina being carried away toward the curb by the young angel as the curtains of her eyes came down.

Valentina, when sighting Emily, hurried her tiny steps and seemed so small against the vast lawn, yet shared a freshness with the new grass. Emily kneeled down and caught her with a hug. She wondered as she looked into Valentina's bright brown eyes if she had ever seen longer and darker eyelashes. Waiting with excitement for a kiss while melting in Emily's arms, her rosy apple cheeks were an easy target. As she locked eyes with Emily she would say, "I see you," and smile. Valentina would release embarrassed giggles and hide her face with her tiny hands. Emily looked down, smiled and said, "Valentina, even the moon gets embarrassed and just sneaks a peak, and at other times he would show his full face, not being shy at all." Valentina then decided to do a funny dance and tilted side to side. She stopped dancing and decided to gather some grass and hand it to Emily, radiating sunshine within the sunshine of the bright day. "Thank you so much for the beautiful blades of grass, Valentina," Emily said as the little girl climbed onto her lap. The moisture of the grass was fun for Valentina's tiny feet as her toes played through the blades as the warmth of the sun felt soothing. Overhead, the lovely pastel of the sky almost seemed to be part of the inhaled fragrance of this spring day. Behind the Great Lawn, the sun's brightness reflected the many pine needles of Pinetum enhancing the trees.

A squirrel perched on its hind legs stopped in front of Valentina, puffed up his caramel and white tail then gave her an expression of puzzlement. She sent kisses to the squirrel and he chirped and bounded away. Emily and Valentina looked at each other and laughed. Emily smiled as she enjoyed becoming part of Valentina's adventures. It seemed that the nature of Central Park was drawn to them. "What is that touch so light on my hand?" said Emily. She bent down and tickled Valentina as she said, "Is someone playing creepy spider?" From the air above there were songs over the treetops, music for the skies, the birds brought the sweet melodies of spring everywhere. Valentina turned to Emily and asked, "What are they singing?"

"Love songs, silly."

"Why do they stay in the trees?"

"They are happy and safe there with their friends and they make new baby birds."

Valentina wanted to know why the birds were singing. Emily answered that they were happy to be part of nature's beauty. Valentina asked, "Can all of nature speak?" Emily thought to herself that it sounded like one of the questions she would ask of her mother in her own youth. Nature's language has many different ways of talking.

"Nature likes to talk in rhythms like the sound of waterfalls rushing down mountains or the wind picking up speed."

"What is the wind saying?"

"Perhaps that rain is coming."

"What is the waterfall saying?"

"Perhaps it's telling us that ice is melting from the mountain tops."

All of a sudden, Valentina was napping and Emily said, "I wouldn't think of waking you, after all, who wants to lose their dreams in a peanut butter and jelly sandwich?"

Emily brought her a few tiny sandwiches remembering how happy they had made her at a recent outing at the Botanical Gardens. Valentina could not stop talking about them.

Valentina, not really sleeping, tugged on Emily's blouse and pointed to the sky. She said, "Look, popcorn and cotton candy!" Emily smiled and looked up to see the ethereal episodes of beauty continue as spring's breezes introduced varied white puffs.

"Where do all the happy puffs go?" asked Valentina.

"Living in the lovely blue is wonderful for them, but eventually they must change to water for the Earth's health. They will always come back as long as there is water on Earth."

Intuitively, Emily started to feel a nascence of a momentum to this day. She noticed an elderly, well-dressed woman walking towards a bench with a large bread baguette. She was quickly surrounded by pigeons and sparrows as they seemed to expect her arrival. Emily turned back toward Valentina as the little girl said, "Look what I made for you." She handed her a picture of a man and a woman holding a little girl's hands walking through a park.

"It's beautiful. Thank you. I'll hang it up as soon as I get home." Valentina told Emily that it was from her favorite coloring book.

Emily told Valentina to look at Matthew's hair as a yellow butterfly decided to land on his head. Matthew heard them laughing at him and turned towards them and powerfully displayed his biceps. They laughed only harder, thinking how silly he looked with this bright yellow butterfly flapping his wings on top of his head. Valentina was so special; Emily knew that their connection had love at its core. She thought to herself, "If only I felt stronger, I would love to adopt Valentina."

As the children gathered around Matthew he knelt down and his huge knees were immediately covered by two of the children. They loved him. His warmth and kindness flourished within his Hollywood charisma. While tossing the ball around and focusing on each child, he made sure that no child would be neglected.

Emily's laughter made him lose his concentration. A West Highland Terrier suddenly bounded through the grass, looking almost like a toy rabbit, heading full speed for Emily and Valentina. This incredibly fast Westie suddenly stopped in its tracks right in front of the blanket and started licking Emily's nose. Having lost his concentration, Matthew got bopped on the head with the ball which was fortunately a sponge ball. Valentina, now seeing this, became more hysterical, which attracted the relentless Westie who started licking her nose. Now, everyone was laughing; the children, the counselors, the passersby, fans that recognized Matthew and Matthew himself. No one could contain themselves.

The sunshine was so innocent and kind; perhaps only the poetry of a rainbow could add to the day's magic spell of beauty.

Chapter 2
Occurrence

The puppy decided that it was having fun and would stay awhile. Valentina, playing in the grass, would run away two or three steps, then turn around and dance back to the puppy. These two were playing inside of a sunny smile.

Valentina yelled to Emily suddenly, with sheer astonishment, pointing her finger, "Look!" It was unbelievable. The Westie was floating up several feet into the air, up and down. People were losing their balance everywhere in the park. Valentina's head tilted upwards with a puzzled expression seeing the dog float by above her head; but then she realized that she had started floating up as well. Emily quickly grabbed her tiny hand as she began to levitate also. Emily spotted a cell phone in the air and reached for it, but was too late as it floated through her hand.

As Matthew caught the ankles of two of the children floating towards him, he noticed his vision seemed affected. Everything he saw seemed enveloped in a sort of transparent steam. While above the ground, for a moment he felt nauseous and disoriented. "What was happening? How could this be possible?"

Emily saw the sky as the floor of the park. The grass field became the park's ceiling as she felt she was walking on the sky. She saw families grabbing soda bottles and blankets floating about them. A fried chicken leg floated by Valentina and she tried to grab it. Balls, cell phones, pretzels from the vendors, people and pets, all were floating slowly up and down several feet above the lawn. It was an incredible sight. It was as if the entire Great Lawn became some sort of trampoline as no one was able to keep their balance. A round, stout woman with her boy, who was round as well, was hovering above a park bench. One of the lady's hands was holding her pocketbook strap which was tangled within the bench. Her other hand was holding on to her child. It would have been comical if it were not for her fearful shrieks. There were some young girls still holding their jump rope, looking silly, as a lot of loose red Jell-O found their hair.

In the distance, Matthew could see people clinging to the tree trunks on the outskirts of the Great Lawn. The air was electric with refracting light. The flashing brightness of what seemed to be thousands of flash bulbs going off was dizzying. Some mothers were heard screaming, "Somebody help my baby." Matthew yelled to one of the orphanage counselors to try her cell phone.

"It's not working."

Valentina, who had first thought that this was all fun started to cry when she heard all the people's fear. Emily pulled her closer saying, "It will be okay." Emily turned, looking towards Pinetum just outside of the Great Lawn, seeing flashing also with a mirror intensity; the white light found all the spaces between the trees and their branches. Their normally triangular bunches of blue-green needles and elegant long and slender drooping needles appeared briefly as lit ornaments.

Suddenly, as quickly as it started, it all stopped. Matthew heard sirens coming toward their area. People could see the park police cars as well as the city police cars coming from every direction. The lawn and park benches were all littered with cell phones, milk bottles, soda cans, chicken salad, bagels, shoes, toys, juice bottles and balls.

At Fifth Avenue and 105th Street there was a similar occurrence. Objects and people were seen floating over the Central Conservatory Garden. The police at Fifth Avenue who communicated to the officer at the Great Lawn said that fortunately, all the people and objects had soft landed. "The only problem we have now is that we can't get the Vanderbilt gate opened."

The police radio transmission continued, "Wait, the gate is opening as we speak, we're going in." The officer in charge at the Great Lawn returned the communication saying, "Keep those people inside of the area to see if any medical attention is needed. Get names and addresses and question all those people that were affected." The officer responded from 105th Street, "Sir, it appears that we're dealing with a large wedding party."

"It doesn't matter how many people you are dealing with, we need facts now!"

In the distance, the senior officer looking out at the lawn saw the chief of police coming into sight. "Is what I heard true?" he asked.

"It's not only true, but amazingly there have been no injuries so far." Then he turned to one of his officers and said, "Get one of the park personnel to get those ducks back to the lake."

Receiving instructions from the chief of police, the senior officer spoke into his megaphone. "Everyone exit the park in the direction of the Obelisk. We are investigating. Anyone injured please head towards Belvedere Castle or wave your hand for assistance."

It was a dazzling delivery of brightness, courtesy of what seemed to be thousands of white rays reflecting off of many mirrors. The rapid flashing left many people crossed-eyed, some temporarily without sight. Others lost their balance, feeling dizzy and falling to the ground.

Emily remembered that she noticed an unusual stillness to the area a few minutes prior to the occurrence. She thought it odd that for a few moments there was not even a slight breeze or a sound of the city.

"Why would there be such quiet and stillness as a prelude to the shock of this occurrence?"

The complexity of the elements involved within this happening was beginning to coalesce in Emily's mind: hyperspace, gravitational effects, refracting lights, all in a confined area. She suddenly had a realization.

"I recognize some of the properties of this event." She looked towards 57th Street while contemplating and noticed that the skyscrapers seemed subservient to the enormous shadows of the slow moving clouds.

Emily, always the scientist, focused her thoughts and turned to Matthew. "Our sensory mechanisms were affected. It was very similar to space sickness that astronauts experience during gravity changes."

"How could that be possible, we are not in outer space?"

Emily's thoughts momentarily jumped to conversations she had with her mentor, Professor Kensington.

"I don't know yet, Matt. In microgravity the brain turns things around. As an example, when the space shuttle is in the microgravity of space, the astronauts can easily become disoriented, losing all sense of balance."

"I did see many people falling down and heard some of the children say that they were dizzy, and I myself felt disoriented."

"Me too. I actually saw the sky and ground reverse around me. Somehow the ground force involved in the event did not counter gravity. Everything points to the same weightlessness that astronaut's experience. These people and objects were somehow caused, to a certain degree, to lose their area of ground support against the gravitational force. Notice the different reactions. There were people who felt queasy, nausea, vertigo, headaches, vomiting, lethargy and an overall malaise. Long hair was lifted and spread out on a woman which is the type of reactions that have been reported at NASA due to weightlessness. This could cause a sickness such as Space Adaption Syndrome."

Everybody gathered themselves from the unexpected and amazing occurrence. The people involved looked at one another with an odd stillness and then continued to straighten out their clothes and belongings. They all had a common bond, an experience shared like no other. There is a certain comfort in the company of others that would be the proof of what would seem to be unbelievable. Emily said to Matthew, "My phone is not working."

"Neither is mine. When we get home, I need to get on the computer and make some calls."

Emily became aware of a tugging on her beige chinos right below her knee. It was Valentina. Matthew said, "Emily, we better get her to the other children." Valentina put both her tiny arms into the air, her large dark sensitive eyes locking with Emily's. She picked her up gently and said, "Who do I see? Is that Mrs. Gibel? I see you Mrs. Gibel." Valentina quickly echoed those words with a smile. Mrs. Gibel was a senior staff member at the orphanage and a more modern-day Mary Poppins would be hard to find.

"Come Valentina, the other children are waiting for you with the counselors," said Mrs. Gibel.

"But I want to stay here."

Spoken with a kind voice, she said, "Come now, we have milk and cookies waiting for us in the game room."

"We'll come and see you real soon," Emily said sincerely.

Mrs. Gibel took Valentina's hand and headed for the rest of the group; but Valentina's head kept looking back at Emily and Matthew.

David, still holding Allison's hand tightly looked blanched and almost not present. In David's other hand was the ever present mirror.

"Is David okay?"

"He seems to have been more shaken by the event than the other children," Allison responded. Matthew and

Emily tried to lift David out of his dark cloud. "I bet you have a beautiful smile, let's see it," said Emily.

Allison said, "I plan to set up an appointment with Dr. Jeffries as soon as possible." Suddenly, David walked directly toward Emily.

"What is it, David?" Emily asked. David looked into his mirror and said to Emily, "I know you understand," as he pointed to exhaust smoke from one of the police cars.

"What do I understand, David?"

"My dreams of fire under red skies, with no clouds and asphalt melting my sneakers while my eyes burn."

David's intensity took Matthew captive. It was the mystery surrounding the boy. "I'm sorry Mrs. Monroe. I think David is very tired and he has been having trouble sleeping," explained Allison. Emily hugged David and Matthew somehow knew that she did understand.

Emily's mind was already at work solving this unusual mystery. Matthew knew that the ride on Metro North would be a quiet one. Once a problem had her focus, all roads had to point to a solution. Emily thought that it was odd how intensely bright the light flashes were. It was as if nature had hidden thousands of tiny crystals and mirrors within the grass and the trees. The entire area seemed encompassed by a light refraction. The speeds and directions of the rays seemed to be bending and changing instantly.

Peace did not come with that night and Manhattan seemed especially empty the next day as the powerful pulse of the city had become unusually quiet. The air was full of mystery and questions reaching the streets of all five boroughs. The unknown has always given birth to a lot of confusion.

Chapter 3
Conference

===

"I'm certainly glad that he's in charge," thought Roger Holmes, the Assistant to the President for Homeland Security. He knew President Hansen's composure had a chilly calm most men and women never find when under extraordinary stress. This man was always reachable and hid from nothing. He would remain resolute till the answers were revealed as he was a truly gifted leader.

"Roger, what have we been able to determine thus far?" asked the President.

"Cameras and videos haven't revealed any clues. We do know that the height above ground stayed constant and weight was not a factor with respect to the people or items involved."

"Were we able to determine the numbers?"

"Yes, the flotation effect seemed to peak at seven feet. The control involved in this event was incredible."

"Can you elaborate?"

"All the people in the affected areas actually experienced a soft landing."

"It leads me to believe that there is an intelligence behind this event, although the early scientific reports that I have received include many other possibilities."

"Mr. President, we now have reports of similar events to the Central Park occurrence taking place across the globe. Sir, it has been determined that they all took place simultaneously."

"Amazing, these occurrences were on a planetary scale."

These questions had an unusual new feeling to them. The atmosphere was saturated with the mystery of the occurrence. There was an eerie feeling in the President's conference room combined with a loud silence. It was as if all the cabinet members were sitting in a dark room not knowing what was going to be revealed.

The phone's ringing actually sounded anxious.

"Excuse me, Mr. President. It's NASA," as a trembling hand passed the President the mobile phone. Hanging up with NASA, the President was connected to a second call.

"Yes, we must investigate all event locations. Call me back when our operatives are in place."

"Yes, Mr. President," answered Tom Franklin, Director of the CIA.

Turning towards his group of advisors, immediate plans for the wording of the press releases had to be carefully considered.

It was easy to recognize the President's voice coming across the car radios and televisions. Each word was shaped with strength sure and powerful as he called for calm and assured the world that the best minds would be investigating the unusual occurrence.

Chapter 4
Orphanage

Once back at Westchester at the Lindale Orphanage, the Head Supervisor Christine Court asked her assistants to accompany the children to see Nurse Patricia. The head of the orphanage, Irving Best, thought it would be a sensible precaution after hearing Mrs. Court's account of the events that took place on their Central Park outing. The children were assured of a lollipop and thought Nurse Patricia was kind.

Mrs. Court asked one of her assistants, Anna Rodriguez, to escort David to his appointment with Dr. Jeffries immediately after seeing the nurse. This would be his second appointment with Dr. Jeffries. A practicing child psychiatrist for over fifteen years, Dr. Amanda Jeffries was a brilliant, as well as an attractive woman. She attended the finest schools and received honors in her field. She established a reputation for breakthroughs with children who have extremely difficult problems. Irving Best spoke to her about David and his complex situation and asked for her help. In all her years as a child psychiatrist, Dr. Jeffries had never encountered a more challenging and unique case.

It was only noticed by a fortunate chance of circumstance that David would only communicate while looking into a mirror. This was an amazing discovery since the orphanage staff, as well as any doctors David came in contact with, never heard him utter a word. David arrived at the orphanage two years ago at age nine. One day, while Allison came for his bedtime check, she noticed that David was making eye contact with her from his dresser mirror.

Ronald Yates

Allison Berman said to David, while maintaining the mirror contact, "Are you ready for bed?"

"Yes, Allison Berman."

Amazed to be hearing his voice and trying to stay calm, she said, "Allison is enough. Everyone just calls me Allison, okay?"

"Okay, Allison," said David while looking at her through the mirror.

Speaking into the mirror, she said, "Okay, come into bed and I'll tuck you in." David climbed into bed and Allison tucked him under the covers, turning off the lights while leaving on a small night light.

"Good night, David," said Allison, as she closed the door. There was no response.

Allison reported the entire incident to Mrs. Court who was amazed and took out David's records from her file cabinet.

"How did his voice sound?" asked Mrs. Court.

"Very soft and somewhat raspy."

"It's no wonder, who knows when he last spoke? Have you ever seen how many Math and Science books David would look at in the library room? More than one of our volunteer teachers has been taken by surprise by David during our learning classes. It was just recently that Mrs. Stafford brought to my attention that he had written a chart of the first four planets circling the sun, showing their distance and how many days were involved in their orbit!"

"I wish I had a memory that good."

"Mr. Best has stated that in the thirty years while being head of our orphanage, he has never seen such a mysterious child. Yet, he firmly believes that David is gifted. I will speak to Mr. Best as soon as possible. He has been in contact with a renowned child psychiatrist and has expressed his concern for David often. Irving Best is a very sensitive man and feels that there is a deep and worried awareness in David's eyes for such a young boy."

David's mind, which has such an intense focus, is always surrounded by fear concerning the real world. Several different medicines and therapies had proved ineffective for his mental health. Hyper reactions to loud noises usually of a mechanical nature, construction type sounds in particular, have caused him to retreat further within the quiet of his room.

"I remember when he first arrived here and could not be found that night for over three hours," said Allison.

"Yes, I remember that there were strong thunder storms and thank goodness one of the children saw him enter a food pantry. David was incredibly afraid of the thunder, and I recall the doctors had a name for this condition: Tontritophobia."

Mrs. Court had installed a large, adjustable mirror extending from his desk in the classroom at the orphanage. She also let Dr. Jeffries use her office for her meetings with David as there was a large wall mirror adjacent to her desk.

"Hello, David," she said as she spoke into the mirror. "My name is Dr. Jeffries." David looked back at her through the mirror and rolled his chair closer to the mirror, about a foot away.

"David, can you hear me?" she asked in a kind and soft tone. "I understand that you don't like thunder." Still, there was no response. Patiently, Dr. Jeffries asked, "Why, David?"

"I'm afraid it will never end," David answered while looking up at Dr. Jeffries in the mirror.

"David, everything that has a beginning, has an end."

"What about time? Do its waves ever reach a shore?"

"Whoa, kind of heavy for a boy who just turned twelve," Dr. Jeffries thought to herself.

"That's an excellent question, David. Do you think of time often?"

"Yes."

"Have you noticed that the thunder booms stop eventually? The fact that you realize that the thunder does stop eventually, why would you feel that there is still a danger?" David turned away from the mirror and stopped talking.

In the next session, David would not sit. Pacing back and forth, his eyes would never leave the mirror.

"David, why don't you tell me about some of your dreams as I understand that you are having difficulty sleeping?"

"You won't understand."

"Perhaps together we can try to understand, I will promise to try my best."

David, looking at Dr. Jeffries' reflection saw that her face and her smile were warm and sincere.

David spoke into the mirror, "I am in a deep crack in the Earth when I see broken tablets of stone before me. They are in the deepest part of the crack. There is important writing on the broken stone. I try to read it, but it is too deep and dark. I become nervous that I won't make it out of the crack. I climb towards the top where there is a very bright light, very white. I pull myself out and everything is sunny and I am on a wide path."

"Is there anything on the path, David?"

"No. But there is a music in the silence of the path."

"Can you explain it?"

"It has to do with the brightness in the area and I really can't explain it now."

"Where is the path leading?"

"I don't know."

"Do you see anything in your dream on either side of the path?"

"Yes, on my left there are endless small hills of grass that lead to a large powerful silver gray stone mountain."

"What about the right side?"

"There is a beautiful bright beach and a very blue ocean."

"David, are there any people on this beach?"

The boy was hesitant and a bit nervous in his response as he said, "Yes."

"Did you know any of the people?"

"No, I ask myself 'who are these people?' But it is difficult to see their faces. They're in the distance and it is very bright, but somehow I know I don't know them. I am alone in the brightness."

"What are you feeling in the dream?"

David started pacing faster and responded, "What's going on and what's ahead for me? Then I wake up."

"It is a very interesting dream, David. Dreams can reflect a healthy imagination. In your dream, I sense a search for answers."

David was still looking at the Doctor, yet remained silent.

"Is something wrong, David? Are you okay?"

"I'm very tired," said David as he turned away from the large wall mirror.

"Okay, we'll talk again some other time."

Dr. Jeffries buzzed her intercom and Allison came in and took David's hand leading him to the entertainment room. Once there, David sat down with his classical CDs and put on his headphones. Dr. Jeffries watched as Allison led David away. David gets disoriented at times and needs escorts to some of the different activity rooms as well as to the cafeteria.

Dr. Jeffries found it difficult not to be preoccupied with David's case. There were many children with problems, but he was so young and yet so cryptic. Thinking, "Is David the mirror and what is he reflecting? Is it reality? David is a complex boy, young and trapped in an intricate abyss, yet fighting for answers in reality's reflection. I am looking forward to the day when he stops hiding in the corners of the mirror, the day he will step forward into what is tangible and know reality. David has a lot to offer and is clearly intelligent well beyond his age. The day will come when he will know and touch the true relationships he deserves."

The next day, Dr. Jeffries headed for her meeting with Irving Best, the head of the orphanage. Mr. Best said, "I understand that it has been discovered that David would only communicate while looking into a mirror. Why is this?"

"There is no fear for David in the world of the mirror. It is my opinion that his mirror, in some way, is holding the world accountable for him. The mirror is his unique view of the world; his reality. It would be difficult, if not impossible, for David to remove himself from his world. He is safe interpreting reality on his own terms. It is also my opinion that we must break through his mistrust of the real world. It is odd that for David, reality is concealed within its own reflection. This is a very intriguing case."

"If I understand you correctly, the mirror stands in response to the real world."

"In response to what? Only within David can the answers be found. To him, by speaking words only to the mirror, David is making a statement. He will not accept or speak to reality as it stands now. Speaking through the mirror he at least acknowledges that there is a reality through the reflection. This is all a form of self preservation for him. There is a path that I must help him find that leads him out of his mirror world to the world of reality. Confronting reality with an alternative world, he is eliminating stresses that are not found within his mirror as it has no edges and serves as his shield."

"I understand from speaking with some of the orphanage staff that David seems often lost and has to be guided to many of the orphanage facilities. A particular staff member noticed that his comfort level is healthiest when he is at the orphanage garden, although he does get very upset when he discovers that a plant has died."

"This information combined with an analysis of his dreams makes me believe that he is searching for a healthier reality."

Chapter 5
After Shocks

Nervous car radios could be heard while walking down any block in New York City. Updates and news alerts by so-called experts with varying degrees of understanding were desperately trying to reel in a rallying point for possible causes for this unprecedented occurrence. People turning on their radios and televisions actually thought that they were hearing an excerpt from a movie trailer rather than a factual event. The talking heads were all expounding different theories. "Would there be clues found by a forensic scientist, such as gravitational residue, perhaps? These events are a bewildering dispensation of power. Who is capable of acting with such audacious authority and to what end? It must be an anomaly of nature. This is a provident force. Something or someone has a future goal in mind, and we better find out quickly. Is it possible that some sort of contagious phantasm could be victimizing all these people? Perhaps someone has created an illusionary game by using brilliant manipulations of reflections, But the game is played by whom?" There were even psychics analyzing the events on television programs as well as giving opinions, such as the astrologists saying that the stars had spoken to them of these events. Realizing the occurrences were a reality, everybody became aware of the frightening fact that changing the channel would not change reality. If only it was a movie.

The power of gravity can be enormous. Light itself cannot escape the gravity of black holes. Power failures and communication interferences are being speculated to be the result of solar flares.

Ronald Yates

The Vice President, speaking from an undisclosed location, sounded shaky as he was talking to the President
who was at the White House. "We are trying to locate the
source. Information seems to be pointing to these events as
a global phenomenon. I have reports coming in from operatives and Heads of States from countless locations, from
Tokyo to Paris. In Tokyo, people have reported to had difficulty breathing and walking. In Paris, people seem to be
unable to function due to extreme nausea. In New York,
specifically in Central Park, there are reports that people,
animals and objects were actually floating a few feet up in
the air for two minutes."

"Please continue," said President Hansen, in a controlled tone.

"Hold on Mr. President. I'm receiving updated reports.
Yes, it has been confirmed. The sensations of disorientation,
falling down and dizziness are coming in from many cities
all over the world," said Vice President, Robert Loren.

President Hansen, knowing of Robert's organizational
and retentive capabilities asked if there was a pattern or
commonality to the time or location of the disturbances.

"These disturbances have occurred all over the planet
simultaneously at an interval of time lasting exactly two minutes. The people in every event location seemed to have
shared a similar visual experience according to our reports.
In Tokyo, the people reported that iridescent, glacial-like,
bright, two-dimensional human shaped forms were leaping and streaking in every direction at incredible speeds. In
Shanghai, bright figures were seen as translucent warriors
outlined with a shiny, glossy glow. In Paris, the people described an electric gallery of shapes, dizzying in their leaps
and their flickering speeds. Icy and distorted light changes
appeared as if being viewed through chiffon. In all of the
reports, no phone communications were possible during
the occurrences. Word travels fast, and out of the confusion
has come a lot of fear. Although the descriptions vary slight-

ly in the different geographical locations, they all shared temporary bright and sometimes blinding reflections. Many reports talk of brilliant, transparent, crystal-like shadows of beings visibly shattering and then reforming everywhere at amazing speeds. There have been reports that the blue clouds surrounding The Smoky Mountains have appeared electrified at times."

"Robert, I want you to call a cabinet meeting, as well as an emergency meeting of the Security Council."

"Right away, Mr. President. I just think you should know that I've been receiving many disturbing calls."

The normally cool diplomats themselves sounded bewildered and confused. More than one of the frightened diplomats asked in genuine fear if there is something they should know. Is the world coming to an end? The President's assistant, Steve Gordon, interrupted, saying, "Excuse me, Sir, I have the Russian Prime Minister on the line, as well as the Prime Minister of France."

The President told the Vice President, "Assure everybody that the United States is working on finding out the cause of this cryptic event."

Hanging up the phone and turning his attention to his assistant Steve, the President asked that the calls be transferred to his office. The Russian Prime Minister, being the first one connected to the President, said, "I am sure your country has nothing to do with these strange happenings as we would not want any problems between us." The President who excelled at languages spoke to the Prime Minister in Russian.

President Hansen looked up at Emanuel Leutzes' painting of Washington crossing the Delaware and thought that having the first President as an advisor couldn't hurt.

In Japan, unusual electronic waves had been detected in the forests surrounding Mount Fuji. Using EMF detectors, engineers discovered and chartered the disturbance of the magnetic fields. At the event at Moscow Park, a Russian newscaster reported an unknown reality with transparent white shadows and figures with extremely bright reflections in the park. Most of the people had difficulty focusing and most witnessed accounts have come from those who were wearing sunglasses. The reporter went on to say that Russian scientists have answered the news of the events saying that there is a scientific explanation for everything, although it may seem supernatural.

The clarity and luminescence of the white reflections were thought to be angels arriving by some people in the European locations. The Paris locations had people reporting what seemed to be a wrinkling of the air around them and thought their eyes might have been playing tricks as it was difficult to see within the bright, radiant reflections. Once again it was the people who were wearing sunglasses that were able to identify some sort of defined boundaries around the crystal lined forms. In Italy, the Italian pines had an unusual illumination as the glowing tree tops were not even common to a sunny day; yet, the surrounding rocky terrain and grasses remained dark.

One of the President's advisors reported that after the London occurrence, scientists found unusually high carbon content in air samples. These samples were taken from Hyde Park and Regents Park. Considering London's lush trees and the green of the surrounding countryside, this was quite bizarre. It is as if all photosynthesis stopped in various parts of England. These parks also had a similar event to Central Park involving the floatation of people and objects. The people in Hyde Park who would normally stand on soap boxes expressing their political points of view were now speaking of the end of time or the next world war.

Chapter 6
Nervous Cabinet

The headlines around the world were weighty: "IS THIS REALLY THE END?" "ARGENT SHADOW BEINGS ATTACK EARTH," "ARE THEY FROM ANOTHER PLANET?"

Scientists across the globe were still baffled, making no sense out of the global occurrences. The laws of physics seemed to have been defied, yet an intelligent presence was likely as all the events were coordinated. People across the globe experienced levitation in the same moment of time. Planetary confusion was starting to turn to fear. Unfortunately, when there were unexplained mysteries certain people felt the answer must be in having a gun nearby. The only problem was, who were they going to point the gun at? It seems that as soon as there is an unexplainable situation, a lot of people become frightened and are ready to take their stand with a gun in hand. Before an explanation is found, an accidental bullet could resound and an innocent creature could be downed. When crowds are losing control across the globe it is difficult to find the tall cowboy that yells, "Break it up!"

President Hansen thought the intensity of concern in the silence of the room was almost painful in its depth. He felt twelve pairs of eyes upon him as he prepared to address the Cabinet. He was facing an incredible test by an unknown, yet clearly formidable power. He felt every nerve pressed, yet his heart was strong and his will unrelenting. The President addressed the Cabinet saying, "We will unravel the surrounding data and stare this mystery directly to its core. To paraphrase Albert Einstein and Bertrand Russell, 'In this situation which confronts humanity, we feel that scientists should assemble in conference to appraise the perils that have arisen.'"

President Hansen continued, "These perils, though not nuclear, are from an unknown source and therefore possibly more threatening to our Earth. We must form an international assembly of scientists in order to achieve intelligent solutions. Whether this is a planned attack or unknown phenomenon; whether our enemy is a hostile country or weather phenomenon; either could be a serious attack on Earth. Scientists that are working in an international cooperation rather than in competitive uncooperation will achieve faster and healthier results."

The members of this Cabinet knew that they were fortunate to have this leader for the United States as well as for the world. Standing under an uncertain sky with gray clouds turning darker, Michael Hansen walked through the Presidential Garden slowly. He thought, "All mysteries unfold. I must move faster than its layers begin to peel. There are certain advisors and ambassadors that believe an attack is eminent with the goal of worldwide domination. Monsters that still want to control the world have surfaced before."

The President looked down at the path and his eyes rested on a juniper peeking between two stones and it brought his mind back to his youth with his friend Ed when they were at Yosemite Park.

Ed Thomas, now a graduate with degrees in Electrical Engineering and Michael Hansen in the process of acquiring his law degree were going camping. Close friends since meeting as undergraduates at Yale, they shared a love for the beauty of nature. Ed Thomas had a vision of a nationwide railroad system that would improve the quality of the environment. Michael Hansen would strive to stop the poisoning of the planet's air and water by achieving a political platform where his voice could be heard and his ideas implemented.

Flashes of emerald rode the watery rapids between the pine-shaped mountains. Behind the mountains dawn began to emerge. Blue lights surrounded the pines as well as the grass lining the river. Bands of beauty's light were bright as more sunbeams lit the sparkling waters. There was an ease to the winds as they passed through the pines and over the grasses. Spring's arrival liberated mountain water falls and forest streams from their frozen boredom. The season's party had begun as the waters splashed across rocks. The poetic artistry of each season oftentimes would amaze Ed Thomas. The water's flows were adapting to large rocks and branches that were in its path as it avoided collisions with a soft and elegant flow that reunited and continued downstream. "Mike, will you look at that?" said Ed, pointing to a tumbling mountain waterfall. To either side of the mountain a radiant soft sun with elegant beams of light were gracing the clouds through to the horizon. "How many of us have looked up at this type of sky, feeling it mirrors the divine?" The sun was reflecting off of high glaciers melting the ice into fresh cold crystal waters rolling in a free-fall as they splashed against the rugged mountain walls. Powerful rocks and trees, at their best, could only slightly divert the rush of the waters. Gravity wasted no time leading the liquid crystal to its destiny as the leaves and the branches would bow to its force.

Michael Hansen remembered suggesting that they stop at this ledge during their hike as the view was magnificent. He climbed a thick shoulder of a trunk extending from a powerful tree approximately five feet over the cliff's edge. "Are you nuts?" Ed said with serious concern.

"I'll be okay, don't worry so much; when I was younger I would swing off of tree-tied ropes twenty feet into the air into a small lake."

"You do realize that this tree is on the cliff of a mountain."

Michael, fearless while adjacent to a powerful waterfall, leaned over for a closer look at the furious plunge of the rolling waters when suddenly a flock of magpies appeared. He slipped momentarily and then regained his balance. Trusting his inner voice, he instinctively shimmied back to the cliff and sheepishly suggested that they continue to head down the mountain.

"Oh, so you don't think it's a good idea to die young?" said Ed. There were different sounds, shapes and shades of color within the mountains, trees and creeks that seemed to all be in its own harmony. A small stream was languidly making its way over some smooth stones next to a dark, large sycamore. Michael and Ed felt they could taste the beauty of Earth's harmony through the fresh mountain creek. The water was clear, naked and wonderful as it passed over the stones and was scooped into their hands. Ed looked up at the fresh, rippling waterfalls and turned to Michael, "Is there a future for our country that can be this fresh and pure?"

"I'll tell you one thing, the next time I decide to shimmy across a tree trunk extending from a cliff to have a conversation with a waterfall, I'll think twice."

"Why not wait for the water to be resting at the bottom first?" They both started laughing.

Heading back down the pine sloped mountain adjacent to a small waterfall, Ed turned to Michael, "The planet cannot continue to replenish its natural resources if humanity continues to abuse its gifts."

"I see what you mean," he responded, as his eyes fell upon a pile of cigarette butts. "The indifference these cigarette butts represent is dangerous and unfortunately, the disrespect to nature continues."

"At least most states have instituted smog alerts for the changing air. Weather changes are causing more particulates in the air we breathe. These tiny particles, from dust storms and forest fires as well as from the burning of fossil fuels from cars and industry are now a strong health hazard.

These tiny particles can affect our lungs and circulatory systems if something is not changed soon. We will be seeing more people in the cities wearing masks to filter out the air due to highly industrialized areas. The dust from construction sites, which is carried by the wind, is yet another source of particle pollution."

Ed continued, "Floating from China to Los Angeles, smoke drifts within gray and black shaded carbon clouds are keeping the land and sea warm and sad. Bellowing out of factories and cars, blobs of gray and black continue to cause strange lightings in our cities. Denver's traffic is turning its once fresh air brown; there are times when the twilight cannot be found. The children should be able to wonder about twilight's beauty with its hidden secrets, not the gray shadows that slip and fold within the dark carbon clouds. There are cities that have a contaminated fog as part of their skyline. We must address those who cause our eyes to tear with their gray discoloration of what were blue skies and night stars. It would be a sad future if we couldn't look up to see moonlit starry skies. There is no pill to cure this situation."

"I know that it is the pollution that is causing a fast rise in temperatures as I continually read that new record highs are being reached across the entire planet."

"We must do everything in our power to make a difference. Certainly we could devise a plan for planetary care on an international basis if we are able to land on the moon. People have to realize that everything and everyone is connected. We are all part of everything, right down to the sub-molecular levels."

"I see your science degrees are emerging. I do know that quantum scientists are showing this to be true."

A majestic moon, evening's emperor surrounded by night's twinkling jewels lit the domain with dark blues and purples in this night in the mountains. This emperor was able to remove darkness with a shot of its moonbeams. It would light rivers, turning them into night's mirrors for nature's insomniacs and for those who have lost their way. Moon flashes could be found even within the ground foliage; perhaps smiling or confusing the fireflies. During the day, the moon and the stars are hidden in plain sight. They are the magicians of our world. The moon seemed to have had a lavender aura at its interior and a mystic blue smoky night cloud drifted by playing with the colors.

Now back at the bottom of the mountain, and at their camp, they looked at the clear night sky from their sleeping bags, amazed by the amount of stars and their pureness in the dark clear. The rare multi-twinkled brightness enhanced Yosemite's beauty to an incredible expression. Starlight lit the mist surrounding the mountain tops, the paths of the mountain streams and the emerald of the big trees. The future President loved the beauty of his country and its stars and stripes. Michael Hansen heard a loud snorting sound. Ed Thomas, scientist, environmentalist, good friend and the future Secretary of Energy was now fast asleep.

Michael Hansen thought to himself, "Our country's dreams, as well as the world's dreams, will not be destroyed by those whose only interest is greed. Our planet will not be exploited and neither will our children's futures."

Remembering the grandeur of the distant Yosemite sky, the President felt the chaos of his office bring him back to the present. He was aware that every state was showing a warming trend and thought that he must do more for a cleaner environment.

"Mr. President, sorry to disturb you, but Ms. Nadar would like a few moments. Shall I show her to the Oval Office?" asked Mr. Gordon.

"Yes, thanks Steve."

The Secretary of Transportation, Sheila Nadar was all business and quite attractive, carrying with her two reputations: A sharp mind and an endless appetite, especially when it came to desserts. Secretary Nadar was often seen munching on a large chocolate doughnut between her phone calls, yet never seemed to gain weight. Secretary Nadar was sitting outside the Oval Office in a dark blue dress with her hair tied back wearing large black-rimmed glasses.

"Hello, Sheila, come in," said the President.

"Mr. President, I am considering advising restricted travel due to the unusual circumstances surrounding these recent events."

"There have been no known problems, thus far, and I don't want to add to a situation that is already lending itself to panic."

"I have just spoken to my counterparts in Paris, London and Moscow and some new information has surfaced. It seems that an odd, heavy howling wind has whipped through the streets surrounding the event locations in these cities. Amazingly, within these event locations, not one person experienced a mild breeze."

"Winds that acknowledge borderlines; what will be next?"

"That's what I'm worried about. There were no reports of these strong winds in Manhattan. I would still like to hold off on any travel restrictions, but please keep me updated."

"Mr. President, may I respectfully disagree. There have been unknown forces worldwide that have the ability to seemingly affect the very gravity of the planet in certain locations. In the interest of safety, I must insist you reconsider travel restrictions."

"You make a powerful point, Sheila. I will leave you in charge of coordinating these restrictions while minimizing any reactions of panic. It will be a difficult balance, but you have my confidence."

"My stomach," said the Secretary of Transportation, as she put her hands on her belly.

"I know how you feel. The stress has been intense."

"Oh, no, it's not that. It's just that my stomach is growling. I'm starving."

"Amazing," thought the President, "some people just never lose their appetite."

Chapter 7
Cabinet

The cause of the occurrence was unknown and even more unnerving, it was unseen. Confusion reined supreme in the conference room and the concern in the air hung heavy. The members of the Cabinet were talking over one another, most of them in panicky tones. Clarity and control, if present, were well hidden. The thoughts of the Secretary of Defense were as narrow as missiles and were exiting through laser eyes, wild and cold with no direction found.

"This is clearly an attack launched by an advanced military, with a highly developed stealth program; clearly a show of power," said General Rudd.

General Jules Rudd, recently appointed Secretary of Defense, was a tall man at six foot seven inches, with a stern demeanor that demanded respect. Many military personnel refer to him as "General Whistling Nose" behind his back, but never to his face. A combat injury aggravated his breathing, but never interfered with his performance in the military.

He continued, "I will not wait for this enemy to reveal itself. This enemy's plan is well concealed and my people will find their identity as they are bound to slip up."

Stealthy glances were exchanged among the Cabinet members upon hearing this comment as they quickly turned their heads in an ornithic manner. "One thing is certain; we have never seen or heard of a power that can suspend thousands of people in the air, at different locations, which are great distances apart."

Sheila Nader, the Secretary of Transportation added, "Not to mention that while these people were hovering several feet above the ground, some reported seeing transparent folds in the air."

The Secretary of Energy, Ed Thomas, said, "We must be open to all possibilities."

General Rudd, as he rolled his eyes toward Ed Thomas exclaimed with sarcasm, "What possibilities; a fucking flying saucer attack; or perhaps it's your global warming attacking? I guess ray guns would explain all the communication problems and electrical disturbances that occurred during the incident."

Ed Thomas had noticed that in the past the General had a habit of releasing obscenities when things didn't fall into place.

"General, you do realize that I hold degrees in electrical engineering."

"Perhaps one of the power nations has conquered invisibility."

"General, you know we are close to that discovery ourselves as it involves certain bending of light waves. The attack was ingenious, as it was difficult to respond to while experiencing swirling sensations in what was originally a familiar environment. It could have been a natural phenomenon and you keep calling it an attack, but no one was actually hurt."

"Not this time."

The conference room's tension was growing more tangible with each moment. The General suddenly stopped his response as the conference room fell quiet. The President had arrived and the confusion seemed to have found its own corner. The President's presence was strong as he addressed each Cabinet member with determined eye contact.

"I will not allow the unknown to take control of my administration."

The lack of fear in Present Hansen's eyes was no disguise. This was the first major challenge in his Presidency, but he had a history of facing all of life's challenges head-on. President Hansen, continued, his voice steely, "We will face this situation with strength and we will find the answers."

The silence in the conference room had an anxious presence as the Cabinet members' mental engines were spinning hard. The President continued, "I have just received an update from Cecilia Washington."

The members of the Cabinet knew this NASA coordinator well. The President and Cecilia Washington go back many years and are good friends. She is a brilliant scientist, as well as communicator.

The President continued, "According to Ms. Washington, many of the cities in question have high pollution levels."

With hearing this comment, Ed Thomas threw a glance at General Rudd's direction.

The President continued, "The people's behavior affected by these events has been investigated for hypoxic influence. The time of useful consciousness will be measured. In the seas, we know aquatic life has already been affected by hypoxia. Pollution dumped in our planet's oceans, as well as in its atmosphere, affects oxygen levels for all life. Thus far, our geologists have determined that there are no major changes in Earth's crest. Current movements in plate tectonics and continental drift are fairly stable. Our scientists have found no unusual occurrences in Earth's inner layers. The seismic wave technology shows our planet's structure is stable. Our geological oceanographers have found normal movement on the ocean's floors. The Atlantic Ocean's floor, for example, is still spreading at the rate of four inches per year."

"Mr. President, if I may speak?" asked the Secretary of Defense. "These events happened simultaneously. In Rome, there were similar reports of dizziness and visual problems and the same was true for Tokyo, Moscow, Paris and London. The unusual light manipulation reported from all of these locations all occurred within the same two minute period. This not only implies control, but a message of authority. It is my belief that Ms. Washington, although very capable, is looking in the wrong direction. The architect of this occurrence may be unknown, but this is an organized attack." The Secretary of Defense, with his voice rising in volume, said, "The country behind this attack is in charge of an advanced technology."

"We don't have all the facts yet, General, and what country could conceal such power from all of our agencies, as well as our satellites?" asked the Secretary of Energy.

"The cryptic nature of these events eliminates all but the most sophisticated and advanced enemies."

The President spoke, "Ladies and gentlemen, the mysterious nature of these events continues to bring more questions, and I need answers. I will consider all possibilities until we have more facts pointing us in a certain direction."

"Sir, if I may?" asked the Secretary of the Treasury, Richard Ginsberg coughed and cleared his throat, as it was his habit.

"Go ahead."

"The stock market is sensitive and does not like mysteries. It is only a matter of time before the worldwide markets are affected."

The President thought that it was only fitting that the Head of the Treasury's comment would be elliptical in nature, yet as accurate as a laser.

"Richard, as our government's Chief Financial Officer, I know that you will monitor the situation. Please keep me posted as to any future recommendations that you feel might be necessary as I know that the markets dislike uncertainty. I will address the events publicly with well chosen words to avoid any panic. The newspapers, television as well as the internet will be scrutinizing every move that we and the other governments of the world take."

President Hansen knew that as the President of the United States, he would be under scrutiny's microscopes in every corner of the globe. President Hansen has a shield of integrity that any attack has yet to penetrate. The President turned to Ed Thomas, "Cecelia Washington, after coordinating information with the various scientists at NASA feels that the odd light reflections could tie-in with the anti-gravity effects that were felt in Central Park, as well as other parts of the globe. She is not ruling out an unknown atmospheric occurrence. The people at all the occurrence locations have all claimed to be practically blinded momentarily by crystal-like images. They were reported to be transparent shadows seen while they were being lifted several feet above the ground."

"Excuse me, Mr. President, I have Ms. Washington on the line," said one of the President's assistants.

"Please transfer her to speakerphone."

"Yes sir."

Cecelia Washington's voice was heard easily throughout the conference room as she said, "The severity of the sensory disruption causing the disorientation was astonishing in its magnitude. Cities across the globe continue to report in and the people are all relating a similar account. The consistent reports of brilliant flashings of white shadows passing through one another at incredible speeds are part of all the reports. Our scientists at NASA are calling these simultaneous events vortexes of abstraction."

"Cecelia, can you elaborate on that?"

"Yes, anyone caught in a gravitational vortex has their senses distorted. These were electromagnetic fields affecting gravity as well as bending light. Vision would be distorted, thus the visual accounts we've been receiving from the occurrence sites should not be assumed to be accurate. People caught within these events surrendered their orientation for two minutes as they found themselves suddenly in unfamiliar surroundings."

Ed Thomas turned to the President with a look of, "May I?" and the President nodded back at him.

"Ms. Washington, this is Ed Thomas speaking. The people that have reported these crystalline figures were very adamant."

"Remember, Mr. Thomas, according to all reports, these bright light beams were bouncing in every direction as if ricocheting between thousands upon thousands of mirrors. The people themselves were bright from the lights and to one another they possibly appeared as white shadows or crystallized figures, so to speak. It is ironic that with all the light, no one could really see correctly, if at all. Consider a continuous two minute attack of countless flash cameras. The assault to the eyes would make witness accounts unreliable."

General Rudd looked towards the President on hearing the word "attack" used in Cecelia Washington's description.

"Cecelia, could this have been a planned attack?" asked the President.

"The confusion in the affected areas does support it as a possibility. Thought patterns would mimic the different directions of the light as the event was possibly electromagnetic in nature. Thoughts electrically jumping from the brain synapses could change thought patterns in those who were affected. There are scientists who are considering a sophisticated computer communication using the light within the vortexes."

"That doesn't explain the flotation and levitation of the people and objects at the occurrence sites."

"No, Mr. President, it does not, which is why I'm leaning towards natural phenomenon involving the sun. Our scientists at NASA feel that there could be a relationship with the occurrences to the weather in space. Magnetic fields twisting on the sun can disrupt our satellite and radio communications. They're called "hot spots," which are areas on the sun's surface that have relatively cool temperatures. Our space weather bureau is very sophisticated. They forecast the weather and the magnetosphere for Earth and the sun as well. The orbiting weather satellites should give us a close to real time imagery of any unusual surface or space developments. Mr. President, considering that we need to study these events all across the globe and quickly, may I make a suggestion? We have a state of the art research center orbiting the planet with some of the world's top scientists aboard her now."

The President agreed, and then said, "Hold on Cecelia," as General Rudd held up his hand.

"What is it, General?"

"Sir, may I remind you that the space station is a collaboration of nations."

"General, what's your point?"

"What if one of the participating nation's scientists, currently working in the space station, has some responsibility for these events?"

"General, I appreciate your caution, but I trust Cecelia's judgment."

Speaking into the speakerphone, the President said, "Cecelia, I think it's time to get some more results from our ninety-six billion dollar investment in the space station."

"I will coordinate all the space stations' resources with all of NASA's data. I will call back as soon as possible, Mr. President."

"Thank you, Cecelia."

The Secretary of Interior, Samuel Muren, always wearing his suspenders, said in his usually slow and deliberate manner, "Mr. President, hallucinations have been found to occur in high level electromagnetic fields; perhaps we should consider that these people witnessing and experiencing similar phenomenon were victims of mass hallucinations.

General Rudd stood up and said, "Are you out of your mind? Next you will be joining Ed Thomas talking about flying saucers."

President Hansen knew full well that Sam was no country bumpkin and a brilliant man. Sam knew every boundary on the planet and could access the geographical and political significance instantly with his incredible photographic memory.

"Please sit down, General Rudd," said the President, with a stern glare. "Cecelia Washington has stated that electromagnetic fields are strongly suspected to relate to every event. We are not yet sure of our facts and how they relate to the events involved. General Rudd, if an enemy has developed this technology and is using it as you say for a show of strength, we are dealing with an adversary with a more advanced technology than we have. I will be counting on you to coordinate and evaluate the decision as it unfolds with every division of our military forces."

The President turned his eyes to Barbara Jolie, the Secretary of Health and Human Services. She was an impressive woman in many ways. Setting up soup kitchens in poor neighborhoods in Detroit as a high school student, Ms. Jolie has championed caring programs for health and welfare. Across the United States, she focused especially on newborns and the elderly.

"Ms. Jolie, do you have any updates on the health of the affected people across the country?"

"Recent reports show that the people most affected were in the Central Park area of Manhattan. They have all been examined and found to be in good health and were left with minor cuts and bruises. There were some cases where the people were very confused and wanted immediate answers as to what happened to them. I thought it would be prudent to take down all their information and correlate it, in case they shared something in common."

"Excellent, please coordinate your results with the reports that are occurring internationally as well."

"Of course, Mr. President."

The President responded to the buzz of his speakerphone. "Mr. President, we have several Heads of State and various Ambassadors wanting to speak with you. Also, Vice President Loren has just arrived and has several updates from NASA," said his assistant, Steve Gordon.

"Tell the Vice President that I'll be right there."

Turning around and addressing the Cabinet, the President said, "It is possible that this has been a worldwide public demonstration of power: a manifestation. This being the case, we must move quickly and make sense of these events. We must unify all the great scientific minds quickly and search for any patterns relative to all of these occurrences."

The same raw restlessness that ran in the Cabinet meeting was reverberating through much of the cities' population. News of the unusual events spread fast, as did uneasiness among the people of the world.

"Will there be a world left for our children to grow up in?" wondered many of the people across the Earth as fear began to spread.

Chapter 8
White House

"Mr. President, I have the updated reports from NASA and from around the globe," said Vice President Loren.

"Let's have it."

"Climate scientists from all parts of the globe have noted freakish weather events that are on the rise."

"Explain."

"Stronger storms have been reported with an unusually large amount of severe sprite lightening. There was one report that told of multiple blue jet lightening shooting out as high as fifty miles into the atmosphere from the tops of the storms."

"Has this been confirmed?"

"Yes, by NASA. The space station picked up the energy readings as the electrical discharges were large scale. NASA has also turned up some frightening information. They discovered that the oxygen levels have lowered a degree on a planetary scale."

"Is this enough to cause breathing problems?"

"According to NASA, it is. Also, Russia is getting unusual gravitational readings. There have been new reports stating that there are volcanic eruptions occurring in many countries."

"Do you see this as being an elaborate terrorist plot?"

"Too powerful and intricate. NASA has reported that there are changes in the magnetic field of Earth's orbit and considered the possibility of some sort of greenhouse effect. This considered, the scientists at NASA found the events occurring too quickly as the content of CO_2 in our atmosphere is rising too fast. This kind of effect would require centuries to take place."

A Presidential assistant interrupted saying that he had an important call: The Prime Minister of Canada was on the line.

"Excuse me Robert, I better take this call."

The Prime Minister, sounding alarmed, spoke with a shaky voice. "Ships have called in from the Northwest Passage. The ice is melting unusually fast and large ice blocks are dissipating from the Arctic Islands."

"I'm sure you have your best people working on the issue, Mr. Prime Minister. I understand from NASA that your Canadian mobile system has installed a robotic assembly to the space station with your fifty-five foot robot arm. Is it functional?"

"Yes, Mr. President, the computer assembly can interpret analysis now."

"We'll keep each other advised. I will speak to you soon and thank you, Mr. Prime Minister."

Steve Gordon informed the President that the First Lady was on the line.

"What's going on darling, this is all so odd. What happened in New York City? It has been so difficult to reach you," said the First Lady.

"We are working fast, Doris. One theory is that solar flares have been causing communication failures. I'll call you as soon as possible. Keep everybody calm."

"What should I tell Elizabeth? She just called from Yale, and you know how sensitive she is."

"Tell her to trust her father. I've got to go now, Doris. I love you," the President said as tenderly as possible as he hung up. Doris nervously hung up the phone. She knew somehow that her husband would find a way.

"Mr. President, I just finished speaking with Ms. Washington," said Mr. Henry, the President's Senior Advisor. "She informs me that our state of the art orbiting research facility is now monitoring the entire planet, and we should have our answers coming soon. The space station can view 85% of our populated areas and circles the planet in 90 minute cycles."

"Good. Who do we currently have up there?"

"According to Ms. Washington, the current crew is phenomenal. Richard Peters, a leading physicist and astronomer specializing in gravity research, as well as a Noble Laureate, is on board from the United States."

The President thought that while considering that the worldwide events have gravitational phenomenon in common, this was a fortunate appointment to the space station.

Mr. Henry continued, "Sue Li, a crew member from Japan, also a physicist and a Noble Laureate on her work for electromagnetic phenomenon; and Vladimir Dar, a Premier Russian scientist specializing in electrical phenomenon within space as well as the cellular level. Dar is so brilliant that he has often been compared to Albert Einstein."

"I know of all of them. Thank you. As soon as Cecelia apprises and coordinates with these scientists, I want a link set up to the oval office with NASA and the space station. Upon the establishment of the link, I want a conference call as soon as possible."

Chapter 9
Vineyard

The village just outside of the town of Castre was quite tiny. A few small stores lined the cobblestoned main street. There were small homes with lots of character and color; flower baskets in the windows with different shapes and sizes. There were several small apartments above the shops. Most of the village tenants were shopkeepers or workers in a neighboring vineyard.

Henri moved to the flat above Madame O'Dous' candy store after his wife disappeared two years ago. Henri knew the stress was too much for her and held no animosity towards Jacqueline; and was sure she would return one day. Henri Jordan worked as many shifts as possible at the vineyard to find more money for traveling and medical expenses; his daughter, Yvette, having a serious blood disorder, meant different hospitals, medical tests and treatments. Henri, although thin, was a sinewy and strong man from many years working in the fields. Henri's face, leathery and dark, showed many lines, some from the sun, most from worry, as he could not love his daughter more.

Yvette was so kind and sweet—"Why her?" he would often think. Yvette would usually stay at the egg store with his sister Anna while he worked at the vineyard. After stopping at the flat to clean up, Henri now refreshed, walked down the stairs and outside, and ran into Madame O'Dous. A more bright and fun personality could not be found. Madame O'Dous had strong, broad shoulders and a wonderful smile with big juicy cheeks. Wearing a white, puffy blouse, with a blue skirt under a bright white apron, with red polka dots, Madame O'Dous looked much younger than her age.

Ronald Yates

Although eighty years young, Henri was quite comfortable leaving Yvette with Madame O'Dous when his sister Anna was not available.

Madame O'Dous was loved by everyone in the village. "I have fresh dark chocolates for your picnic with Yvette," Madame O'Dous said with a smile. Henri arrived at the egg store to pick up Yvette for an afternoon picnic. Anna made a picnic basket and gave Henri a yellow fleece blanket. "Papa," Yvette said happily as Henri lifted her carefully as she was so light and fragile. Yvette's smile gave a brightness to her presence, and the joy of life shone through her. Henri connected with Yvette's eyes and was sure of the love meant for a father's eyes. Henri knew as she looked up at him, chances were that one day she would leave him. Unfortunately, it would not be for college or marriage. Henri often cried for the days and future love she would never know, yet her eyes stayed bright and fearless, yet her world was so small. Would she ever get to see the Alps, Paris or Cannes? "Papa, why are you crying?"

"I just have something in my eye. Are you ready to go to the park?"

Yvette loved playing in the forest area which was not too far from the vineyard where Henri worked. "First we'll stop at the bread store, as Madame O'Dous gave us some nice pieces of chocolate for our dessert, and you know how much you love chocolate sandwiches."

Everyone in the small village knew Henri and Yvette and waved with warm smiles as they walked the cobblestone street. Henri drove the car on the gravelly road leading towards the vineyards and the adjacent woods. He turned right, and followed the road up to the hill that began the forest area. He parked and helped Yvette out of the car, grabbing the picnic basket and blanket as well as her little red wagon. They slowly walked along the path, as Henri pulled Yvette in her wagon towards the edge of the woods. Henri paused a moment admiring the beauty of the vineyards where he and his fellow companions worked so hard.

He lifted Yvette, "See, that's where Papa works," pointing towards the vines.

"In the flowers, Papa?"

There was a fairly large sunflower field between the vineyards and the hill at the start of the forest. It was a magnificent sight in its own right, with all the flowers standing tall facing the sun.

"Past the flowers, see all the vines and how small the people look that are working."

"I see, Papa."

He recognized Yvette's beautiful smile, expressing a pure amour de la vie. Henri thought the child's smile more beautiful than all the sunflowers in the world. Only the love he had for Yvette kept her from seeing the fears and worries in his eyes, as his heart ached at the thought of losing her.

This area of forest was always quiet, as few people came close to the vineyard area from the village. Access to other parts of the forest was much easier. Henri again looked down at the sun-drenched vineyard, and then continued on the forest path, still pulling Yvette in her little red wagon. The path became more shaded as they entered the beginning of the forest with some large dark cedars partially blocking the sun. Yvette left the wagon and her father took her tiny, fragile and soft hand in his large calloused hands. Henri could not help but notice the dryness of the forest path, wondering if the draught would help or hurt the grapes; yet, the juniper branches along the path were rich with berries. This particular part of the woods always seemed deep green and vibrant as far back as Henri could remember.

The entrance seemed narrower than Henri remembered with more brambly areas. It had been a while since their last picnic here as Yvette had become weaker since last spring. This new medicine from Dr. Bollard seemed promising and Henri thought her strong enough now to enjoy a picnic. Thicket areas surrounded boulders along the path as well as a small creek. Henri couldn't remember the forest having so many shades of vibrant green. The beauty of these woods, "Ce n'est pas possible," thought Henri. These woods were breathing scents of evergreen and wild roses; many of the woodland trees and shrubs displaying colorful baccate branches; plentiful plump berries bursting thorny briar with deep vibrant reds and purples.

Yvette approached the small round greens of a forest bush and touched them. "Ils sont mouilles, Papa."

"In the small round green circles, the roses are born; for now they wait in their bud for their time to appear."

"Are they still babies?"

"Yes darling, but soon they will all burst out, with lovely colors and scents and be young and vibrant."

At the village flower shop, Yvette always seemed drawn to the roses as her favorite flower. Henri inhaled as the breadth of the breezes brought wild bouquets from the woods. "Where else could forest shrubbery have such a wonderful presence? It must be France," thought Henri anticipating a great year for the wine grape. The path brightened a bit as sun beams pierced through some tree tops and found a sweet patch of grass. A few feet adjacent to a narrow creek, they could hear the water playing. Henri, looking into the creek, saw smooth stones through the clear water's tranquility. He thought this was a good place to stop.

"Yvette, come sit on the blanket. Tante Anna made you your favorite, tuna salad and cucumber." Too late, Yvette found a butterfly to amaze her.

"Elle est si mignonne," he thought as he watched her play. Henri fought back a tear and thought to himself that he must stay strong and hold positive thoughts as a bright future must be hers. Yvette giggled as she tried to catch the yellow butterfly. Unsteady in her foot work, she fell down on her derriere and giggled some more. Yvette's attention then turned to the creek. Her father thought how small Yvette was as he watched her crouch at the creek, giggling as water wiggled through her little fingers.

"C'est froid, Papa."

Henri looked at his watch and saw that it was time for her medicine. Knowing her time was short, he was always thinking of what he could do for her that was new and exciting. Yvette's eyebrows lifted; her famous frown face arrived. Now she'll start to stomp her tiny feet, thought her father.

"Vien manger."

"Je n'ai pas faim, Papa."

Yvette really loved the woods. Last spring she brought back some flower petals, small stones, pieces of bark and several pine cones. She would stroll about the blanket and bring back different discoveries from the woods.

"Ne vas pas trop loin, ma petite."

A light flower shower came with a breeze. The blossoms landed on tree branches and small shrubs and appeared as if they belonged. The breeze brought petals to the tiny brooks following its soft current until captured by border moss or a large stone. The fickle breeze even adorned Yvette's curly blond hair with petals, before disappearing. Henri, now a bit hungry, found Anna's basket; pulled out a piece of the baguette and broke a piece off to have with the tuna salad. He turned around and pulled the picnic basket closer to him. In the basket, he found the tuna salad as well as a string bean salad on top of a red and white checkered cloth napkin. Henri loved her salade haricot verte as Anna always found the perfect amount of mustard and lemon to toss the salad in. There were also sliced cucumbers and carrots.

"Yvette, come see what Anna made. Where are you? Are you hiding?"

Looking in every direction, he could not see her, and she should be easy to spot with her blond hair and yellow blouse, not to mention her blue suspendered pants. Henri stood up, and being it was the middle of the day, twinkling leaves blinked in every direction from the bright sun. Walking towards the deeper, denser and darker part of this area of the forest, Henri briefly saw Yvette turn past a large tree surrounded by big stones and thick shrubs lacing the area. He quickened his step while yelling her name.

Approaching the shrubs, he had a noticeable mysterious feeling. Although they looked like wild rose shrubs they were unfamiliar to Henri. He was well acquainted with this forest and most of its growth, as he had many walks through the area growing up. Turning right around the large tree as Yvette did, Henri found no paths, just dense forest as he stumbled over low growth branches. Clearly, no one has walked here for some time as the grass and moss were undisturbed. He knew something was different in this area as it did not have common growth.

He continued forward and the growth became lusher. Henri heard the unmistakable sound of his daughter's laughter. Moving towards the sound, he encounted a very large hybrid oak tree, seemingly leaning on a huge boulder while giving cover to very strong brambles. The thick brambles which also were sharing the boulder were leaning on it until meeting the forest floor. Henri noticed scents of ripe fruits on fresh forest breezes. Yvette's voice was singing, but from where? The way was becoming darker due to dense foliage.

As Henri moved forward, it appeared that the brambles became a deeper emerald color and formed a dense barrier with tree branches that were extending over the stones. He thought that it was possible that no one had passed this way before. Seeing light behind a sweeping drape of leaves, he pulled the trees' branches aside and was able to see through a small opening between two boulders. There was Yvette, singing and playing her imaginary games. Behind Yvette was an unusual grove of small trees that appeared as pines. These trees carried a lavender and pink oval shaped fruit; or perhaps it was a cone or a flower. There were more of these trees further back; approximately twenty or more. The tallest tree appeared to be approximately seven or eight feet. Henri noticed a crooked brook with large smooth stones negotiating through and around this group of pine trees. He looked for an opening to the area which Yvette had discovered. "How did she find this path through these boulders which were entwined with all these twisting branches?" he wondered.

Yvette was far too weak and small to climb the large rocks or trees; indeed it would even be difficult for him, if not impossible. Walking further along the side of this wall of nature, a large moss green boulder was holding back a thicket of stubborn, woody brambles. Bending his still agile body to a lower level, Henri found a narrow opening under the brambles between a corky trunk and a boulder. Although the opening was tight, Henri was sure Yvette could have crawled through. Henri, although he may have to incur scratches, felt that he was thin enough to pass through the opening if he moved some branches. Head first he crawled halfway through the opening, but he could not see her. It was then that he heard a song. Yvette loved to sing while playing in nature's surroundings. It was her songs that made her possible to locate while playing hide and seek in the vineyards. Turning his head towards the sound he saw Yvette had gone further into the unusual growth of trees. These pine-like trees were compact and rich emerald green, making the lavender and pink flowers stand out brightly.

"Yvette."

"Tu m'as trouvee."

Henri pulled himself through the opening, his foot becoming entangled in the creeping bramble and he was momentarily trapped.

"Regarde Papa, n'est-ce pas beau."

Ronald Yates

Now free and standing, he stepped across the narrow creek which was bordered with flat stones, green with
moss and slipping slightly he yelled, "No" to Yvette. What
was in her hand? It was one of the lavender flowers and
Yvette was bringing it to her mouth. "No," he yelled again. It
was too late! Yvette had bitten into the oval flower and was
chewing. Henri rushed to her yelling "Spit it out!" Yvette had
swallowed the flower. Henri took it from her hand and found
that it was more like a fruit with its shape and soft texture. It
resembled a large, thick, single rose petal; a deep lavender
color on both sides with a bright, pink line of color outlining its width. Yvette's attraction to the fruit was understandable due to the rose petal shape and colors. Henri noticed
that the small pine-like trees formed an "S" pattern leading
deeper into the forest. He wondered how long these unusual trees have gone unnoticed.

"What is it, Papa?" Yvette looked up at her father with
an inquisitive look.

The movement of Henri's hands was a blur. He was prepared to rush Yvette to the doctor. He took Yvette into his
arms taking the leftover piece of fruit as well as picking a
whole fruit from the unusual trees and put them in his pocket. Henri was very frightened.

"Yvette, we must go see Dr. Bollard." Stepping gingerly
across the creek and past the remaining strange trees, he
headed out of the area.

Yvette was very comfortable with Dr. Bollard; a kind
man and an excellent doctor. Henri's mind kept going back
to the fruit. Yvette appeared to be fine.

"How do you feel?" asked Henri.

"Papa, cette pomme est delicieuse."

"What did it taste like?" asked her father.

"It tasted like thousands of different candies kissing my
tongue; like all the candies from Madame O'Dous' store
tous en meme temps dans ma bouche. The flavors are still
jumping on my tongue."

Henri sighting the picnic blanket knew he was close to the car. Henri turned the car into the narrow dirt road and glanced at Yvette as she turned to him, her face luminous for a kiss.

"Yvette, you must stay in your seat," Henri said, amazed at her rosy cheeks. "Papa, can I have another bite of the kissing fruit?"

Quickly down the main road and arriving at Dr. Bollard, he picked up Yvette and rushed in.

"Thank God you're still here."

"What's the matter?"

The rest was history. Yvette's physical readings were perfect and her blood count came back normal.

Dr. Bollard said, "This grove of fruit trees is a gift of restoration. Trees are often a source of cures. The aspirin from their bark, good health from their foods, such as fruits and nuts, are well documented. The power in this fruit is unprecedented. Yvette, it seems, has tasted from the arbor vitae."

Chapter 10
Bulldozers

Danielle could see the driver's eyes set as his large hand pulled down a control lever. The mechanical teeth of the large bulldozer cut into the earth sending up sparks as it hit rocks and dislodged living roots. This would be just one of the beautiful beings that would be torn from this section of land. A being that is a caretaker and giver of shelter to other life forms, as well as one of Earth's lungs, would be tossed and shredded. The bulldozer continued ramming magnificent trees with ruthless, rotten, rusty metallic teeth with tires trampling the land. These machines would force subterranean waters out of their stone beds leaving behind dead roots as well as dry land. How many tracks of nature's irrigation have been permanently lost? How many stretches of land would no longer support life?

Danielle thought, "What arrogance we have to decide what species the world has room for." She wondered what ghouls in development disguises were behind the clearance of this ancient forest. Danielle's tears were filled with fury as she watched the machines that ripped the beauty of the land with their steel. She thought that Fred F. Barry must be the sycophant that is behind this new land clearing. He was a master Greed that knew what tactics would gain lands that were the most difficult to acquire. Fred F. Barry had many different types of weapons: Some would blow up the land, some would be machines that would rip and ravage life from the land and some tactics would grease the right hands for his purposes.

Danielle knew that the number of corporate and state leaders that refused to march in the Greed's parade were few. This would not stop her from taking stands to preserve the planet's life and resources.

Earth's beauty has always been available to all with no need to hide, for who would trample kind life with uncaring steel? The land's beauty seemed to be crying to Danielle as she watched a clearing machine crushing, crunching and cracking the land, rolling over harmless conifers that anchored the land with support against floods. The bulldozer continued to roar as it squelched Earth's beauty in every sense. No longer would people hear bird songs or breezes rustling through the leaves in this location.

Wrinkles of anger surrounded Danielle's eyes and the tension attacked her forehead as well. It was difficult to deal with the piercing pain as the beauty of the trees was one of the loves of her life; this was what sent her to college to study dendrology. She knew that the Greeds of certain industries were aware of alternatives to destroying what was left of the world's ancient forests. There are only twenty percent of the planet's ancient forests remaining, but the Greeds don't care.

PAST

Chapter 11
Ogunquit

They came from the horizon, an endless unrelenting army of liquid shape-shifters, saline soldiers altering the world shores as time is their ally and therefore, their history is one of superiority. The waves of the ocean rarely have had their confidence shaken.

There are certain shore lines and towns that just don't surrender easily to the oceans. One borders the town of Ogunquit along the rocky shore of Maine. Half a billion years of history can be found in the layered rocks beneath this town. A short walk from this beautiful little town was Marginal Way. Along this winding footpath was a show of nature one would never forget. Deep green brambles and small conifers found their way alongside the path and between the cliff openings. Looking down from the spiraling path, proud gold and amber boulders laden with aged algae stood guard at the shore; the ocean rudely testing their resolution with powerful slaps of surf. Defiant and proud protectors of Ogunquit, the boulders held stubbornly. Weathered, smoothened but not yet succumbing.

Matthew inhaled the misty ocean air as he neared Ogunquit's windy horseshoe path that was Marginal Way. Matt felt the soulful, soft winds of dawn as he looked out to the waves. A trumpet shaped shell found the shore as if an ocean announcement was eminent. The horseshoe cliffs formed artistic ridges with almost haunting beauty beneath and extending from the side of the windy path. The energy and beauty of this rocky shore was just what the doctor ordered. To be a starting pitcher for the New York

Yankees was incredible, but with this stardom also came incredible stress.

There was little movement in the mist with the exception of light swirls due to the sea breeze, or perhaps a gull's path being momentarily chartered. Matthew thought the fog had added an extra enchantment to an already mystical path. At the path's beginning, Matthew noticed the small evergreen and briar that lined the walkway as well as penetrating parts of the powerful rocky cliffs all along the way to the shoreline. The sound of the sea waves announcing themselves to the proud stones drew his eyes to the ocean.

Every morning brought a new beauty to Marginal Way, yet this morning seemed unusual. The clouds were in mysterious, varied gray-blue shades brightened by the yawning beams of dawn. Matthew looked down the cliffs toward the water seeing the ocean sprays leaping against and above the stones where they temporarily captured flashes of morning light in the soaring water droplets. He walked further down the path and the view over the cliffs became more panoramic. The entire area was bathed in a morning mist of opalescence. Differing beams of dawn piercing the unusual sky bouncing off the sea and mist caused an eerie obscureness that made the surroundings seem unreal.

Matthew had walked a quarter of the way along the horseshoe path that was part of Ogunquit. At this point he could see to the inside of the path and well below its edges. There were boulders that were flattened and designed to varying shapes by the authoritative pounding of the surf through the years. To the outside of the path, forming the horseshoe, there were small evergreen trees with lovely homes peeking out from behind them. The lucky few who could afford them were privy to a view that is often found in paintings. A few of the small evergreen trees had found their way to the inside of the path as well, perhaps between some very large rocks and boulders. Although these small trees did not soften the power of the boulders, they did balance the beauty of the area and lend their presence perfectly to the symmetry that was Ogunquit.

Rounding a large brambly evergreen, Matthew noticed a lone figure in the distance. He could not really tell if it was a man or a woman due to the smokiness of the mist. Strange, he rarely encountered other people at this time of day. Matthew thought, "Let's hope it's not another Yankee fan," as he came to Ogunquit to avoid more questions about his fitness. Matthew thought that perhaps he should turn around. "No, on second thought, the air is fresh and not everyone is a baseball fan." He continued on deciding to just enjoy the magnificent morning. Looking toward the sea, each wave was seemingly pushing for more space as high, soaring sprays would integrate with the dawn's morning mist. Matthew's eyes caught by a flock of seagulls looked skyward as they slowly glided higher, leaving traces through the mist.

As Matthew passed a bench, well situated midway on the spiraling path, the figure he previously saw became clearer. He moved closer and saw that it was a woman. It seemed that they were alone within one of the sea's spectacular courtyards. The woman was gazing out to the misty blue-gray gambrel roof, where the sea meets the horizon.

Emily watched the waves bring winding rapids in a multitude of miniature rivers moving as if in a race between the boulders on the shore line. She thought how the stubborn stones would not surrender to the sea, yet always the next wave would come. Waves, wild and young, trying to break free and leave, but were always called back. The sea is a patient power and in time the boulders would become sand, As the stones are not immutable: Always wave warriors will come seeking shores. There is no choice; they will continue making changes to the land. They will disintegrate the rocks into a granular soil.

Emily felt everything she saw: The beauty, the power, the exhilaration. When she came into Matthew's view, he experienced a surreal feeling. This was the kind of woman that appears only in those rare dreams. In certain of these dreams, he could see her face somewhat clearer than in others. He wondered who she was. Is she from a former life? He knows from the dream that they were meant to be together. There she stands before him, never seen clearly in his dreams, her presence is unmistakable. When he awakens from these dreams, he wonders if this woman will really ever exist for him. Will he ever be able to touch her, or know her in his waking life? When he wakes up, he tries to hold the image of this woman, but the image would remain somewhat wavy and fleeting. He wonders if this is true for all people: To have a love known from their dreams. Perhaps it was the silvery lights reflecting off the surf and through the fog.

He walked closer. The woman's hair, dancing back with ocean breezes and with the brightness around her was intoxicating. Dazed, he rubbed his eyes hoping to clear them. Perhaps the anti-inflammatory medicine was playing tricks with his head. He looked back towards her. She was still there; a vision perhaps, so delicate and graceful, yet present among all of nature's power. He felt his heart pounding. "This never happens to me," Matthew thought. "How could I feel nervous? I was cool as a cucumber pitching game seven of the World Series."

The trail was descending slightly, winding down closer to the edge of the cliffs. Matthew turned past a group of small conifers and suddenly he was within twenty feet of the woman. He froze slightly, and then pulled back to the conifers. Remaining still, it was as if he spotted a rare beauty on an Audubon outing. He stared as the slender woman elegantly opened her arms slowly, parting the mist gracefully with her movement. The fog outlining her silhouette gave her a mystical aura as she breathed in the sea air. Matthew moved slightly closer. "What is it about her?" he thought.

"This woman's stance has an ease, a sweet balance, more graceful than most. It is almost as if she is not touching the ground."

The sea breezes continually bring a sense of freedom to the movement of her long cascade of amber hair. The early sunbeams piercing the mist and bouncing about the moist air seemed part of her spell. Who was she? Matthew noticed some ships in the distance as if he were looking at an old painting through the mist. "Are the shores of Ogunquit enchanted?" Matthew wondered. "Most women worry about the winds undoing their hair and insulting their appearance. These sea breezes only complimented the woman's hair with a wildness that agreed with the surroundings." Thick, rich, deep auburn was alive and playing with the wind. The sky, now showing some strawberry tones, seemed to be accommodating the woman's astonishing hair with bright ginger highlights. Her wild hair calmed momentarily as the sea wind settled. She glided both hands through her hair, her face becoming more revealed. Turning her head to take in the beauty of the morning scenery, Matthew now had a clear view of her face. The woman had a lovely complexion with large eyes, high cheek bones and was somewhat pale. Matthew, having dated some beautiful women thought he must be dreaming.

Time itself became still. He found himself in that area between time, where it passes slowly, or not at all. Hers was a beauty defying typical definitions, yet unquestionable. A nervous excitement he had not felt since Diane had accepted his invitation to the high school prom came upon him. It was a feeling that comes with first love when you think you could touch the stars. He knew in his gut that everything before this moment did not count. He thought, "I don't even know her name." The unknown excitement dancing in his heart fed his nervousness. This woman surrounded by the light from above and within this misty morning gazed past the shore's kingdom out to dawn's horizon. To Matthew, this day delivered a dawn only found in dreams, yet unbelievably, the woman was still there. This woman was one with the morning, the day's beginning, and perhaps Matthew's beginning: Perhaps part of many important new mornings.

"I must speak to her," he thought. Matthew's knees felt unsteady. "I am a starting pitcher for the New York Yankees, how could I possibly still be nervous? I must go forward, I must know this woman. I must speak to her." This morning was hers; her world, her home. She had become part of the beauty of the surroundings. Yet Matthew knew he must knock on morning's door. He moved towards her as she was still unaware of his presence, seemingly lost in thought. He struggled to say "hello." The woman was so much a part of the morning beauty that he actually felt he was intruding. Matthew hoped for a glance from her. Closer now, the radiance of her beauty was real. He thought that the weak raspy sound from his throat that struggled to find the air might not have been enough to catch her attention. The woman turned around and made eye contact and spoke in a kindly tone that smiled. "I didn't quite hear you, did you say something?" Matthew, now captured and captivated, tried to clear his throat as well as the trembling in his voice. The woman's eyes, an amazing shade of turquoise, with a lovely shape were intensely intelligent as well as enchanting. Matthew thought the unusual lighting in the mist was victimizing his vision. Her beauty, somehow frail and understated, was very cerebral.

"Matthew."

"What?" The woman laughed. Even her laughter was so light that it seemed to sail on the ocean breezes.

"Hello, I'm Matthew. Matthew Monroe," he said smiling, as he put out his hand. The woman extended her slender hand and said, "I'm Emily Westwood." Matthew could see that she had no clue as to who he was.

Emily thought to herself, "He's very handsome with a great smile. But, wait, I never say things like that to myself; but at least it was to myself."

Matthew felt his heart beating loud and fast, more so than the most important pitch he delivered in the World Series. His hands felt cold. He felt nervous; a nervous excitement. The cliffs, the boulders, the briars, and the ocean— he no longer saw them. There was only this woman and the mist. He felt like he was floating; living in a dream. Matthew's throat and mouth, still managing to stay dry, within this misty morning, would not deter him. Clearing his throat he said," What a beautiful morning."

Matthew felt his heart racing and his face blushing. Emily moved toward him, her hair abandoning all control now and moving wildly with the return of stronger morning sea breezes. The cascade of color similar to a tropical mahogany laced with ginger brought a certain wildness surrounding her frail elegance.

"It is a magical morning."

The only sound Matthew heard was Emily's voice, the pounding surf and seagulls. Matthew's nervousness continued to have a strangling effect on his voice, yet he knew he must continue speaking. "Do you come here often?"

"I can't believe I said that, it sounds like I'm one of those characters in a bar," Matthew thought. Matthew exhaled a large sigh and saw his breath temporarily part the mist. He felt dazed, as if in a waking dream.

"It's my first time in Maine, and I'm so happy I found this town."

A strange sound broke into their aubade. The moment was broken. A voice came from beyond the mist. Matthew looked up the path and spotted an older man with a large grey beard.

"Come Emily, we must prepare to leave," the man yelled down towards them.

Emily, putting up the hood of her light green jacket, turned and waved as the morning fog turned into a light drizzle.

"I have to go now, it was nice meeting you," Emily smiled.

He felt helpless as he smiled back with some difficulty. Matthew watched, locked in time as she walked away up the path, softly parting the morning fog with a gentle consideration. He heard Emily's voice, "Coming Professor."

Matthew thought, "This unknown man was intrusive and interruptive, but how could he know? How could he know that I must spend more time with this woman?"

"Yes, yes, great meeting you."

As he watched Emily turn around and walk up the winding path, although still somewhat spellbound, he noticed a lovely balance to her slender, yet shapely body.

Matthew thought, "I must stop her, but how? What do I do? What am I talking about? I don't even know her, but her eyes."

The emotions within him felt close to overwhelming. Matthew was nervous. She disappeared into Ogunquit's mystical fog. Matthew thought that he had made his strongest acquaintance with desire when he met Diane as a teenager or when he discovered baseball. This was different. This desire was found at the core and somehow he knew he must find her again.

Emily walked up the path back to the village with Professor Kensington. The Professor opened his umbrella as the spring rain began.

"Good thing I always carry one of these."

"That's the London in you."

"It appears that I called for you just in time as you would have been soaked and we have a long drive to New York. We have research to document for the laboratories at the New York Botanical Gardens before next week's seminar."

Maine had always been one of the Professor's favorite states as there was uninhabited forest to explore.

"You're right, of course," yet her mind was still at the cliffs of Marginal Way, thinking of the man she had just met. Emily felt a kind feeling from Matthew although he seemed shy. She should only know that he was usually quite the opposite. The Professor started the car as Emily turned and looked back through the rear window.

Matthew thought that when he spoke to Emily he must have been blushing. "Could she hear his breathing?" Matthew worried. When she walked away, disappearing into the lifting fog he desperately wanted to say something to stop her. "I said nothing to make her remember me," thought Matthew. "I might as well jump off this cliff into the boulders." Now overcome by a feeling of emptiness, he turned to walk back towards the town. He was a New York Yankee, idolized, surrounded by great teammates, family, fans, and girlfriends; now there was this empty feeling. There was no fullness to his breathing. He heard his heart's voice say, "Find her." He looked towards the ocean and saw the waves attacking the cliffs and then retreating. It seemed nature itself was upset with her leaving.

Matthew thought back to Diane, his first love and high school sweetheart. They talked of being married and what a wonderful romantic future they would have. They dated exclusively for four years. Suddenly, she was engaged to Peter McLain, son of one of Ohio's wealthiest businessmen. Matt confronted her and she called him a dreamer. "One in a million becomes a pro athlete."

Matthew's heart was crushed, "But you always said I could do it and supported me."

"I'm sorry Matt, I did love you, but we were immature and my parents wanted me to be with someone like Peter, who already was established."

Matthew looked towards the shore, his heart felt young and alive again. The weight of Diane's memories disappeared along with the pain she had left in his heart. "How could this be?" he thought. Matt hadn't had a strong emotional tie to any woman since his relationship with Diane. Matthew erected a strong wall to prevent pain and hurt from entering his heart; yet only several moments with Emily and his heart was set free.

There are many men who dream of that special woman. In their dreams, they try to zoom in on the woman's face, yet the clarity always escapes them. Men rarely search for this woman of their dreams, as after all, it's just a dream. Matthew thought, "Was it a dream? Was I really with her?"

The excitement in his heart was real. His mind was doing somersaults. "I must fill the new, challenging emptiness by seeing her again. Where, when and how? She is wonderful, she is beautiful. Calm down, Matt."

Matt thought that he must figure this out. Emily, part of this mystical spring morning, fully entered his heart with her loveliness. He felt that the morning missed her as well. Emily though, couldn't be envied by this magical dawn, as she was part of its symmetry. If ever a woman was possessed by beauty, it was Emily. Her eyes were unbelievable, like staring at love, yet somehow with an intelligence impossible not to notice. He remembered feeling his lips tremble as he tried to speak, a strangled incoherent sound. Matthew thought back to the first sight of her, seeing her gazing towards the sea and how it had a dreamy quality to it. He thought of the older man who had called for her, and how Emily had referred to him as "Professor."

Walking back to the inn alone, Matthew was left with a mystery. "Thank God for Linda," he thought. Matthew could always count on his sister for support. It was Linda that recommended the town of Ogunquit to recuperate and have some down time. Linda lived in Manhattan in a small apartment on the West Side. Working as a Sales Assistant in a large finance company, she knew what stress could do to a person. The town situated on Maine's coastline with its beautiful walkway would be the best medicine for Matthew.

Matthew looked around as the rain began to fall. The path of gold that appeared on the sea started to darken as did nature's ceiling. Behind him, the small conifers began to stir.

"Perhaps I'll see Emily in the morning at breakfast," he thought. Matthew had a delirious impatience. He could not stop thinking about her. Normally a huge appetite for breakfast, he couldn't eat, yet he never felt more alive. Although he had a new contract for millions, as a starting pitcher he now knew he was lacking. He shared but a few moments with Emily, yet every thought led back to her. Emily was the cynosure of his mind.

The April shower now replaced by sunshine, he thought he would stroll by the shops around the village. With luck, he might run into her and the elderly man that she left with. Matthew visited every art store, the ice cream parlor and restaurants; no Emily. He decided to go back to the inn as his arm was now aching a bit from the surgery.

"Odd, if I hadn't torn a tendon, I would be in spring training and never have met her. Oh, what am I talking about? I just met this woman for five minutes."

Lying in his motel bed, he closed his eyes. It was evening and Emily was fourteen hours in the past, yet Matthew's mind was still filled with their morning. He knew he would not sleep. He called Linda. "Matt, do you know what time it is?" Matt looked at the clock: 2:00 AM.

"I'm sorry, but..."

"What is it Matthew, you sound different?"

Matthew told her of his encounter. "I've only seen her once yet I feel like I'm losing something every moment that I'm not with her. How could this be possible?"

"Sounds like you have been hit with the thunderbolt."

"What's that?"

Ronald Yates

"You know, the thunderbolt effect is the term used by the people of Italy when you are totally smitten and you meet the most special person. Didn't you ever see the God-father? Don't forget what Mom used to say." Matthew remembered his Mom's favorite saying whenever he had girl problems growing up in Canton, Ohio. "Love always finds a way, dear; just ask your father."

"Well it's good to know that you could be excited again after your experience with Diane."

"Who's Diane?"

"That's great Matt."

"I'm sorry I woke you. I didn't know what to do after I was searching for her all day; any ideas?"

"Well clearly she's not a baseball fan. Try Marginal Way again. Perhaps she'll be back."

"Thank you. I'm really sorry I woke you."

"Don't worry about it, it will all work out, and I have a good feeling about this. I love you."

"I love you too."

A few hours passed, and although earlier than usual Matt decided to start his morning walk. Though a new day for Matthew, it was still yesterday. The power of Emily's beauty and aura still seemed like a dream. Matthew's fear: "What if I don't find her?"

Matthew arrived at Marginal Way embracing hope. A path of bluish moonlight defined the waves from the horizon to the shore. As he viewed the beauty of the area, he could not help but feel that the nature around him shared his desire for her return. Suddenly, he felt nervous, unworthy. "What if she were here? What would I say?" Matthew almost felt in a crisis mode; in a panic. He realized it was Emily's inner beauty that was the most tangible; it brought the radiance that merged her being with the magic of the morning. He must find her.

Chapter 12
Bullies

There was a group of children who were horrible to Emily in elementary school. She was glad that sixth grade would soon be over and looked forward to the summer. Emily was smart and pretty, yet she was also frail and thus was not strong enough to play sports. She really loved to learn and enjoyed books and school classes. This made Emily a target for the school bullies since the fourth grade. Most children stayed in the apartment complex during the summer; sleep away camps were costly and many parents were leery of the day camps that were available.

It was a quiet day at the apartment complex's playground. The square playground was situated between four of the large brick apartment buildings. Tree-lined lawns bordered all of the fourteen story apartment buildings on three sides. The twelve buildings surrounded one large rectangular shaped lawn which was at the center of the entire apartment complex. Tall maples approximately nine stories high and twenty feet apart bordered the rectangular lawn. There were benches surrounding the playground on the exterior of the concrete path as well as several benches in the playgrounds interior. These interior benches were usually occupied by mothers or grandmothers keeping an eye on their small children.

Emily looked across the playground and could see large saucer like flowers now fully opened on the two enormous magnolia trees situated at the front of the center lawn. The magnolia tree blossoms were many with plentiful pods; fuzzy like kiwis looking like long one inch eggs were ready to add more flowers to the beautiful tree. From these tiny containers there would eventually come sweet scents with the white cherry pink flowers.

Breezes would bring petals down to the concrete paths softening them with their beauty. The long bench facing the east side of the playground always seemed to be the most popular. Emily knew why and gave it the name "the windless bench." She would investigate different birds and trees and would imagine all sorts of things. One summer morning while following a beautiful large yellow butterfly between the two large magnolia trees, she made a discovery. The butterfly entered through the foliage to the interior of a witch hazel tree that was recessed about fifteen feet from the center of the two magnolia trees. The tree which was about twenty two feet tall had long entwining branches forming a sort of umbrella of laced foliage which swept all the way down to the grass. Emily, still chasing the butterfly fell to the grass against the tree's foliage. She lifted a branch full of leaves and rolled on the grass and under into the interior section of the tree's umbrella. From behind the tree's curtain of leaves, Emily moved a few to the side and could see the smooth light gray bark of the two magnolia trees. She found that she was able to stand up within the tree's canopy. She parted a few of the higher leaves and the pink white shades of the magnolia's flowers were revealed. Directly ahead between and past the magnolia trees was the extra long windless bench and the view of the playground.

Emily released the leaves and turned around just in time to see the butterfly disappear through an opening in the umbrella's foliage. Dappled light made for a warm secure feeling within the tree. She circled the grayish trunk of the tree noting that it was somewhat darker in color than that of the smooth gray magnolia trunks. Emily sat against the trunk and looked up at the foliage that was her roof. Becoming quite comfortable within the tree, it occurred to her that this could become a great hideout. She was happy for the leaks of blue as beams of summer sky were welcomed in what would become her sanctuary. Depending on what angle she looked up at the roof composed of branches, and the time of day, it would sometimes appear as if there were many suns trapped within them.

She decided to look closely at a fallen leaf which was about five inches in size. She noted that the uneven, rugged, jagged edged oval leaf had a large center vein with other veins branching outward; the leaf seemed to have a picture of a tree within it. One side of the leaf was a deeper green than the other.

In time, while at the library, Emily would learn to recognize trees by their leaf size and shape, as well as their trunks' character and color. She would also discover that the witch hazel trees were thought to be bewitched by early Europeans. They were amazed when the trees launched its seeds sometimes thirty feet into the air. She would also learn that during droughts it was said that the branches of this tree could actually locate underground water. The tree is most famous for its medicinal qualities. She would also learn that its leaves would turn yellow at the beginning of December and odd, curly flowers would appear on the branches as the weather became even colder. Funny, hairy, oval like pods seemed to always be on the branches. She discovered that her sanctuary was the only witch hazel on the entire block. Finding a sanctuary in this unusual tree might turn out to be a good thing since she was having problems with bullies.

Nature's world was magical and exciting to her. Her connection with nature grew more comfortable. Emily's curiosity about nature and especially trees continued to grow. While back at the library, she was surprised to learn that aspirin and even chocolate came from trees. An ancient race called The Mayans would prize chocolate drinks from the cocoa trees.

Suddenly, while examining one of the leaves, Emily jumped as she heard, "Where's that nerd, Emily?" bellowed a strong girl's voice.

"Oh no, it's Mary Ellen," thought Emily.

"Yeah, where is that twerp?" asked a loud second voice.

"Susan," thought Emily. "The two meanest bullies in the neighborhood."

Emily couldn't help but think back to what had occurred last weekend while she was reading on a bench avoiding the playground. Mary Ellen and her followers appeared in front of her laughing. "What are you doing on our bench?" said Mary Ellen.

Emily looked up at the other girls snickering at her and said, "I'll leave."

"You better leave and take your little pink school bag with you," said Susan as she threw it off the bench and onto the concrete path.

Emily's drawing pad and crayons fell out of the bag. Sliding off the bench, she put her drawing pad and crayons away while the group of girls continued laughing. Emily stood up and Mary Ellen was directly in front of her. "You forgot to pay the toll, nerd," said Mary Ellen.

"I only have a nickel."

"Oh, that's going to be a problem. That's not enough for the toll, so I'm going to have to punch you," threatened Mary Ellen.

Mary Ellen punched Emily on the shoulder, "Hand over the nickel."

Emily hurried over to the other side of the lawn towards the playground and sat near two elderly women who were chatting. They smiled at her kindly. She took out her pad and crayons and decided to draw the sky. There were lots of very large white clouds with narrow rivers of blue finding their way through. Emily tried to hold back her own river of tears.

While in her sanctuary, Emily thought, "They don't know I'm here."

She peeked through the leaves and heard Susan say, "Let's check out the other side of the playground, that twerp Emily owes us some tolls."

Emily was safely hidden within the tree. While still in her sanctuary, she thought back to an incident last year while in the fifth grade. One of the girls that stayed in the shadows seemed alone just like herself. Emily spoke to her and thought her kind as she seemed quite friendly. She confided in her and told her how much she loved nature and even trusted her about having no father at home. Emily thought that this girl could be her first good friend.

"Perhaps sixth grade would be different," she thought.

The girl was Susan and now everybody knew all about her, at school and in the neighborhood. The silence of her thoughts was broken as a sudden summer rain tapped the leaves of her newly found enclave. The morning rain was lenient and Emily felt secure in her shelter. Trickling over the leaves of the witch hazel tree, and listening to the gentle rain it was as if the cold brick apartment buildings of the complex didn't exist. Emily parted a group of sweeping leaves and saw people scurrying under the building porches and umbrellas were opening. Several young children were laughing as they hid from the rain in the playground's large concrete barrels. Most of the children were already wet from playing in the sprinkler. Emily was totally dry within her foliage umbrella. The sweeping curtains that surrounded her began to sway. The arriving raindrops grew stronger and sounded like many peas bouncing off the leaves. Emily thought it was time to go home.

Emily started to walk around the playground as the rain began to subside. She decided to take notice of the shape and texture of some of the other leaves around her. Some of the trees' leaves were jagged edged and wide while others were heart shaped or oval. One tiny tree, only three feet high, had silvery leaves that were shimmering with the breeze against the side of one of the apartment buildings over a small adjacent lawn. The grass seemed tickled by the breeze. Emily became more arboreal and happily decided to re-enter her sanctuary before people returned and might see her. A tall, thin grounds keeper walking down the path adjacent to the lawn had a large, artistically shaped branch in one hand and an axe in the other. The branch, a likely victim of last night's rain storm. The winds were strong and easily pruned many of the trees' branches. Emily watched the grounds keeper as he tossed the branch on a stack with the storm's other victims.

The next morning, Emily's mother was up early for the breakfast shift. Emily gathered her notebook, crayons, a book and a jelly sandwich as well as a blue towel and left the apartment, excited about her new enclave. The early morning silence was broken by a couple of impromptu bathers and thirsty travelers taking advantage of left over rain puddles. The sparrows and pigeons ignored each other as they drank, yet there was a lot of excited tweeting going on whenever there was a new arrival. Emily laughed as a squirrel temporarily disrupted the puddle party with a jump from one of the benches. She continued walking and from the center of the playground she looked across to the large maple trees which were on either side of the two magnolia trees. These trees which were lined up next to each other almost totally blocked the view of the large center lawn. It was quiet and she decided to study the curtain that was formed by the trees from this side of the playground. Gazing at nature's curtain of green from a bench, she thought that it was thicker than ever. She could not even see the large rectangular center lawn on the other side. The top of the green curtain seemed to have new trees forming within the larger trees' top branches reaching even higher. It seemed that the trees were always reaching higher as if to touch something. Emily wondered if it was the sky.

The curtain was being formed by different types of trees which were at varying distances from each other. This caused recessions in the green of the curtain at different levels. These different stages of curtain changed the color in the tones of the foliage due to the different lighting within the curtain's depth. The partition of green had taken on a strong character. Maples and oaks were the tallest trees in the complex; they were full of July green and formed the sides of nature's partition. In the center of this curtain of green, Emily could just about see sections of her sanctuary.

The witch hazel, although recessed several feet from the two large magnolia and maple trees, still seemed to be part of the large curtain of green. From the distance she watched as a bird soared away through an opening in the wall of green flying away from the playground while disappearing from sight. It was now probably flying somewhere on the other side, over the large rectangular lawn. Envious of its flight through the green partition, Emily thought how wonderful it must be to fly around the treetops and enter through shaded portals to another side. This graceful partition of beauty was no two dimensional curtain as it contained many deep and dark passageways through its sweeping cascades of foliage. The layers of green with the ramification of branches, some intertwined with the adjacent tree would form shaded tunnels; each tunnel a different depth of shade's darkness: A different shade of shade.

Emily enjoyed watching the birds enter these portals wondering if some chose to stay within nature's curtain or continue on through to the other side. In a way the curtain was a world unto itself. There were also the high flyers that chose to soar over the large ten story green divide. Why negotiate a tricky branch portal within the green curtain when the route over the top only has clear skies to navigate?

Emily decided to walk to the other side of the playground. She squeezed between the side of the windless bench and a large bush and made her way in between the two magnolias and into the witch hazel tree. Like the bird, Emily was now on the other side of the enormous green curtain. She noticed the shaded portals in the curtain from the sanctuary window as a butterfly crossed over to the playground side, or did he?

"Perhaps he is resting between his worlds in the curtain portal," she thought.

Emily leaned forward peeking out of her sanctuary. The robust leaves of hanging branches framed her little face. She saw so many dramas unfold from her alcove windows. The mean girls led by Mary Ellen and Susan were causing trouble; mothers and grandmothers were keeping an eye on babies and small children; the ground keepers were mowing and growing new lawn. A recently planted bare spot within the lawn had begun a small grass forest which seemed to spring up in no time. Emily thought that perhaps it served as a forest world for a fire fly or ladybug. Her witch hazel tree became her home away from home. She would look forward to bending beneath the tree's green drapes and entering her safe haven.

Early Saturday morning, Emily took off to her new hideaway. The air on this summer's day was still. Even the countless blades of grass showed no movement, patiently waiting for a maestro to lift breezes' baton. In a prelude of non-movement, every blade and every leaf stood waiting in position. Finally, the baton was lifted by the breeze. The grass and leaves began a synchronized sway with the leaves rustling on cue. All the flowers were now fully opened on the magnolia trees.

There was not a person in sight. A squirrel stepped up to her, posed on his hind legs to stare directly at Emily. This squirrel with a larger than usual black nose and matching mascara like stripes on its belly caused Emily to laugh and say," I have no food for you." The squirrel, after a brief hesitation took off across the lawn. Lying on the grass below one of the magnolia trees, she took in the beauty of the large pink and white flowers against the sky. Emily thought that the scent of the morning seemed to come from summer's blue beauty that only these flowers could know and are kind enough to share. Anyone that had put a flower to their nose knew that their scents were made of smiles. Emily was upset the other day as she saw two older girls tear several beautiful orange lilies from the ground. These flowers were supposed to be for everyone to enjoy.

At times the foliage brought tiny tunes; sparrows chirping invisibly within the leafy crowns. Emily would try very hard to locate the singers above her, but most times to no avail. Emily decided to enter her sanctuary. For some reason, a group of sparrows were causing a noisy stir at the back of her witch hazel tree. She walked around the trunk, pulled aside some leaves and saw that the water sprinklers were activated, flying drops of opal in the sunlight. She loved when the circles of water would meet, momentarily causing droplet collisions in their rotations and it made her smile. She noticed the exposed roots of a nearby tree were rippled and powerful as they held tiny lakes of water, courtesy of the sprinklers. Emily thought that the powerful roots which were holding this beautiful tree stable had a calming character. Her eyes followed the trunk up from its roots to its crown.

"Such elegance to its trunk tapering tall and stretching to the sky," thought Emily.

The sunlight revealed momentary clouds formed by the sprinklers as well. On the edges of the spray these wispy formations would dissipate in just seconds, yet Emily found the occasional rainbows within those seconds.

"These water sprinklers were not only pretty to watch but were helpful to the thirsty birds as well as the grass and the trees," she thought. She now experienced the trees, the grass, the bushes and the flowers all as one magnificent connection to the surroundings of nature, and felt energized.

One summer morning, Emily felt something touch her shoulder.

"Just a branch within the tree that was her sanctuary adjusting itself in the breezes," thought Emily. Her ears were alerted by a whistling voice. "Strange, a voice. After all, I'm alone in the sanctuary, it must be the wind."

The wind picked up and she heard the whispering voice again and listened carefully. The voice seemed to be saying, "Music of the winds. Was it really simply breezes whistling through the leaves of this witch hazel tree?"

When outside of her sanctuary, if possible, the mean bullies would still attack her. At times, Emily found it difficult to keep rising above the pain. She thought that how in the sixth grade they were taught the Golden Rule: "Do unto others as you would have them do unto you." This came from Confucius who called for a society based upon kindness. She was safe in her sanctuary and avoided any assaults by the bullies, but knew her shelter was not invincible. Still, for Emily, there was a feeling of inviolableness while inside. Although alone in her sanctuary there was never emptiness as she would always be amazed with nature's visit.

Chapter 13
The Chase

A streaky darkness was dripping down a weird evening sky. The light rain had stopped and it was time to head home as it was nearly 8:30. Emily felt safe as Broadway was still crowded with people coming home from work. Excited about the box of chocolates and the card she made for her mother's birthday, she would hide them in her draw as soon as she arrived home. Emily's mother worked until 9:00 on Wednesdays, so there would be plenty of time to hide her present.

She felt that the eerie night lighting with its dim shadows was not to be trusted. Two of these shadows crossed by her while she was waiting for the light to change. She looked up and was greeted with two menacing smiles from older men. Although they were in sports jackets something told her that they were not to be trusted. Now walking off Broadway with less lights and people around, anxiety heightened her senses. Darkness was filling the streets and these nameless faces were still following her. Emily quickened her pace, stumbling as her shoe caught on an uneven sidewalk. They were closer, laughing and talking loudly as well as moving faster. She now knew that these were not nice men as her mother always taught her to trust the feeling in her stomach.

Emily hurried to cross Crescent Street as she saw her apartment complex, but did not see the speeding car, as she was thinking of her sanctuary. The car was almost upon her and somehow as if a wind floated her body forward, she narrowly avoided being hit. She heard her heart beating and her toe really hurt. She reached the playground, turned around and saw that they were on Crescent Street.

Emily sensed that the two large unknown figures were aware that she knew that they were following her. These men were uncaring as they were powerful compared to this frail little girl. The pumpkin moon seemed to light Emily's path with a strange yellow orange color. The after rain haze refracted the pumpkin lighting, somehow giving Emily a certain comfort. The sound of their shoes attacking the pavement was loud and she could tell that their pace had quickened even more. She was in danger.

Emily thought she heard a voice and said to herself that it must be the wind. Bending low against the bushes that lined the playground she walked even faster, as she turned and looked back. The men were entering the projects looking to their left and right. Emily knew they were searching for her and looked for help, but there was no one around. Running in between the two magnolia trees, she rolled under the witch hazel's drape of leaves and was in her sanctuary. She realized that the bag which contained the chocolate had been caught on a low branch. Taking a deep breath, she extended her arm and wiggled the bag free and pulled it in to her sanctuary. She looked against the brick buildings and saw shadows that seemed to hold secrets.

Emily peeked out from the front of her alcove toward the playground area and saw that it was clear, but heard a mumbling to her far left. The darkness that drenched the artificial lights of the apartment buildings caused a warping of shadows. She ducked, seeing big, convinced shadows against the brick of the apartment building grow even larger. She drew further back within her sanctuary. After waiting two minutes, she peeked out again and the mean shadows were missing as well as the muttering sounds of the menacing men. She lied on her back and released a big sigh of relief. Looking through the leaves she felt comfort seeing the tall, adjacent trees she knew so well.

In the surrounding grass there were tiny lime and white sparkles flashing on and off. She loved the little bright-winged lights of the night. She felt the leaves of her sanctuary stir and knew that the strange wind whispers would come again. She thought the whispers were saying, "We must bring the music of the winds." It did not scare her and she decided not to tell her mother or her teacher, but what did it mean? They would just tell her that it was her imagination once again.

Unseen and unknown birds of darkness passed over the building's grass and walkways; their shadows were speedy night phantoms. Emily would walk briskly home with the box of chocolates in hand.

Chapter 14
Miss Mulligan

Emily looked forward to her new school in Astoria, Queens. She was quite happy to put elementary school behind her and begin junior high school. She thought the teachers and kids at the elementary school tried their very best to make her as miserable as possible. In the sixth grade, her last year at elementary school, she remembered approaching her stern homeroom teacher, Mrs. Leyton, to finally report the bullies that were tormenting her. Mrs. Leyton just told her to toughen up.

Emily's homeroom teacher for the seventh grade at her new school was Miss Mulligan, a kind woman with a lovely smile that seemed to fit with her curly salt and pepper hair. She loved her new classes and already learned a lot in just three months, but the bullies still picked on her constantly.

"Okay class, reading period is over; let's get to know more about one another. Emily, let's start with you. What activities do you enjoy doing after school?"

Emily continued reading. "Emily," said Miss Mulligan. The boy next to Emily touched her shoulder. She looked up and the class started laughing.

"Class, you should not be laughing at Emily as she has excellent concentration skills."

"Emily is too weak to do anything," said Mary Ellen out loud, as a few kids snickered and giggled that were sitting near Mary Ellen.

"Please wait your turn, Mary Ellen. I asked the question to Emily. Go on, Emily. What are your favorite school activities?"

"I enjoy reading books about nature at the library."

"Why is that?"

"It makes me wonder about things, such as what it would be like to fly above the trees like a bird."

"Oh, she wants to be a bird and play with trees," laughed Susan, Mary Ellen's best friend.

"What a nerd," yelled Mary Ellen.

"Emily, I think you have a wonderful imagination," said the teacher with a kind smile.

Miss Mulligan, turning towards Mary Ellen, "Okay, what's your favorite after school activity?"

"I like to hang out in front of the candy store with my friends, not with stupid birds and trees." Several of the students in the class laughed, as she said this.

"My father says trees are just a pain because there are too many leaves to clean up and birds just crap on people from them," added Susan to more class laughter.

"Yeah, why don't you make like a tree and leave," said Mary Ellen to Emily as several other girls started chanting, "Leave. Leave."

The bell rang and the kids scrambled out of the classroom.

Miss Mulligan walked up to Emily who was still in her seat crying. "Emily, it's okay, they're just jealous because you get such good grades."

Emily looked up at Miss Mulligan with her large amazing turquoise eyes full of water. "When I answer a question in science class, the kids start to call me Professor Emily, and they all laugh at me."

"I can speak to Assistant Principal Mr. Laseter on your behalf."

"No, no, if you do that, the bullies will beat me up after school."

"I've seen this before, Emily, there are bullies in every school; shall I have a monitor escort you to your next class?"

"I'll be okay," Emily answered, standing up and looking frail holding all her school books. Miss Mulligan watched the small girl walk away—her books seemed so large next to her body.

"I hope I have a daughter like you some day, Emily."

Emily smiled; her unusually bright eyes seemed even brighter when she answered with her smile, "Thank you Miss Mulligan."

Miss Mulligan noted in her records to speak to her parents on open school week. She will suggest taking Emily to the Metropolitan Museum of Art. At the Met, paintings will show the importance nature holds to the great artists throughout history; then when her classmates laugh at her due to her love of nature, it will seem unimportant, and she will realize that she is far from alone. Miss Mulligan also thought to suggest an outing to the Botanical Gardens or perhaps Central Park.

At times, when coming home from school, Emily thought that it was good that her mother was working. If she were home Emily would have to say that she got bruised and dirty while playing in the school yard. A lot of the school kids lived in the same large apartment complex and shared the same playground. Just hearing one of the kids saying, "Here comes Mary Ellen," would send shivers through Emily.

Her love of school did not seem to be shared by any of the other children. Every day Emily had to find a new way to escape Mary Ellen as she was the biggest and meanest girl in her grade and the leader of the bullies. Emily would try to enter and leave school from different paths to avoid being caught by the bullies, or else it was a punch or a drink thrown on her dress or hair. She often wondered if Mary Ellen's group of followers were really that mean or were they just too afraid not to be her friend. To make matters worse, Mary Ellen lived in the building directly across from Emily's. To escape, Emily turned to the world of nature, where she would cultivate friends of a different kind.

Chapter 15
Fire Escape

Cathy experienced some very scary times as a single mother with no man in the house. New neighbors moved into the apartment next door with which they shared a fire escape. Mrs. Mello, the former tenant was a widower and a very kind lady. She loved to listen to the big band singers, such as Frank Sinatra and Helen Forest. Cathy would always check on her neighbor during a bad storm to see if she needed something from the store. The new neighbors, a big man about 27 years old with a dark-haired girlfriend had many parties. There were times that there would be over 25 men and women screaming and acting strange. More than once there would be up to five or six men drinking and yelling while standing on the adjoining fire escape which extended to the windows in front of Cathy's bedroom.

Cathy tucked Emily into bed and wished her sweet dreams. The City Housing apartment had decent sized rooms. The windows faced another building which was across the way; also there was a parking lot which had a small grass area at the top of the lot with two benches. There were tall trees on the side of the two buildings just out of reach of the fire escapes.

Cathy's thoughts went to the horror of last Saturday night. Loud and foul language woke her with a start. There were men on her fire escape. Emily heard her mother scream and ran into her bedroom. "Mommy, what are those two large men doing in front of our windows?" The two men were holding beers and grinning at them in response to their fear. Cathy not only heard, but felt loud music vibrating the apartment; obviously there was another party getting out of hand.

One man with a mustache knocked on Cathy's bedroom window with a cigarette dangling from his lips and a beer in his hand. She walked up to the windows, slammed them down and locked them. The clock said 2:00 AM and Cathy went to the kitchen to call the police precinct.

"There is no law against being on a shared fire escape, Miss."

"There's a knocking on our window and these people are scaring my young daughter, and they look very dangerous."

"I'll dispatch a car, Miss, but it's going to be awhile, as this is Saturday night and we have our hands full."

Cathy hung up and started crying. Emily tugged at her pajamas and Cathy said, "I'm not a good mother. I don't know what to do or how to take care of you."

"It's not your fault, Mom, and remember that you said God watches over everyone."

Cathy looked down at her frail and wonderful daughter, and thought, "Was it any wonder Emily was her source of strength."

Cathy and her daughter pulled down the blinds and went into the bed and hugged. Emily felt her mother's heart break. There were five large silhouettes now and loud voices filled the bedroom, making each passing moment mean and long. They were fear's prisoners. Instead of twinkling stars, there was no moonlight, no night sky, just sinister silhouettes haunting their bedroom through the shades. The room was becoming stuffy as smells of beer and cigarette smoke made it through the cracks.

Emily, feeling her mother's pain said, "Don't worry, Mom, we'll be okay. Can we have tuna sandwiches tomorrow?"

Cathy knew it was Emily's way to ease her tension. At times Cathy was amazed at the hope and strength that came from her fragile daughter. Crying, Cathy pulled her daughter closer and thought what a special gift life gave her. Emily would have the success she deserves. Cathy would make sure of that. At times she felt that if not for Emily she wouldn't make it. She also thought it ironic that a fire escape would trap them with danger. "It was baffling that the law would not address this issue," she thought. These men seemed to have no sense of time. Are they stupid and selfish as well as unkind? Pulling the covers over their heads, they kissed goodnight and Cathy assured Emily that it would pass.

Cathy was so tired from the work week that she was actually able to fall asleep. Emily saw the shadows leaving and softly rolled out of her mother's bed. Lifting the blinds slightly, Emily smiled and said, "I thought I heard rain."

A kind morning light found its way through the window between the cracked blinds. Walking over to the bed, Emily saw that her mother was still asleep. Their night of fears that seem to be flying and bouncing off the walls was finally over.

Coming home from her shift at the restaurant, although exhausted, Cathy decided to go to the police precinct. After waiting half an hour, she was told the Sergeant was ready to see her. Sergeant Rice looked up and was taken by the beauty of her eyes, as he asked, "How can I help you?" Cathy explained the situation and Sergeant Rice asked if she had spoken to her landlord.

"I called the office at City Housing, and they just told me that all you can do is phone the police. When the police do arrive, it's quiet for a few moments, but as soon as they leave the music starts blasting and there are people on our fire escape. It actually sounds like these men are in my bedroom and my daughter and I are terrified. Is it possible for the officers to stay longer?"

"I wish we could spare them but there are so many burglaries and violent crimes that we don't have a force large enough for noise control."

Cathy started crying, "My daughter is so young and very frail."

Sergeant Rice noticed that her face, although strong, became very vulnerable, as he responded, "Unfortunately, there are bad people that use fire escapes to gain entry into people's homes. Usually it's to steal for drug money.

"These idiots actually think it's their personal terrace to drink and smoke on. We live here and it's not right," Cathy started to cry.

"Now, now, I'm going to ring their bell and have a talk with your neighbors."

Cathy's turquoise eyes were like two ponds as she looked at Sergeant Rice and thanked him.

"I'm really not supposed to do this, but here's my card; I wrote my phone number down. Call me the next time this occurs and I'll come over and see what I can do."

Cathy, bending over in tears in her wooden chair said, "I'm sorry, I'm so tired."

"It's okay, I understand."

The next night, Cathy decided to peek in on Emily before going to sleep. After what occurred the night before, she was happy to see Emily's face serene and smiling. She knew she was having her happy dream. Emily had this dream more than once, and after telling her mother about it, they decided to name it "The Happy Dream."

In Emily's dream, it is a bright, sunny day with pastel skies and white puff clouds. Cathy's daughter sees herself running up a meadow surrounded by many waves of small green hills. These hills have flowers with the colors of the rainbow everywhere. The flowers lift Emily to the top of the hill bouncing under her bare feet and springing back to their original bright happy form. Emily giggles at the hilltop alive with the flower fun and brightness of the day.

Emily's mother would say, "How lucky you are to have a dream with colors."

"Don't your dreams have colors?"

"I think they're in black and white, kind of like our television."

Chapter 16
Open School Week

Emily had no need for validation from others as her thoughts were occupied with the mysteries of her environment, in particular, nature. There seemed to always be calloused children in all her grades. She knew that she was not as strong as all her classmates and many of the bullies would tease her and call her a "wimp" or a "teacher's pet," as it was obvious Emily enjoyed learning. She tried not to cry, but would break down occasionally while in her sanctuary. She would never tell her mother because she thought she had enough problems working hard as a waitress and being a single parent.

One day after class, Emily asked Miss Mulligan, "Why don't the other children see the beauty of nature that's around them? They make fun of me for enjoying beautiful skies, birds, squirrels and trees."

"Emily, all these children want to impress each other. Being different and unique makes you a target. You enjoy learning about what's around you instead of trying to be with the in crowd. Unfortunately, by going against what the other children think is cool, will probably cause you to be picked on."

Miss Mulligan thought to herself that Emily had an awareness and sensitivity to the nature in her surroundings that were not realized by many children or adults. Emily cherished the beauty of nature.

"Why are they so mean?"

"Remember Emily, they are this way for a reason. Perhaps they can't even understand why they act this way. Bullies need to hurt others in order to feel better about themselves."

"I don't understand; just because I'm not as good as them in sports or as strong, why hurt me?"

"Emily, there are adults that are bullies too. They will pick on a co-worker and laugh at them and bully them as well just for lacking certain skills; when someone hurts them they feel that they should hurt someone else. They could be compensating for shortcomings that you don't know about. Do you understand, Emily?"

"I think so, a little bit."

"I will speak to some of the girls if you would like."

"No, that would make them madder and they'll say that I'm a tattletale."

"I know I've suggested this before; maybe it would be good to put it on the record."

"I think I'll just try to avoid them."

Emily's mother had arrived for open school week. Miss Mulligan looked at the woman's face and saw brightness behind a remarkable shade of turquoise colored eyes.

"I've seen those eyes before. You're Emily's mother," said Miss Mulligan as she extended her hand. Cathy Westwood smiled. "I'm guessing your husband works nights and couldn't make it to open school week. I know Wednesday evenings is not always good for parents."

"Emily's father left me when he found out I was pregnant." Mrs. Westwood was not at all upset with the question as she felt a kindness from Emily's teacher and Emily had spoken very highly of her.

"I'm sorry, I didn't know."

"How could you."

"You should be very proud, Mrs. Westwood. Emily has a great curiosity as her questions dig deep; this opens paths to new thoughts and ideas. Unfortunately, some of the students inhibit her from expressing herself in class. They take advantage of her frailty and intimidate her."

104

"I know that Emily speaks to you after class and I appreciate that you're taking the extra time with her. I work most of the week full time, but thankfully her grandmother is near and can watch her most of the time."

"Emily will ask a question often and some are very difficult to answer. My answers usually will bring Emily to another question. She does not accept boundaries as she will continue to probe. I have never had a student like Emily before. Although her classmates are very tough on her, somehow she rises above them. I wish I could have a daughter like her one day. Many of her fellow students bully her. When she asks a question in class, they will call her "Professor Emily" and start laughing. This has caused her to retreat and save her questions for me after class. Emily has a very precocious mind."

"What do you mean precocious?"

"She is unusually advanced for her age, far ahead of the other children in her thought processes. Emily, being so delicate physically, combined with her fellow students' difficulty in understanding her, makes yet another reason for her to be targeted by bullies. Mrs. Westwood, is there any way you could afford a private school?"

"I'm a waitress and I'm lucky I can pay the rent." Every penny Cathy Westwood had went to Emily's needs.

Back at home Cathy Westwood had a talk with her daughter. "Emily, why didn't you tell me that the children were unkind to you at school?"

"I'm okay and I didn't want to worry you."

"Miss Mulligan thinks very highly of you and I'm very proud. She knows that you appreciate nature, yet your classmates think that it makes you un-cool and tease you. Emily, I think you and I should go into Manhattan to the Metropolitan Museum of Art."

"We are?"

"Yes, as well as Central Park. Miss Mulligan is sure that you will love it."

"It's okay Mom, I know you have to work."

"Emily, I'm taking off a Saturday and we're going and that's final, okay?" Emily's eyes filled with tears. "I love you, Mom."

Emily's father had just got up one day, left and never returned. Cathy was only six months pregnant at the time; twenty-one years old and without a job. A friend of hers told her about a job at a neighborhood restaurant called "Johns" and she took it. She worked hard as a waitress, vowing she would never let Emily down. Soon after Emily was able to speak, she would ask why her father left. When Emily was a bit older, Cathy would explain, "He just needed to go away, as he never felt well here. We'll pray for him at church."

The people at John's diner became like family to Emily. At times Emily would go there after school when her mother only had one hour left to her shift which, in most cases, ended at 4:00. John, the owner, would see her arrive and say, "Why is it brighter in my restaurant? Did a ball of sunshine just come in?" Emily would sit at a single booth and do her homework and John would always bring her a glass of milk and a freshly baked chocolate cupcake. "Little girls need lots of milk to get big and strong," he would say.

Cathy's friend Carolyn, also a waitress, would always have a little present to give to Emily. Amazingly, Carolyn made Emily a bird from the paper placemat on the diner table. Emily laughed and thanked her.

Cathy has a bank account for Emily's future education. Any possible extra shifts at the restaurant she viewed as Emily's future. Emily would not be denied her chance in life. Cathy was still attractive, just older looking than her years. Lines weathered her face, thus it bore the stigmatization of hard times. Worry was responsible for most of her lines and long working hours were responsible for the hardness of her beauty; still her kind smile warmed her.

On other days, Emily went straight to the supermarket from school to pick up milk, eggs and cereal. Her mother would be a little late, as she would stop to give soup and bread to the homeless shelter from the restaurant. Cathy was tired as her shift started at 6:00 in the morning for breakfast, yet she knew how important her trips to the shelter were. There was a strength to Cathy's beauty. Her turquoise eyes were bright and smiling set over full cheeks and under blazing red hair. She still attracted a lot of attention from customers at the diner. She always kept a distance that she balanced with smiles and humor as her job was important and her experience with Anthony was not completely forgotten.

Trusting, popular and pretty, Cathy became a victim of her youth and beauty by a selfish man whose lies brought her to his bed. Emily's father Anthony had dark, black, curly hair, long eye lashes and green eyes. There was not a girl in the neighborhood that didn't fall for him. Anthony eventually left them all, including Emily's mother. Although he abused Cathy, she still felt intimidated and fearful when she was alone, even though it was mixed with feelings of relief. Were it not for Emily, she would have remained bitter after being deserted and left to this difficult life. As Emily grew, Cathy realized that she was a lucky woman and Emily was the best part of her heart. Cathy used her anger towards her husband's desertion to hide her fear of being alone. As her love for Emily grew, her anger dissipated, and her courage as a single mom was fed by this love. Cathy would do whatever it took for Emily to have a successful future, no matter how exhausting waitressing could be. College would be able to help Emily answer all those endless questions that she was always asking.

Emily arrived at the apartment and put down the groceries.

"My, my, such a heavy bag of groceries for a little girl," said Mrs. Kelly, the elder lady who lived across the hall.

Emily smiled, "It's not so bad, Mrs. Kelly." Mrs. Kelly dropped her cane and Emily scooted over and picked it up.

"Thank you, dear. It's my darn arthritis. I'm going to bake you and your mom one of my special peach pies."

"Wow, that's great. Thanks Mrs. Kelly." Emily's mom would say that one taste of Mrs. Kelly's pie and you were transported to a sunny country day.

Emily put the groceries away and began to set the table. She heard the door open and ran to greet her mother. They hugged and kissed and Cathy asked Emily how school was. Emily didn't want to worry her mom about the bullies so she didn't mention any of the incidents.

"We learned about Martin Luther King Day."

"Oh," replied Emily's mother.

Chapter 17
Grandma Grace

"Mom, why is it that a man who spoke about peace and said that everyone should be kind to one another would be killed?" asked Emily. Young Emily's questions were endless. On a clear starry night she asked, "Can the stars fall down?"

"No darling."

"Why?"

"I'm not totally sure, but when it snows, stardust comes down with each flake."

"Can I see it?"

"If you catch a snowflake in your hand and look quickly you might see some of the stars twinkle."

"Mom, why is snow white?"

Emily's questions were endless about all that surrounded her. Though her mother had difficulty keeping up, she tried to do her best.

"Emily, why don't you write down all your questions, and then I'm going to take you to the library. But to answer your first question, Martin Luther King was a special person. Unfortunately, there are people that think violence is the answer when they want things a certain way. Martin Luther King knew his life was threatened, yet he stood up for what he believed in."

As Emily's connection to nature grew stronger, new doors opened. There was much to learn. She felt an oneness and an awareness of nature's harmony. Using her imagination, there were times when she could see miniature creeks and rocky knolls within her apartment complex. At night she would often retreat in her beautiful imaginary lands before falling asleep. In Emily's thoughts, nature's beauty surrounded everything and everybody. All was integrated and everyone was kind and helpful. There were no bullies at all. Emily would fall asleep with a smile.

Since her mother introduced Emily to the neighborhood library, there were new books in the apartment on a constant basis. Usually the books related to nature. Her mother picked up one of the books and started to thumb through it. It told of Carl Linnaeus, an extremely well respected Swedish botanist. This made Cathy happy as Emily would realize her interest in plants and science could turn out to be very important. The other children who made fun of her interests just didn't understand.

"Emily, don't forget these books have due dates."

At times, her mother would have to call to Emily two or three times as she would be so absorbed in her reading. At the library, Emily found an enormous amount of information on nature. She learned that the great conifer forest south of the North Pole produces much of the oxygen that keeps the Earth healthy. Before the rise of the Rocky Mountains, as well as the Swiss Alps, these trees existed; they were thousands of years old. There are pines that are still living that were born before the building of the Pyramids.

Emily learned of the Monkey Puzzle trees, the trees of the forests of Russia, Eastern Europe and all over the world as sanctuaries for precious life. She learned that trees could survive all of Earth's seasons and many trees would store water in their trunks and would help feed dependent forest life. Their lives were in the earth as well as on its surface. Water and minerals from the planet are drawn to their branches where they hold carbon dioxide and breathe out oxygen. These beings were interacting with the sun and the planet's atmosphere through a process called photosynthesis. They absorbed pollution from the atmosphere; they fertilized the earth with their leaves and sheltered many species from harm. Emily continued to learn as much as possible about the largest life forms on our planet.

When Cathy had the breakfast shift on the weekends, Emily's grandmother Grace would pick her up and they would meet Cathy at the coffee shop. Grace Westwood, a widow since Cathy was twelve, tried to help with Emily as often as possible.

Emily took her grandmother's hand and noticed that she was coughing. "Are you okay?"

"Yes, it's these incinerators, darling," she responded, while seeing that the air was being filled with white ash.

"It looks like snowflakes, Granny."

"It's not good; these are polluted flakes that dirty the air and make people cough."

"Is it everywhere in the world?"

"I'm sure there are high levels of particle pollution in many of the cities of the world. Look at the top of the apartment building across from ours. Do you see the ash shooting out from the roof causing the soot showers? The building incinerators burn the garbage and the ash and cinders are released into the atmosphere."

"That doesn't sound good, Grandma."

"Often large fires will send soot storms into the air just as the incinerators do."

"Someone should start to do something about that problem. I don't like it when you cough."

"Your grandfather used to say, 'Tus maith leath na hoibre: A good start is half the work.' This is an old Irish proverb. Your thoughts of solving the problem are a start, as something has to be done to the corruptors of people's lungs. The soot in the air is one of the reasons people have to wash their cars almost every day, but what of their lungs? There must be a better way of disposing garbage. Maybe you'll think of something, Emily."

"Grandma, could you tell me more about Grandpa?"

Ronald Yates

"Your grandfather loved to teach Irish dancing and he really loved to eat, especially my Irish stew. What he loved most was to tell a good story."

"Can you tell me some of the stories, Grandma?"

"One story your grandpa told was of a field of shamrocks where tiny yellow flowers grew that lit each and every clover. There have been many who searched for this meadow as it is said that it would bring great fortune. But in order to discover the fortune, you must run barefoot through the clovers without laughing."

"Well that's not hard."

"Oh, but it is. The shamrocks tickle the toes to an unbelievable degree."

Emily laughed and said, "Tell me the story about the green knight again."

"You certainly love that story, but I think it will scare you."

"No, it won't scare me. I know he's just made of vegetables."

Grandma Grace laughed and said, "Okay, I'll tell it to you this evening, just as long as you don't get scared."

"Why did you and Grandpa come to the United States?" asked Emily.

"We came because of the mighty woman with the torch. One day we'll take a trip to meet her and read a poem."

"What poem?"

"The poem is called 'The New Colossus' which was written by Emma Lazarus."

"What does that mean?"

"When you meet her I'll be able to explain better, but we knew that in the United States there would be opportunity for people to better their lives."

"Mom always says that she could feel Grandfather watching over her. Grandma, how is this possible? Can the past, present and future be in the same room?"

112

Grandma Grace thought, "Such questions; some of these questions are impossible to answer."

Arriving at the coffee shop a bit early Emily's Grandma picked a booth and sat down. Cathy smiled when she saw them and put up ten fingers.

"How does Mommy do it, Grandma?" asked Emily.

"Do what?"

"Find smiles for everyone."

"Emily, when you serve the public you have to realize that they have hard days as well and you must keep your sense of humor."

Cathy kissed them both and they went off to see Emilio the baker. Emilio was immense, a man mountain with a heart just as big. At the bakery they would pick up a large cardboard box filled with Italian bread such as semolina rolls and baguettes for the restaurant. Emily loved the fresh smell and sometimes Emilio would give her a freshly baked chocolate chip cookie. They entered the store and saw Emilio kneading dough with his massive arms. Emilio's large and hearty laugh filled the air with his good nature when he spotted Emily. Emily smiled at him and he melted. He winked and pulled out a big round cookie. Emilio liked to wear a beige cap with grey stripes turned on his head so that the visor would be against the back of his massive neck. Emily smiled and thought that he was wearing his train engineer's hat again. Emilio's voice could be recognized anywhere. The last syllable of each of his sentences seemed to stretch.

"Do I see somebody that would like a cookieeeee? Do I see Emilyyyyyyy?" Looking at Cathy, Emilio said, "You didn't say your sister was coming."

Granny Grace smiled and said, "Flattery will get you nowhere."

"Then how about a fresh semolina bread?" Granny smiled while Cathy and Emily were giggling.

"Emily, it's getting late, we should get going."

"Okay, Mom."

Back at the house as they were getting ready to take Grandma Grace to the bus stop, there was a sudden loud crashing sound and screaming in the building's hallway. Most of the time it would turn out to be disrespectful tenants or teenagers ringing doorbells. Cathy's adrenaline kept her guard up as she peeked into the hallway. There she saw Vinny sprawled against the hallway wall, practically passed out next to a smashed liquor bottle. As the three of them left for the elevator, Vinny's sister was cleaning the broken glass as she apologized when seeing them. On the other side of the long hallway a group of young boys were playing a game called "scully" on the floor with bottle caps. Funny how the building would always become very quiet when Sergeant Rice arrived on a stop-off from his patrol.

While walking to the bus stop, Emily thought that it was amazing how tiny blades of grass, as well as tiny yellow flowers, would find a way through the cracks of the concrete slabs that made up the sidewalk. Their delicacy seemed to actually soften the concrete even though they were tiny presences.

"Emily, what are you investigating?" asked Grandma Grace.

"What's in the cracks."

Cathy, Emily and Grace walked down Crescent Street and Grandma Grace bordered the bus at Broadway. Back at the apartment, the phone rang and Emily picked it up. It was Grandma Grace letting them know that she arrived home safely.

"Mom, Grandma said that she's going to make us one of her special dishes for our next dinner: cabbage with bacon."

Cathy Westwood thought back to her youth, and said, "Good, that was one of my favorites."

Chapter 18
The Metropolitan Museum

Cathy preferred her outings with Emily to be at a movie, as she was on her feet so much, but knew that this was an important outing for Emily, especially after speaking with Miss Mulligan. "Emily," she said, as she bent her loving face down to kiss her, "Are you ready to go to the Metropolitan Museum of Art dear?"

Emily's eyes opened to her brightening room. She thought, "Wow, a day with Mom at the art museum, no bullies today."

"You'll meet many works from famous artists who see and feel as you do."

"What do you mean, Mom?"

"Wait and see."

Emily was breathless with anticipation as she walked up the concrete stairs which led to the entrance of the magnificent building that was the Metropolitan. After walking up another huge staircase they found themselves in the Impressionist section.

"Mom, why are there men in uniforms everywhere?"

"These paintings are very important and valuable and they should not be touched. These men protect the paintings."

Emily, with an extraordinary awareness as well as sensitivity started to take in the paintings. "Every painting is expressing love," thought Emily as she felt the beauty and devotion of each artist. She threw her arms up in the air and started a slow spin.

Ronald Yates

"Emily, what are you doing?" asked her mother.

"Isn't it wonderful, Mom? I'm surrounded by love and beauty."

Cathy smiled, knowing what a sensitive and intelligent audience Emily would be. "I knew you would enjoy the Met, as did Miss Mulligan."

Emily spun towards her mother and fell into her arms saying, "Thank you."

Beauty was everywhere in these paintings. The artists that were capturing special moments in nature were Emily's favorites. The importance of nature to all of these artists made her know that she was not alone. To many of the artists, trees were an important focus within their work. She watched trees interact with breezes in a painting by Camille Corot. In 1871, the French painter created an oil on canvas called "A Woman Gathering Faggots at Vielle/D'Avray." The breezes were apparent to Emily as the leaves were swirling in a lovely woodland area. Upon reading notes about the artist, she discovered that even in 1871 Corot felt the effects of industrialization and feared a loss of the beauty of the trees to the countryside of France.

Emily saw a painting by a Belgium artist, Simon Denis, called "Study of Clouds," which put her in a temporary spell. There were many European paintings which Emily found out were called Masterpieces. Camille Pissarro captured the beauty of chestnut trees in his painting "The Garden of the Teulberries on a Winter Afternoon." Many of the painters and photographers found the Bodmer Oak an excellent subject. Claude Monet painted a section of a forest highlighting this tree. The painting was called "Bodmer Oak, Fountainebleau Forest." Emily thought how lovely it would be to enter these woods and did so in her imagination.

In the future, she would revisit these paintings often as they affected her deeply. A particular painting called "The Four Trees," by Claude Monet, painted in 1891 puzzled Emily with its meaning and beauty. In the background of the

116

painting there were vague ethereal trees seemingly composed of the haze of the sun. Her future considerations of this painting would bring many questions.

"Why were they in an order, perhaps in size place," Emily thought. "The Four Trees," with their mirror image in the water brought her much contemplation. "Where were the tops of the trees? Were they hidden in mystery? Which were the real trees to Monet? The watery reflection of the four trees was seemingly more substantial than even the structure of the background trees composed of the haze."

In her studies of the painting, Emily felt Monet was showing more dimensions to the trees or perhaps to reality itself. In the water a mirror image is seen showing the physicality of the trees which is the form they present in the natural or physical world. The fluidity of the water in the mirror image could be showing the beauty of the spirit of their natural form. In the water the fluidity will always return with the rain. Is the truth of the appearance of the natural world more valid in the reflection of their beauty? Is the reflection showing the transient or perhaps the divinity of who they really are? Was Monet challenging the physical form? Is what the viewer is seeing an interpretation of the physical as being the intelligent energy that makes up everything? More than the beauty of the trees and water, the painting was an interpretation of life's compositions.

Emily thought that the painting showed life relative to time represented by the river's liquid. The different lights in the painting perhaps exposed truths in reality's appearance through the water's reflections. Can time be touched? Is it tangible in the reflection? Lift the water in your hands and it runs back into the river and the reflection stays. How deep did Monet's mind go? Was his stream of consciousness ongoing as was the river's flow: The water of time? Is time ongoing into the depths of forever as does the poetry in Monet's painting? There is no finish line to eternity.

Emily's thoughts would coalesce over time when considering this painting. In the future, it would occur to her that Monet had consciously or subconsciously entered the world of quantum physics. The feature of the trees, the lilies, the grass, and the bushes formed a reality which was in a changing state before our eyes. There is a math in the spacing of the four trees and their posture.

Which were real, and is there more beyond the reflection? In Monet's painting "Ice Flows," painted in 1893, the reflection of the trees seem to be more alive than the trees themselves. Is there more beyond the trees made of reflection; beauty's source? Could the reflection itself be a symbol of the spirit? Emily thought that the artist was acknowledging not only the physical, but the spiritual, as the painting's observer becomes aware of intuitive feelings. These feelings are real and takes us to life's other dimensions. She found that Monet, as well as many of the other artist's paintings not only captured nature but its spirit as well.

Emily was not alone as these artists felt the same aliveness of the trees as she did. She also learned that most of these artists wrote poetry as well. Much poetry could be found in some of the artist's sketch books. Paintings are poetry and poetry is painting. Both depend on knowledge from deep inspirational sources. She thought to herself that she also writes poems at times. In the future, perhaps the great statesmen will be artists and poets. They appreciate the importance of nature. A poet as President would realize that the Earth sustains us, and not only physically. This President would emphasize our important connections to nature and would know the spirit of the land.

Emily became enormously excited when she came upon T.H. Rousseau's painting called "The Edge of the Woods at Monts-Girard, Fontainebleau." Reading the panel describing the painting, she was amazed at the subject matter. This man, a century before she was born, was protesting the destruction of ancient trees. According to the museum notes, Rousseau bitterly opposed the harvesting of these trees. The open space in the painting is the edge of the area of the ancient woods that were threatened with further cutting.

In 1881, a Frenchman named George Seurat painted "The Forest at Pontaubert." This painting showed an integration of the oneness of the forest as it encompassed the air itself.

Emily's mother interrupted her saying that she was getting tired. "We can come back another time."

Just then a security guard seeing Emily's enjoyment said, "There are more paintings of nature in the American Landscape section."

"Oh Mom, let's go. How do we get there, sir?" asked an excited Emily.

"Aren't you tired yet, darling?" asked Cathy as she looked around for a place to sit.

"There are seats in the Landscape area," said the security guard. Cathy thought to herself, "How nice of him to notice that she was ready to collapse from exhaustion."

Emily loved the large size of the paintings in the American Landscape section. The "Heart of the Andes," sold for the highest price ever paid to an American landscape artist in 1859. The painter was Frederic Church, a painter from Connecticut who wanted to bring out a spiritual dimension he felt through nature. The painting had beautiful large trees to the right and in front of a large mountain overlooking the water. Its large size amazed Emily. The landscape painting that affected her most was titled, "Pine Grove of the Barberini Villa," by the artist George Inness painted in 1876. There was a dream-like presence to the painting as it appeared that the trees were marching towards the viewer with a sense of purpose.

"Okay, Emily, you might not be tired and hungry, but I am," said her mother.

"I could make you spaghetti when we get home."

Ronald Yates

Cathy smiled and thought to herself, "She's never seen Emily so happy."

Once home, Emily tried to recapture all the visual experiences from the Met. These painters were much like her, cherishing beautiful events in nature; visual poems they were. This museum was a home for treasures in time.

Chapter 19
Dreams After the Met

From the top of the hill Emily could see the beautiful city and its surroundings. Meadows were alive with violet wild flowers and the magnificent stone buildings were a natural balance with the beauty of the outlining trees and gardens. The sun bathed everything with a golden radiant light. Bountiful berries and other types of fruits bright with color were everywhere, highlighting the city's aura of happiness. As Emily continued looking down from the top of the hill, she thought to herself that the city must be ancient. Weeds and flowers found their way between the weathered paths of stone that were navigating around the trees, buildings and gardens. The people were lovely looking with a healthy glow.

"Mom, I had my dream again, and this time I saw a beautiful city from the top of the hill filled with happy people."

"It sounds lovely, Emily, but you should get dressed or we'll be late to meet Grandma."

The next night the dream came again to Emily. She bounded easily up small rolling hills of bright green with resilient and brilliant rainbow colored wild flowers. The flowers seemed enchanted by the sun as each was surrounded by a brightness that highlighted their color. Each halo of brightness merged in the radiance of the entire flower fields. Smiling, she kept bouncing higher and easily made it to the top of the largest hill. She looked to the other side expecting more wonderful flowers. They were there lining a brook that ran down the hill all the way to the city. She could not stop smiling. This time the city appeared to be surrounded by

Ronald Yates

a very bright blue narrow river with an equally bright blue aqueduct running through the center of the city. The fruits on the trees were like none she had ever seen, due to their extraordinary large size and varied colors.

The people seemed to float about the city as if on some sort of cushion of air, with no aid from the bouncing flowers. This time the city's buildings seemed to be composed of some sort of translucent crystal-like material; a sort of white silver in coloration rather than stone. Each building could be a sculpture in perfect balance with the large trees. As Emily continued to gaze out at the city, her eyes were greeted with many lovely fountains with crystalline reflections in their light and elegant sprays. Emily thought to herself that only an architect of unusual creative ability and awareness of functional harmony could have designed such a city. "How do I think in these advanced terms?" Emily heard herself say during the dream.

After relaying the dream to her mother, Cathy responded, "What an imagination. You probably created this lovely city from experiencing all the paintings you saw at the Met." Emily's mother thought to herself that the people and city in Emily's dream were perfect; all is gentle and there is harmony. Is it just a creation of Emily's kind imagination or is it a real geographical location? Perhaps she saw pictures in the library of this city as it is so very clear to her.

Cathy, glancing outside through the windows of the room, noticed that the colors of the trees were marking time's forward walk. The tips of the leaves were beginning to show shades of brown, orange and red. The trees were stunning in their autumn designs but would eventually stand naked. They would drop their autumn gowns and leave them to energize the Earth.

Chapter 20
Autumn

Across the playground, Emily saw that the windless bench was empty. Behind it the curtain's core was almost totally revealed by autumn to be a labyrinth of branches. Seeing birds fly through the curtain would continually amaze her. The speed in which they navigated the intricate passageways was incredible.

Sitting on the windless bench, Emily took in the beauty of the trees that were surrounding the playground. Most of the leaves were a gold color that was sparkling bright in the sun. The paths of the complex sparkled with gold as well, due to the many fallen leaves. She thought smiling, "I'm rich as I am totally surrounded by gold." She recalled a lesson in school that spoke of certain explorers such as Cortes, who searched for cities that were said to be rich with gold. At about the same time, roughly the year 1530, the President of New Spain had heard tales of cities with streets that were paved with gold. Perhaps it was the gold leaves of autumn.

Tippity-tap was the sound of the small group of leaves that brushed the asphalt. Autumn leaves were happily surrendering to the season and were enjoying their wind rides, flaunting their colors as they eventually made it to the ground. Emily thought it was a sort of autumn snow fall. Unfortunately, there was a poverty of grass fields and trees in most of the city, yet still the leaves' mission to fertilize a new territory would continue.

The light winds of October would cause the leaves to swirl within with dizzying spins to the ground as they could no longer cling to their home branches. Emily smiled as one chocolate leaf, upon landing to the ground turned out not to be a leaf at all, but a small sparrow. She was fooled many times by the autumn leaves and sparrows impersonating each other. Walking slowly around the grounds of the apartment complex, she would spot many different small birds. A chubby finch jumped from a patch of tall grass briefly revealing splashes of yellow on its chest. The bird would not stay in one spot long enough to see all of its colors, but Emily thought that she saw a flash of crimson. She heard a pecking sound and when she looked up was greeted by a dark bird with a red head pecking the side of one of the branches.

Sitting on a bench by herself in front of a medium sized crab apple tree, Emily heard a sound. Turning around and looking deeply into the trees' complex maze, a branch configuration, she spotted a lime green bird enjoying some autumn sunshine. A strong wind helped many of the trees continue to disrobe revealing the beauty of the poetic poses of their bodies. There were so many leaves swirling in the breezes that Emily thought it was like a snowfall of many colors.

Emily decided to gather some of the different falling leaves and study them in her sanctuary where there were no threats from bullies. Examining the leaves she was amazed by the variety of color and size. Suddenly her concentration was broken as she heard a lady shriek at the windless bench. The lady's friend started laughing as it turned out to be a squirrel that seemed to be enjoying the crinkly sound of the ripe fallen foliage. Focusing back on the leaves, Emily was able to recognize the different shapes from her library studies. A maple leaf with green veins and chocolate burgundy tones seemed jagged compared to a leaf that was peach in color. She suddenly sat straight up as she heard a stirring inside of her bower. An unusual sparrow, with raccoon-type circles around his eyes, with a lime colored chest, looked directly at her. Emily giggled as the sparrow found a crack in the roof and popped out.

While continuing to examine the leaves in her bower, Emily's thoughts went back to school. Mary Ellen and her group of girls would even affect lunch time at the school. Many of the students were afraid to walk in certain areas of the cafeteria. It was not only Emily that was bullied; many of the other children's movements at times were tied down by cords of fear.

A sound like intense crying distracted Emily from continuing to examine her fallen leaves. She crouched and waddled lightly to the edge of her enclosure. Lifting a large leaf, she was able to see the person sobbing on the long windless bench across from the playground. It was Mary Ellen! The bullies looked so big and frightening whenever they approached her in a group. Recently, while crossing the street from the supermarket, Emily spotted them on the far corner and they were heading her way. It was too late to run. "Hey Emily, we need some candy money." Emily handed over the change from the supermarket. Maybe these bullies did her a favor as she was closer than ever to nature's world. Mean girls like Mary Ellen brought her to this sanctuary of nature.

Mary Ellen did not look as scary as usual. Maybe it was her crying. Emily remembered her last conversation with Miss Mulligan. She lightly lifted the cascading branch of her sanctuary and walked towards Mary Ellen. Mary Ellen's head was down, hiding in her arms and she was still sobbing. Emily surprised Mary Ellen when she touched her shoulder softly. Mary Ellen looked up at Emily with her bruised face and said, "What do you want, twerp?"

"What is it?" asked Emily.

"Why would you care? Maybe I'll just kill myself."

"I do care. Whatever it is can't be that bad."

"No one can help me. My parents beat me every day, and I heard them say that they were sorry they ever had a child," continued Mary Ellen sobbing.

Emily thought that while Mary Ellen had tormented her as well as other children, ironically, while at her home, she was the one being abused.

"Your friends like you," said Emily.

"Not really. They're just scared of me."

"Why don't you come with me to my house for lunch, Mary Ellen? My Mom makes the best tuna sandwiches."

"I love tuna sandwiches. You would do that for me after I've been so mean to you?"

Emily opened her arms and Mary Ellen dropped her head on her shoulder. Crying, she said, "I'm so sorry, Emily."

"Come on, Mary Ellen," and they slid off the bench and walked around the playground toward Emily's lobby.

Chapter 21
Lincoln Center

"If this stack of bills gets any higher it might hit the ceiling," said Cathy Westwood.

"Will we be okay, Mom?"

"We'll manage darling, but I may have to work a couple of extra weekends at the diner. Guess what, Emily? I won't be working next Saturday as we'll be going to a place called Lincoln Center. A good customer of mine gave me two tickets for a Saturday night concert as he was called away on business. Emily, do you think you could stay up until 10:00 or 11:00 PM?"

"Of course Mom; but if it's at night, why are you taking a day off?"

"Emily, do you think you would enjoy visiting Central Park before we go to Lincoln Center?" said Cathy smiling. Emily remembered the huge park surrounding the Met and ran into her mother's arms.

Emily held the handrail of the subway stairs tightly at Astoria's Broadway station. The many steel beams were tall at this elevated subway. Her walk was tentative along the subway's platform even though it was not her first train ride. Emily wondered if she would ever become comfortable taking the subway.

"It's okay, people ride these subways every day," said her Mother.

Through dark tunnels with rolling steely thunder sounds the subway arrived at the Fifth Avenue station. Nearing the top of the subway stairs Emily heard bird songs and soon before her eyes there was a beautiful promenade called Fifth Avenue that seemed to stretch forever along the magnificent park. Compared to her neighborhood's tiny areas of grass and trees, Central Park's large landscape filled Emily with excitement. It didn't matter whether the trees were large or small; they all maintained their own unique beauty and grace. The elm trees of Literary Walk brought Emily to a brief standstill. She took a deep breath and said, "Wow."

"Pretty, isn't it?" her mother said smiling as she saw her daughter's happy expression.

Walking down the path surrounded by the magnificent elms, Emily asked, "Mom, is this what heaven looks like?"

"Emily, I knew you would love it here."

The magnificent elms with their dark boughs intersecting and reaching for the sky had Emily amazed. Their power as well as their beauty and sensitivity were very special and Emily marveled at the gracefulness of these beings. The grass with its lemony green tones was lively with the breeze as the blades danced for the sun. The tree branches with their leaves orchestrated light shows in their collaboration with the breezes. Alternating rays of sun highlighted all the color tones of the lawn's cast. A new day, a new sky, rain, snow: The show was always original. These rhythms of nature's happiness coursed through and about Emily as she absorbed everything. Even the ripples and the richness of the deep red, brown and black tones that were the bark of the surrounding trees did not elude her.

Later that night before going to sleep, Emily would remember to thank God for Central Park. After her outing at the park she knew she must visit as many of the wild woodlands as possible and meet all they had to offer; but now it was time to experience Lincoln Center.

Emily closed her eyes; soft notes fell gently around her and then seemed to rise and travel delightfully over blue lakes. She opened her eyes and saw in front of her the New York Philharmonic Orchestra. Listening to Shubert's "Unfinished 1822 Symphony," she felt the beauty that was within Avery Fisher Hall. The music seemed to take her everywhere, riding above oceans, penetrating unimagined doors that led to wonderful thoughts. Emily turned to her mother and smiled.

After leaving Lincoln Center, Emily and her mother walked adjacent to the park on their way to 57th Street so they could take the subway back to Queens. Emily noticed the evening light darker now giving home to darker shadows. She saw a young man lying on a burly bag with some newspapers streaking out of his shirt. "Mom, his clothes are all torn and there are holes in his shoes."

A dim moon added an eerie light to all of the surroundings. Emily held her mother's hand more tightly. "Does anybody wonder who he is? Perhaps he lost his family and friends. Is he lonely? How does he live?" she asked her mother.

"He asks for money in the street."

"Was he always this poor?"

"It's hard to say, dear. Let's hope he finds a happy path."

"Why doesn't this man sleep at home?"

"He has no home; the park bench is his bed."

"Doesn't anybody wonder who he is?"

"I wish I could answer all your questions."

Emily noticed the night sky as she walked down the subway steps in Queens.

"Mom, why doesn't anybody stop and look up at the stars? It's such a beautiful roof."

"People are afraid in the cities and just want to get home safely."

At that point, Emily remembered the two men who were following her when she went to buy her mother chocolates for her birthday. Then she understood what her mother was saying. Cathy went on to say, "People are afraid to come back out and take their cities back. Unfortunately, at night the people are not comfortable."

Emily thought back to the bullies that were around during the day and understood people's fear. Ironically, they were just halfway down the block from the subway when three large nasty looking teenagers surrounded Emily and her mother. As they circled them laughing, they asked if they had anything for them.

"Please leave us alone," Emily said as she was clinging to her mother's raincoat.

"Oh, poor little girl, we just need some money," said the taller of the three teenagers. All of a sudden two of the delinquents were six inches off the ground as an enormous man lifted them up by their collars. It was Emilio.

"Please let us go. We didn't mean anything," said one of the teenagers as he was dangling in the air while watching the taller boy run away.

Emily was lying in bed trying to stay awake as she thought of her wonderful day's experience. She thought back to the power and excitement of Manhattan; the beauty of the park and the glorious symphony. Her eyes began to close as sleep's grasp was too strong to resist. She went to sleep hearing echoes of string instruments. Cathy looked in on Emily as she slept and saw a smile on her face. "It has to be her hilltop dream," she thought to herself. Cathy sat softly on the side of the bed and knelt towards her and kissed her child's cheek; a kiss known only to mothers and angels.

The tree on top of the hill somehow had a calming character. The large lower branch extended a welcome as Emily moved closer. Reaching out to the warm, rich caramel trunk, she let her fingers feel the ripples in its bark. She noticed movement behind the tree. Stepping further down to the other side of the hill she parted some large ferns. The air was very fresh with scents of evergreen and wild flowers. Beyond the hilltop and down the long slope of bright grass there stood an incredible beauty; a city within forest and gardens. Crystal buildings, shaped in large ovals and connecting geometric shapes flowed as architectural beauty.

Each building was a unique sculpture that complemented the poetry of the magnificent trees and gardens; all part of each other, all balanced.

There were children enjoying beautiful parks and colorful playgrounds. People appeared kind and smiling as their movement seemed to be floating on air. "Where am I? What is this special place? Is there a map? Is it a secret location?" These were questions that Emily heard herself thinking in her dream.

The next day from her sanctuary Emily peeked at the lawn and saw each blade of grass move in unison with the breeze. Up and down, just like the bows of the violin at the symphony, her mind shifted to the buildings of Manhattan, "These partition blocks of buildings with cement boundaries are structures containing many layers of people." Emily noticed that most of the windows had a view of another building across the way. It was not balanced with the beauty of nature. "In my dream the people did not have to search for a sectioned land called a 'park.'"

In the solitude of her sanctuary, Emily heard a familiar whistle rustling through the leaves. It sounded once again like music of the winds, and Emily thought that it must be her imagination playing tricks on her. The winds continued to whisper within the leaves; the sound repeated, music swish, the winds swish. Even while walking in Central Park with her mother the sound occurred.

"Did you hear that, Mom?"

"Hear what?"

"Like a voice from the wind going through the leaves."

"Emily, I wish I had your imagination."

It was starting to sound clearer to her now and at times she heard a different sentence. It sounded like, "Send the ants, Emily." In time the sound was clearer and she realized the word was "sentience." Emily vowed to go to a dictionary or speak to her teacher. "Was it a word?" Emily would ask her teacher. She would not say how she heard it as she didn't want her mother called into the school. Her ears alert and straining, the words became clearer especially within her sanctuary. Could her mind be so foreign that only she could hear these voices in the wind while she would spend her days marveling at nature's beauty? Emily decided to write some thoughts about the wind in her notebook:

"Does it have memories of travel?
Does it only know the moment?
Does it have something to reveal?
Does it speak within the trees?"

Emily made a holiday tree collecting some falling branches and arranging them in a large jar. She adorned the branches with ribbons. Drawing a tree on a large piece of oak tag, she scotch taped some fallen leaves to her creation.

"What lovely trees you make, Emily. Since we have each other why not bring one to our neighbor, Mrs. O'Reilly? You know how much she likes them," said Cathy.

Throughout the year, Emily would always come home with a fallen leaf or a sprig from a pine tree and carefully study them. Many were the time Cathy would see her daughter staring at a leaf for over ten minutes as if she were in a trance.

"Emily, what are you doing?"

"Just studying this leaf and investigating its construction."

Her mother almost sensed an exchange between the leaf and her daughter as her focus was so intense.

"It's not talking to you, is it honey?" her mother asked smiling.

"Very funny, Mom."

Chapter 22
Lost Branches

Emily loved the new adventures that came with the new seasons; always surprised by what nature would reveal. The changing skies would affect the lighting everywhere. She especially loved the days that the snow would fall silently elegant, softly and undisturbed by even a breeze. She would catch a snowflake and while watching it dissipate a song from the second grade came to mind: "Catch a falling star and put it in your pocket never let it fade away." Emily smiled as she remembered Grandma Grace saying, "Starlight is captured by the cold then tumbles to Earth in snowflakes." Emily was chilly but she felt a vibrant happiness to the winter day. Most of the branches were now totally bare, with the soft whitish light of winter brushing their branches and becoming part of their beauty. She noticed that some of the leaves were refusing to fall and they remained ornaments for the beauty of the nakedness of the trees.

The few leaves that were left were mostly a bronze gold in color, quivering while clinging to a few branches. A late December wind whirled under a large tree bringing leaves twirling high among the branches with the bright sun reflecting their remaining gold hues. Emily momentarily thought them to be a group of butterflies, and then quickly realized that they were stubborn autumn leaves. The leaves did seem alive as they fluttered their beauty within the frosty and sunny breeze. Emily thought that the grace of the tree doesn't fade in the winter, it becomes a new poem as the leaves fall away revealing a different type of elegance. The ballet poses of their bodies were revealed in the beauty of their shadows as well. She smiled and thought, "Beauty in a dark reflection was being brought by the light of the sun."

It turned out to be a very cold and snowy winter in New York. A January blizzard would turn the apartment complex lawns into carpets of snow. Emily thought it appeared surreal and another one of nature's spells: A terrain belonging to a fantasy. Sections of the lawns were encompassed by clear ice drifts. The sun's reflection would play with the prism of colors that the ice crystal revealed. The ice captured small seas of blue-green grass that appeared as waves frozen in time. She looked up at the sky and saw thick white clouds moving in the blue that considered adding more snow. The trees appeared more elegant than ever as the white of nature adorned their ballet-posed bodies. She would look around imagining tiny landscapes. Water that was dribbling lazily from a snow mound would become a mountain brook. The winds, getting restless, would send small twigs into these brooks and she would imagine that they were bridges. The brooks would then meet small meadows within strange prairies of snow.

To Emily, the housing grounds became a new world. The center lawn appeared as a snow prairie with patches of grass showing in fractal type patterns. She imagined these patches as tiny islands in the carpet of white. It reminded her of a painting she saw at the Met. There were lily pads appearing as lovely islands in the blue water. The sun illuminated the trees whose forms were now outlined with ice and snow. As Emily looked at their poses of an icy elegance she thought they appeared as trees from another world. One tree top had twin branches with lovely ramification extending past the twelfth floor towards the sky. Although the tree was totally barren of all leaves it still softened the adjacent brick structure. The sun found and filled most of the inter-branch space with brilliant gold. She thought there was no end to the seasonal presentations of the beauty of these magnificent beings.

Nature's poetry bewitched Emily. There was so much snowfall this winter that she started to think the lawns would forever stay white. Strong winter winds would prune many branches from the large trees. She couldn't help but stare at one particular long, thin-forked branch lying in the center of the white within the large lawn. She saw many different shaped branches spaced apart appearing lost and lonely on the white, yet lovely in their shapes and in their softness lying on the snow.

Emily was happy to realize that when she read about trees in the library, they were the largest and longest living beings on Earth. Down deep her intuition told her that important answers would eventually come after studying these proud and powerful beings. A strong wind sent a squirrel scrambling to the shelter of its nest in between some strong branches. Night's curtain was starting to come down; she thought it was time to return to her apartment. She walked briskly, noticing the still appearance of unusual gray shadows. She looked up and saw a misty crescent moon.

That night Emily dreamt about the magnificent trees in a city of crystal structures. These structures had translucent coral colors with soft blues, yellows and oranges which were outlined with silver and white. Although differing in size, they were in perfect balance and scale which complemented the beauty of the landscape. These buildings actually reflected the light of day, softly bouncing rays against the trees which were holding their rainbow of colored fruits. The lighting which reflected from the buildings seemed to have a nourishing effect on the trees and gardens of the city. Emily felt transformed by the spectacular beauty of the city that was so compatible with its surroundings. "Why couldn't all cities be in balance with nature? Surely there are builders sensitive to the beauty and importance that is the nature of our planet," she thought. Once again, as in her past dreams, the people all seemed happy as they actually floated among the city of crystal buildings.

As Emily continued to gaze at the city she spotted a couple of orange colored squirrels in the distance climbing up one of the enormous trees. These trees lined a silvery river that formed an enormous avenue in the center of the city. The beautifully sculptured buildings easily became part of the symmetry of life in this city of symbiosis.

Chapter 23
The Gardens

The return of spring brought several of Emily's favorite outings. Dewy grass scented the silence of their first early morning arrival at the New York Botanical Gardens. Rainy sunbeams seemed still within a morning mist. It was as if a pause button was pressed and affected time in the morning's presentation.

Emily saw the trees spreading their branches wide, stretching for more sun. After releasing the water's weight the clouds had carried the night before, only light streaks of white remained within the pastel. She could feel the love in the breezes that were carrying the nascence of buds filling the branches everywhere. Swirly breezes caused flowers to dance. It was easy for Emily to see that the poetic poses of surrounding tree branches were in accordance with their shining guide. Cathy looked down at her daughter and saw such brightness in her eyes that it made her smile.

"Mom, it's so wonderful here, we can touch spring."

Emily was sensitive at an early age about the wonders of nature and its creation. Emily would wonder, "Where could such a varied array of beauty come from?"

"Mom, where does this beauty come from?"

"The Earth, Emily."

"The planet?"

"Well, yes, the planet."

"Where does the planet come from?"

"God, he made the world."

"Has he made other worlds?"

"All I can say, darling, is that he is the intelligence behind the whole universe."

Ronald Yates

They turned right between two large red oaks and soon found themselves in front of the Perennial Garden. It was beautiful. Flower tops were gently unfolding for the morning. The colors of April's rain would soon be revealed. Sun sparkled through the droplets of dew that lingered on the opening precious, and gave the area a special radiance. Emily thought that she was walking through an enchanted garden. She thought that this area of riches should be cherished. She knelt down to caress the petal of a flower; it seemed to glow while channeling a sunbeam.

Unexpectantly, a dazzling flash of lime-green with a bright orange stripe buzzed by the flower Emily was captured by. Just as suddenly, it returned, paused for a second, and then zipped away. She overheard two elderly ladies saying with disbelief that they had been coming to the Gardens for ten years and it's the first time that they have ever seen a hummingbird. They went on to say that they were supposed to be most easily spotted in the month of September.

"How wonderful," Emily thought, realizing how lucky she was to see the tiny bird upon overhearing the ladies' conversation.

A zephyr was momentarily sweetened by cherry blossoms as it captured and lifted them from their tree. The graceful visits from the breeze were brief. Most of the blossoms' journey ended up in the grass near Emily, though some of the petals found her hair. All of the scents of stored beauty were being released. Nature's renaissance had filled the air.

"Mom, this area is so happy."

"What do you mean?"

"Look at all the flowers. I love it here."

"I can see that; maybe one day you could work here."

"To be here every day, through every season, wouldn't that be wonderful?"

Emily felt everything she saw. Each trip to the Gardens would bring a different experience. She would see the freshness of the rapid waters of the Bronx River from the Hester Bridge. She would learn about the different species of plants at the Haupt Conservatory. She would marvel at the beauty of the pines along Lily Way with their cone jewelry, which was first blue then turned caramel colored.

Looking up from the flowers at the Perennial Garden, Emily's eyes were drawn to a tree that had a special character. It was located in the center of the garden area. The tree had a power containing an unusual combination of elegance and wildness. It appeared to be part wind as its foliage seemed swept up through its crown in a heavenly reach. She walked up to the tree and read that it was called a Pinus Strobus. She would see this tree's beauty survive and thrive through all the seasons.

They decided to stop for a snack at the garden café. To the path's right, Emily spotted a familiar tree and smiled; a large Ozark Witch Hazel. Choosing a table that was outside, Emily heard some of spring's voices. Turning left, she spotted a couple of banana-yellow colored birds picking up some leftover crumbs on a nearby table. They quickly disappeared within a richly colored emerald dark pine. It happened so quickly that her mother had missed the whole thing. Coming back from the cafeteria with a full tray, she said to Emily, "Sorry I missed it, but I was concentrating on balancing the tray."

The sky's pastel colors made the rain in the sun shower seem blue, causing an enchanting atmosphere at the Gardens. Emily thought that perhaps Galileo felt this same rain, or perhaps Plato drank it from his fountain. She learned, during one of her library visits, that the rains of the Earth's past return due to evaporation. She caught a few of the drops in her hand and thought, "I hold the past and the future in my hand. Time itself has been captured in raindrops."

"Emily, we should go now."

"Must we?"

Her mother smiled, "We can come back you know; we are a bit wet. Next time, perhaps we'll visit the Rock Garden. A nice man at the gift shop told me that it was his favorite part of the Gardens."

Walking down the Garden Way path toward the train, Emily looked in the direction of the Mertz Library and thought, "Perhaps I can study there one day." Looking at the large tulip trees that lined the path to the library, she could feel their power.

"Those trees are really something. Aren't they beautiful, Mom?"

"You know what, they really are beautiful, and you know what else is really something?"

"What, Mom?"

"You, darling." Emily giggled.

Chapter 24
Children

It is the children who in the end must pay the bill as the planet's land and resources are raped. Fred F. Barry knew how to manipulate people with shiny lights and glitz appealing to unaware parents. Greed can be a powerful ruler of people's minds. Fred F. Barry had no need for a concept of time because how could time stretch further than his own existence?

The sun's gifts of warmth and kindness to Earth's garden could be turned into a deadly weapon by the Greeds. The sun shines its life-giving rays in innocence, not preparing for the pollution that the Greeds leave that alters its purpose. The Greeds of industry have not just clouded the atmosphere with pollution, but their minds as well. Is there no room left in their hearts for their own offspring?

They are a dangerous group of people who align themselves with indifference to enable them to use the environment for their own causes. They reengineer rivers and wetlands causing the impact of storms to be more severe, as the land can no longer absorb the storm's power.

The songs of the woodland sunrise are brought to a halt by monstrous engines. The Greeds level forest after forest along with its many varieties of plant and flower species, possibly eliminating future cures for their own health and life span. The fruits, berries and barks contain powerful components supplied by these trees. These components are loaded with antioxidant compounds and medicines that are important for the immune system's defenses against many diseases. Tumor growths have been inhibited by antioxidants supplied from these living beings called trees.

These antioxidants have been proven to help our bodies deactivate certain carcinogens which slow cancer cells' reproduction.

There are acid rains that are killing plant and tree species and affecting the population of song birds in the forests. The Greeds surround themselves in superficial luxury and care not that they miss the romance and celebration of the Earth as the song birds disappear; as the habitats disappear so do their life-lifting songs of joy. The leafy, shaded roads that fit within the beautiful surroundings of the rolling green hills and lovely woods are being eliminated. In the future, the children may only be viewing large concrete highways that cut and scar the views of the rolling green. They are unaware that all life is interdependent, that all life benefits from keeping the members of Earth's biodiversity thriving. There are no new ideas for energy found in the banality of thoughts of avarice. Membership in Earth's ecosystems has decreased not voluntarily, but due to extinction as Greeds do not consider their habitats.

Corporate axes continue felling the forest frontiers. If Fred F. Barry had a heart he would notice the lonesome place that is left after he brings down a tree. The masters of greed are absent of real character and morality as they continue to add to their material possessions. They reduce their ethics and stab at beauty's soul. Lacking all judgment for the children's future, their instant gratification is built on a shallowness that holds the stem of their martini glass and ignores the hand of their child. If the Greed's minds were not swirling in the joys of more monies perhaps there would be a place in their thoughts that would see their destruction of Earth's habitats. There could be a beautiful balance accomplished that respected the environment when building new cities. Instead, their canyons of concrete can only be viewed from other large towering steel and concrete structures. The leaders of greed that bully and manipulate Earth's garden in the name of progress and civilization must be stopped. The combined accumulated monies of these masters of greed will not restore our Earth or their souls.

Fred F. Barry and other masters of greed feed the lady in black who paints the brightness of day with large carbon strokes. They are not haunted by the biosphere's tragic death and the lady in black's strength will continue to grow from thoughtless polluters. Smog swollen clouds darken the cities. The lady in black smiles as fresh crystal rivers runs black into the Earth's seas. Greeds, with all their arrogance, continue to turn their heads away from the Earth's pain. They continue to conceal new secrets to feed their greed, as if the planet was here to serve them. They have no thoughts for the unborn; yet all of their money will not be able to turn back the course of time.

Danielle vowed to do everything within her power to keep the environment protected from the Greeds and encourage industries to choose healthier paths. She would write a letter to the press called "Oceans Warning":

"Trumpets from the ocean are coming to the world's shores in waves. They announce a call of warning to take stands against pollutions' armies. Life on land and in the sea, as well as the air, is being destroyed.

The past is always first on the endless line that is time. Our present will soon take the spots at the front of this line. It is up to us to allow those, who are at the end of the line, to attend life's concert. As we all know, the future is always last on this line. It is essential that it holds its place.

We will bend within dark disregard no longer. The road that the human race is taking will lead us to a fall that extends far down. Where is the appreciation of this magical world that we all share? Who is outfitting certain humans with shells of indifference? Is it Fred F. Barry? Who was it that said, 'It's nice to be important, but more important to be nice?'"

Chapter 25
The Professor, Danielle and Emily

Professor Kensington was standing in the area of forest adjacent to the corkscrew branches in Northeast France when he heard astonishing news from his Assistant Danielle Gabay. It seems that a new species from the conifer family was discovered in the Southwest of France, supposedly bearing a special fruit. Conifers have been around for three hundred million years. Their fruit is usually a cone with seeds that resemble a flower. Professor Kensington told Danielle, "It is most likely a rare type of pine, yet some of the descriptions resemble a hawthorne, we must make travel plans."

"I have already booked travel to Toulouse and reserved a car to get us to the outskirts of Castre."

Professor Kensington could not contain his excitement when he arrived in the Southwest of France at the forest outside of Castre. It was in this forest that the new species of tree was found and more amazing was the story of its fruit. The fruit was Named "La Baiser" by the French vineyard worker whose daughter came upon it. The doctor who was treating the worker's daughter for leukemia thought the fruit had come from the Tree of Life as it cured the young girl of her disease.

The officer in charge was quite urbane with a commanding presence. The Professor approached him with his credentials in hand as did Danielle. Being French, Danielle attended many conferences in Toulouse on environmental issues, but was not familiar with all the small neighboring cities and villages. More than once, Danielle was escorted out of business conferences for protesting environmental pollution. At a certain conference one of the executives in charge yelled to Danielle, "Yes, we strip the Earth of the woods, but we do not leave it barren. We build factories, stores and create jobs."

"You can create jobs preserving the environment," Danielle screamed back.

Professor Kensington walked gingerly towards the hill. Doctor Bollard, as well as Henri had spoken to many people. Word was out and it was only a matter of time before the situation would become world news. The area had been cordoned off by at least one hundred gendarmes surrounding the area directly below the hill. Danielle thought it was odd seeing the officers standing erectly with the vineyards behind them. The Professor thought of what these trees could mean to the world of medicine. More than half the planet depends on medicinal plants in some way toward healthcare. It would be logical to preserve all forests, especially since the health of our species depends on them. Powerful cancer drugs have been found in the bark of the Yew tree.

They already have given much to the world: Quinine to treat malaria from the Cinchona tree, fruits to treat scurvy, aspirin and an endless list of bark, root and leaf derived medications, many of which we are still discovering. At times, plant information has come from our ancient ancestors' accounts. We still tamper with ecosystems, fragment habitats, and transform landscapes causing interdependent species to collapse. It is important that any species collected from woodlands be substantially harvested. Professor Kensington, being a doctor, worried every time trees were felled, forests cleared, without investigating all the possible gifts humanity could be destroying. More forest species are continually disappearing every day while botanists and dendrologists haven't even begun to find out what's out there.

Professor Kensington and Danielle were granted access to the forest road but would be escorted by two officers. Professor Kensington turned to Danielle, who recently completed her schooling, and was now a Professor of Dendrology herself. They all walked towards the woodlands entrance as Danielle smiled to the Professor saying, "We'll soon be there."

From the top of the hill you could see the vineyards below the forests. Professor Kensington knew that Danielle loved a good wine. She would say that an aged wine represents drinking history from a glass; the wine having been stored in cellars or caverns for years and then released into the present in someone's wine glass.

"I feel that we will have a good reason to toast this discovery with the best wine in France," Professor Kensington said to Danielle. Danielle immediately thought of one of her favorite wines and said, "If all turns out to be true, then we could toast the discovery with a Cheval Blanc."

The Professor said smiling, "Hopefully."

Danielle thought of mentioning that they can now grow wine grapes in Southern England due to the warmer temperatures caused by climate change, but decided that it was not the right time. It was while studying in California that Danielle was introduced to a very special wine. Attending a lecture on climate change, Danielle remembered that one of the speakers was a physics professor. He was discussing the importance of environmental awareness and its relation to planetary physics; in particular, the Earth's axis. Danielle remembered him saying that we all share the same spinning sphere and we should avoid changing its rotation. She also remembered him saying, "Nuclear plants or explosions on the faults of the planet must be avoided at all costs." It turned out that he sponsored this event and in closing had opened a rare Ausone to the delight of all the guests.

As they continued deeper into the forest the Professor and Danielle exchanged glances; never had they seen such varying shades of deep green and brilliant colored berries. Walking carefully, negotiating the unusually rich growth of the forest, the Professor noticed heavy equipment as they arrived closer to the site. The officer explained the equipment was necessary to clear a path through a dense area of boulders and briars. Now at the site, the Professor immediately saw a difference in these trees. It was as if a ponderosa pine had been shrunk. Although the tree was only about twelve feet tall, its trunk was quite thick. The Professor could see at least twenty-two trees. The bark was pinker than the ponderosa, a tree that is plentiful in the mountains of Western North America.

"This lavender fruit against the deep green bristles is enchanting," said Danielle.

Upon looking closer, the Professor noticed overlapping, compressed scale-type leaves which usually indicated the pine family. There were some tiny white flowers surrounded by soft thorns under each cluster of bristles. "A new species?" he asked himself.

"Perhaps hawthorne/conifer inter-breeding," Danielle said aloud, as if she heard the Professor's thoughts. "These boles have unusual color," she added. "The fruit is not drupe, feel its exterior. Velvety it's not. These fruits are bursting with bioflavonoid, see the depth of color." The Professor, happy with the way Danielle is always analyzing a specimen, thinks that she would become a great dendrologist.

When Danielle entered Professor Kensington's office for the first time, he had not expected such a strong presence. Danielle had long, thick, straight black hair and was a very tall young lady. Only the second apprentice he had taken under his wing; many graduates applied with fine credentials, but none with higher scholastic achievements than Danielle. Rising from his desk he had to look up at Danielle to make eye contact. Dark sensitive eyes, yet happy, "Les yeux qui rieurs," Professor Kensington thought. Her French accent was apparent as she said, "Very happy to meet you." Danielle's resume was quite good, Hebrew University, Harvard undergrad, and some Sorbonne; but it was her excitement that struck him most. When Professor Kensington asked Danielle about the genus populous her reaction was one of disbelief. Danielle thought that the poplar tree, especially the Quaking Aspen most interesting. When in Colorado during a student exchange program at age sixteen she was taken aback when seeing a grove of hundreds of these trees during her visit. Danielle's Professor at the time had explained that these poplar trees were all one single living organism connected by one enormous root system. It was the poplar tree that made her decide dendrology would be her field of study. Her love of trees radiated as she said to Professor Kensington, "I cannot believe that this is the tree you chose to ask me about."

"We have much work to do and much to learn." At that moment, Danielle knew she had gotten her dream apprenticeship.

Professor Kensington thought back to his own youth in England and a smile came to his face. He remembered creating quite a stir at his high school just outside of London. To Tom Kensington trees were an important part of his life; at ten years old they held his first home away from home. He would sit in his tree house, perhaps just studying the components of a leaf, its veins or its texture, while other children were playing games. Tom would gaze out of his tree house and wonder why every tree had a different shape, with branches reaching to the sky at different angles and positions. Later he would learn in school that they were sexually conceived. An ordinary tree did not exist for Tom; they were a giving life form: Cleaning the air, supplying shelter as well as food and medicine to many species of life. He thought early on in life that we are all connected and part of Earth's beauty. Industries' assault on the life of the land must stop now. He also learned that these were the largest beings on the planet. He learned about General Sherman, the largest tree in the world that lived in Sequoia National Park. The General weighed fifteen hundred tons with fifty-five thousand cubic feet in volume. One day he knew he must visit the General and as many of these spectacular beings as possible.

Tom Kensington attended a very strict and upstanding high school where he had caused quite a stir. The incident was an unprecedented protest; the very first tree-in. The school wanted to clear away a huge and beautiful elm to make way for a larger cafeteria. Tom knew he could not sit idly by. He climbed to the top of the tree with a megaphone and refused to come down. The Dean threatened to expel him and it was not long before the newspapers heard what was taking place. Tom thought that someone should shine a light on what trees have to offer, someone has to help these beings. We have a lot to learn from them. Tom Kensington had the courage to take a stand against what he thought was unacceptable.

"We must take action against a growing wave of inconsiderate industrialization," he yelled through his megaphone. "Warning," Tom yelled. "Our planet is in danger because too many people look the other way and nature's destruction continues. Lost time cannot be found."

Although not having many supporters he still knew the justification of his cause to be true and not made false by the lack of numbers. "The future of this planet is in saving the lives of these beings," he yelled from his megaphone from the tree top.

Tom heard the sounds of large machines in the distance. "Perhaps a tractor or bulldozer," he thought. Alone in his protest except for the company of his convictions, Tom's focus and purpose remained strong.

"Trees are the breath of the Earth as they absorb the air's impurities and release fresh oxygen keeping our air pure. When we kill them we are killing ourselves," Tom continued yelling through the megaphone.

The large bulldozer and tractor pulled up and parked close to a growing crowd. The bulldozer's driver moving forward towards the tree yelled, "It's just a tree, you dumbass," as he wedged out a cigar butt on the school lawn with his foot; then spitting, some saliva landing on his chin as he yelled to the young student, "You're wasting everyone's time."

"This tree is alive, a being older than you are."

The driver threw his arms up and gestured obscenely at Tom with an ignorant authority in his eyes. He then yelled with an unsympathetic voice laced with hostility, "We're going to bring down the tree with you in it."

Below the tree, on another part of the lawn, two teachers were talking, "He lives in a state of heterodoxy. Notice he is the only student in the tree impeding progress."

The other teacher responded, "The reason is simply because he wants to be noticed, as how could someone attach that much importance to a tree?"

Tom continued with his megaphone, "Each tree must be preserved when possible as they are a symbol for peace, health and the importance of nature to the planet."

Word spread quickly and soon there were hundreds of students cheering him on. His mother who was always supportive started a petition to save the tree. Finally the school board acquiesced and the cafeteria was extended around the mighty elm. Even today students know and discussed the legend of this tree while having lunch and seeing the elm through the cafeteria's windows. The large elm helped the students as it gave shade for eating and studying on hot, sunny days; its beauty and majesty only grows stronger.

Danielle brought his thoughts back to his London office as she asked, "When do we start?"

"Yes, yes, Danielle. Can you be ready on Tuesday? We will be going to the Greek island of Kos to study the Plane Tree of Hippocrates."

Danielle's face lit up as she said, "I can't wait."

Professor Kensington loved her enthusiasm. He hadn't been so excited about an apprentice since his last and first apprentice, Emily. Danielle was brilliant, but Emily was unequaled and unique in her knowledge. After interviewing Emily for ten minutes he found himself thinking, "If only I were thirty years younger as she was exceptional and in more ways than one."

After speaking with a couple of Emily's Professors at Harvard, Professor Kensington heard comments such as, "Emily's intelligence can be so dazzling that there were times that I had to take a moment." The head of the botany sciences at Harvard said that she had an incredibly nuclear mind. She saw everything connected to a problem and immediately absorbed and coalesced the information into a new and exciting approach.

"There is no doubt that you'll find her intelligence impressive," said her Harvard Professor.

Professor Kensington, when looking up from his desk, was momentarily taken aback by the incredible beauty of this young woman's eyes. The bright turquoise blue within their magnificent large almond contour were shining with intelligence. Emily found the Professor's penetrating stare carrying a lot of energy while making eye contact. She became nervous; this was a brilliant man and she wanted the apprenticeship badly. The lingering silence seemed like a minute long, but it was actually just a few seconds. "Strongylodon Macrobotrys," said the Professor. Slender and frail with a cerebral aura surrounding her presence, Emily said, "The Jade Vine; a tropical vine from the pea family with turquoise flowers hanging down up to three feet. It's native to the Philippines and bees pollinate the vines' flowers."

The Professor responded smiling, "I'm not testing you; it's the color of your eyes. They're the same turquoise as the Strongylodon Macrobotrys."

Emily was nervous as she was about to meet Thomas Kensington at the Royal Botanical Gardens in London. She could not believe her fortune; at only twenty-four years old and to possibly have the opportunity to study with her hero, the foremost dendrologist in the world. "I, Emily Westwood, am the luckiest woman on the planet," she said to herself. Professor Kensington is not just a dendrologist and scientist but a known visionary. Emily studied his books and was aware of his history as an environmentalist which began well before his first degree. She heard of some of his exploits from her college Professors. This included the story of his tree-in which made her think of a Rousseau painting with the subject of protest at the Metropolitan Museum.

The Professor's expertise in DNA studies at the Jodrell Labs at the Royal Botanical Gardens brought about some exciting discoveries.

Emily walked to her interview, under an orange-gold sunset which was part of England. She noticed the large mushroom shaped staddle stones to the side of the path. Ladened with moss, these old stones fit perfectly in this lovely garden. Emily remembered from her studies that their early purpose was to lift grain and protect it from floods.

The first question the Professor asked Emily turned out to be the only question he would need. "What is your greatest fear?"

Emily didn't hesitate, "The clearing of our world's forests. In my studies I learned that this could possibly affect the planet's magnetic field relative to their sap flow; a weakened magnetic field would not shield the planet effectively from particle radiation, not to mention that they are the Earth's lungs. We must increase the awareness of the importance of the world's forests. They are an inexhaustible reservoir for carbon dioxide. Respecting these beings is an important way that we could start to repair the greenhouse effect of our planet. The world must let avaricious business and political leaders know that it is not their world. Entire cities have been founded on their pillars of greed."

The Professor noticed that her thoughts came fast with a passion sprung from her heart with an incredible knowledge of the importance of trees. To understand the magnetic affect they could have on the planet through sap flow particularly impressed him. The bodies of trees are electromagnetic phenomenon like human bodies. The forest recharges our planet's magnetic field. The Professor thought her mind, and perhaps Emily, belonged in a time yet to come. This woman's face showed such an intelligent beauty accompanied with an elegant presence. Even her movement as she reached for his hand seemed ballet-like, somewhere in between normal movements. This would be no ordinary apprentice. Professor Kensington knew he had found his partner in the field of dendrology as well as a fellow environmentalist.

The first tree that they studied was the Angel Oak at John's Island, South Carolina. While they were there they were told of rumors of visible energy that was emitting from this tree. People even said that they saw apparitions at times.

While lying in his bed back at the South Carolina inn where they were staying, the Professor looked out the window and thought back to a conference that he had attended by himself in upstate New York. He enjoyed staying at this particular inn because it was very close to a forest and very quiet and enabled him to concentrate on his work. While jotting notes to himself at the desk of the inn, he thought that he heard some unusual sounds. Rising from his chair and looking out to the dense snow-coated woodlands, there they were—white deer! One deer had stopped and seemed to look towards the Professor at his window with a startled expression. Suddenly leaping with elusive gaits in the adjacent forest they appeared apparitional. In a blink they were bounding away, out of sight and into the depth of the snowy woodlands.

The Professor and Emily found no energy readings that were unusual coming from the Angel Oak, although Emily kept insisting she sensed an unusual energy during their visit. One thing was certain: They both were affected by the enormous oak's beauty and power.

Their studies and adventures were many. Together they found the Beech Tree, significant in trapping airborne dust particles with their leaves. The rain then washed the dust from the leaves to the ground. These trees cleaned the air with powerful photosynthesis as well. They discovered that one Beech Tree could supply the oxygen requirements needed for ten people.

Chapter 26
Fred F. Barry

How civilized the Greeds are in their tailored suits. Fred F. Barry, sitting at the head of the long rectangular table looked upon all the faces and said, as he let out a billow of smoke from his large cigar, "Gentlemen, we continue to purchase the rights for more development on new lands. We will be measured by our actions of these acquisitions for future developments."

A Vice President rising from his seat spoke, "If I may sir, we are getting more protests from several environmentalist groups."

"Calm down. It will all work out as we'll grease the wheels of progress with some more green and I don't mean the kind the environmentalists love."

Fred F. Barry was a master of greed. Denial was purchased and more of the future destroyed. It was with ease that he could conceal his true intentions. The Vice President continued, "They're talking about their beautiful woods disappearing."

Fred F. Barry responded while laughing, "Don't worry; we'll leave some trees in the new parking lot areas to mark off the different sections. These people won't be complaining when they see their new jobs and the shops in the malls. They'll drive on new boulevards and be able to find the things they need in less time. These wasted acres of woods will no longer be just empty scenery and bugs. We as builders know how to turn the past into a future of progress." One could hear the evil in his voice and easily recognize it in his eyes.

Ronald Yates

The proud pinstriped laden Greeds flaunted their progress and the avarice of their deeds. They had acquired
more woodland to pave in the name of progress. Concrete
will crush the life of the land. The cold cement will cover
more of the Earth's green. Total greed overwhelming his fa-
cial expression magnified the repulsiveness of his physicality
and the shallowness of his mind. As heavy as his large gold
ID bracelet was, he was able to lift his arm for the toast. Fat
jowls vibrating from his avaricious laughter and over-sized
implants were seemingly prepared to vampire a bison. With
an egotistical boom, his voice celebrated the conquest of
the new spoils. There was no strength or valor, only a shield
composed of shallowness surrounding this conqueror.

Fred F. Barry continued to laugh, "The people will find
the green in a mall, perhaps in a new dress."

These busy businessmen build on the land and will
shred and cut with no thought to any of life's devastation.
Many of these boardrooms are full of Greeds who will make
time to celebrate with the wines of Earth's seeds. The residents that protest of losing the view of the lakes and the
trees will fall on deaf ears.

Fred F. Barry will never miss the sight of green as his favorite green lines his pockets and turns to wicked wealth.
Fred F. Barry has said, "The well of the world's worth is endless, and so we seek our large monies with a clear con-
science."

His tone grew more lascivious as he stated, "We have
our values; we value our possessions. These environmentalists claim that just because we have the power to clear a
wilderness or drill for oil in an ocean, we ignore the resulting
pollutions we leave behind. I say that when we run out of
forest, we could smash through the Rockies for our oil; after
all, who needs clean air or melodious forest birds when we
have air conditioners and cable television? These environmentalists should never concern anyone at this table. Science will figure out new ways. In our boardrooms we will

always be healthy and wealthy without regret as we represent progress. These so-called knowing minds that disagree with us will be quieted because in this conference room we know that it's all about boosting the economy."

Each Greed seated at the conference room table was secretly envious of the other's possessions, and most of all they wanted to be Fred F. Barry. Celebrating with drinks from their goblets of greed, they toast their new investments in concrete. The holes in their hearts are filled with rot as they added to already darkening clouds; meaningless ownerships with promise of money and power and plenty of leftover pollution.

Excited to sign their new contracts when their negotiations were done, their decency showed as they proposed to build something big for a neighboring town. There would be new stores and large complexes of homes and factories as soon as they cleared more of the land.

They called out the bulldozers saying, "There are new lands waiting for us to civilize with concrete and modern designs." The Greeds lifted their glasses once again, "A toast to the flowers and the bees." The Greeds laughed as their toast denounced honey smells not as sweet as money and they continued to bask in false glory.

Fred F. Barry said, "Why should people have to walk for a picnic and risk a fall or a bee sting; why should they miss out on a drive to the mall and a food court full of choices that could never be found in one picnic basket?"

Fred F. Barry thought, "Wouldn't the planet look better if it was entirely paved and contained only skyscrapers, bridges and road networks; a planet of concrete and steel. What a powerful world it would be." Fred F. Barry winked at his fellow Greeds as he signed new contracts with plump fingers in very black ink.

"That really annoying environmentalist, Danielle Gabay, has given me an idea for a new emblem for a line of leisure shirts. The emblem would be of a bulldozer that would symbolize our power. It is easy to buy the right intelligence and ride the politics of confusion and they will always lead to new resources." Fred F. Barry, the master of greed, was quite secure in his extremely costly suit of respectability, as it cloaked his evil intentions.

There were times when Danielle wished she had the money to buy the land that held the targets for ruthless developers. Perhaps then she could save some species of animal or plant; it was unrealistic. She would fight to break the impure links that made up the chains of avarice. The only hope was to continue her quest for worldwide aware-ness of how precious and important the environment was. The knowledge of the danger of harming any part of the planet's balance must be known. Every species has been found to have a connection to another species; whether it is a plant, animal or mineral. The balance of the planet and its relationship to the solar system and the universe is a gift. Every aspect of life is connected under the Great Intel-ligence.

How many views of magnificent beauty are interrupt-ed by enormous nasty steel monstrosities? The Greeds con-tinue to keep tearing at the Earth without even a thought as to how many plants and animals have been lost to their mining operations. War with the Earth cannot be won and Fred F. Barry cannot buy back the damage done.

Chapter 27
Singularity

One of the most magnificent experiences Emily shared with Professor Kensington was visiting the ancient forests of the west coast. Emily was brought to tears upon seeing the cathedrals; they were reaching up through the azure, touching celestial portals. Contained within these magnificent beings are the former glories of human and Earth's history. The height and strength of these trees were imposing. To say the least, they were nature's skyscrapers.

Our species are actually audacious enough to invade and destroy their lives and the lives dependent upon them, with steel vehicles of destruction. The members of our so-called evolved species are oblivious to their importance. Unattended fools across the world are tearing down the lungs of our home called Earth.

Age and disease seem powerless against the ancients. These living beings have been strong for over five thousand years. They are older than the Bible, and it is not only the Sequoia species of the West Coast of the United States that has this incredible longevity. Homer himself must have walked among these giants, at least in his dreams, to write of such power in his works. To be present near a gathering of beings of such commanding stature is humbling; awesome ancient kings assembled in a realm marked by nobility. Their ancient lineage goes back to the time when even larger beings inhabited the Earth: The dinosaurs.

The Redwood Forests are a race of unsurpassed regality; the eldest beings with over fifty centuries of longevity were actually living poetry. The power of their beauty and incredible stature captures your heart. Where else is an authority of these proportions found other than in these towers of strength that are the ancients? Walk among these titans and share their mighty presence while breathing in the reverence in the air.

We share the Earth with them during our lives, yet they have shared time with our father's fathers; and will share time with our children's children. Through the centuries, from their ancestor's seeds of over ninety million years ago, this family of trees lived and cleansed the air for countless of our lifetimes. They have fed and sheltered the lives of many species throughout time and continue to do so. Our species that are killing them and taking their gifts for granted are in severe need of enlightenment. The arrogance of our species is embarrassing; too few are aware of their kindness; too few will give them a hug. If our supposedly evolved species doesn't continue to destroy them in the name of civilization then they will continue to stand. There is decorum found in the orderly power of these forests that are dramatically emphasized by their stature.

As Emily and the Professor stepped forward into the ancient woodland they felt themselves entering a special world within their own world. The trees' towering canopies were separating the sun's light giving the appearance of green hyphens.

The Professor remarked, "It looks like an alphabet from another world."

Emily thought back to the shadow symbols on the trees she witnessed as a young girl. The forest floor was receiving its light codes in varying locations depending upon the winds. The sun beams filtered in this manner made for a surreal lighting.

Emily said to the Professor, "Isn't this mist unusual as it seems to be everywhere?"

"Emily, I see no mist."

"Look around, it's everywhere, like transparent steam."

"I see no mist and it is quite dry this morning. There are those who have remarked to me about seeing energy within the forest. This could be what you are experiencing."

The winds eventually became quiet and the dashes of light began to settle. Emily and the Professor felt a refreshing glow in the light breezes of scented evergreen.

"I'm hungry," said Emily.

"I believe this is the first time I've ever heard you say that. I do have some figs. Will that do until we have dinner?

"That's fine, I like figs."

"This place seems powered with the excitement of possibility. There is a feeling of hope that much that is unknown can be known within this woodland kingdom."

The endurance of the trees over time and seasons gave Emily a feeling of a steadfast wisdom. Surely this intelligence must not only be in her imagination.

"Connecting with the forest does seem to open avenues that could lead to higher understandings of what is the essential balance of our universe," observed Emily.

"Imagine the wonders that could be learned if they could talk, as these ancients are almost immortal. Perhaps it is the historic power we feel in the airs of this forest."

Emily could not only feel her heart, but the heart of the forest as well. The Professor said, "We are actually standing in history's presence as these tree beings have been marking time since before the great pyramids. Their venerableness brings an authority unique to their being. I feel the deep mysteries within the energy of this forest. I do not believe the energies I'm feeling correspond with their atmospheric activities and their exchange of water and minerals."

Emily looked up for the sky, but these giant beings were the sky. Their ceiling of green allowed for some dappled blue. Looking up, she began to spin while extending her arms within the energy and beauty of the forest. The Professor seeing her reacting to the surroundings smiled. Streams of shine explored the tree tops and continued to find numerous portals leading to the floor of the forest. Smaller species of greens delight and bathe brightly in the light. The forestial beams of light within these woodlands created a phantasmagoria of nature.

Emily, while talking to the Professor about the compassion of these beings noticed that he was a few feet away. She then remembered that while they were in a park in Moscow when the Professor was in an excited conversation, his walk became a winding kind of a zigzag. Emily realized that she would have to make volume adjustments in her conversations.

She continued with a louder voice, "These trees are everything at once: Kind, peaceful, self-sufficient, sharing, living poetry and possibly, beings in some ways that are more advanced than ourselves."

She noticed a silver winking in the distance and realized that it was a shiny forest stream reflecting some of the brightness of the day. The Professor looked behind him and in the distance, at the edge of the forest, he saw the sky's blue being broken by a flock of eagles, gracefully soaring over the summits of the tree beings.

As Emily said, "Let's go much deeper into the forest," she noticed the professor smiling. Instinctively she knew this would not be a problem as they both shared the awe of their surroundings. The power of the forest at times held them spellbound and captured their being.

"Professor, I feel as if time has stopped and we are one with the living power of the poetry of these ancient trees."

A light trickling of a brook within a small clearing between three pine trees seemed a tranquil spot for a break in their walk.

Sitting on a flat stone, Emily decided to look up to find the very tops of these giants and thought, "The summits of these beings seem unattainable when looking up from the ground." Just searching for their pinnacles became a dizzying prospect for her as she started to feel lightheaded. The

Professor, noticing that she seemed a bit disoriented, asked if she was okay. "Yes, yes. When I looked up at them I found their size staggering."

Scents of pine and wildflower found paths about the forest hitching rides on spring breezes. The Professor turned to Emily and asked if she noticed a symbiosis between the large stones and the trees.

"What do you mean?"

"Look at the shadows of the branches on the stone and the beauty of their togetherness. Do you see the elegance of the branch against the power of the stone?"

Emily thought to herself how close she felt to the Professor and how there would be no doubt of her support at his college tree-in protest in his past.

She said smiling, "Who says science and poetry aren't related?"

"There has always been a presence in nature that most have experienced when entering a forest. People who have taken walks within the woods have felt a connection to its wisdom."

"This feeling of intelligence seems much more intense among these woods; I sense a powerful presence."

She thought back to the time she was overwhelmed within the presence of the beauty of the elms in Central Park; is it possible that the beauty was also a reflection of intelligence? The beauty and intelligence of the Creator must be close to incomprehensible. A whistling sound came through the woodlands as winds played through the pines.

"Did you hear that sound?" asked Emily.

The Professor continued, "The strong intelligence that we are connected with comes from these trees as well as our intuitive selves and perhaps our real source of intelligence comes through our intuition and our soul. These trees are connected to the land as well as the atmosphere which is partially why we are feeling a depth that goes beyond the visual. The tranquility within these standing giants contains a power and reveals an awareness that seems to touch truth."

Another whistling sound of the wind seemed to punctuate the Professor's sentence. "It seems like the wind is joining our conversation."

Emily thought about the sentences she heard as a child in her sanctuary when the winds entered the witch hazel tree and considered confiding in him. Instead, she replied, "Perhaps there is truth to these winds; it does seem that there is awareness among this large council of elders."

Emily, staring deeply into the beauty of the surroundings seemed fixed and unmoving in a sort of trance. She continued sensing the presence that she remembered as a child in her enclave when she heard the sentences from the wind. She decided to trust the Professor and told him the story of the wind voices within her enclave as a child.

The Professor responded to her story saying, "Here within the ancient forest I sense more than the three dimensions we see. There is another force here, perhaps a fourth dimension. Emily, you have a strong awareness and intuition and are extremely sensitive to all your surroundings; perhaps your experience did have some sort of meaning to you on an intuitive basis. It is the strength of nature and the aura of beauty that penetrated your heart. You are like me, in that the balance and gracefulness of our world leads you to go beyond the appearance of its shapes."

Emily thought back to the painting, "The Four Trees," by Monet. The Professor continued, "We know through quantum physics that everything is in movement and thus insubstantial. The energy at the core of the area is the true level of being and all my intuitive senses are aware of this. There is a presence within this ancient land of beings and within the silence there are many tranches to its depth. I too have felt the tangibility and a sort of communication within the tranquility of nature's silence. Unknown and unseen, it is difficult to define the depth and its significance in response to this realization. The wilderness singularity is on some level felt by most people, yet it is usually overlooked and attributed to being part of nature's visual experience. To say we see, thus we know, is an unfortunate assumption. Most people's focus in the woodlands is to the rustling of the leaves or negotiating a new path through the woods for physical exercise and the beauty of the surroundings. Investing the mind into the complexities of what is unseen is usually left for poets and quantum physicists."

Emily continued to listen attentively. "The translation of what intuition's sense of a reality is that which is unseen yet present should be pursued with diligence and not dismissed. Our intuitions and imaginations can lead to wonderful possibilities. Often it has been found that what can be imagined has turned out to have actually existed. The scientist often cracks the surface of a problem that seems to be surrounded with an impenetrable wall. Frustrated by this lack of total clarity, one scientist says that there is no answer. To another scientist this impasse will often be penetrated with intuition. Intuition's path will allow a scientist to go places where certain equations would have difficulty negotiating."

The Professor continued, "Trees have communicated in fashions that have already been documented. There are species of oak that use a chemical communication to inform the other trees that an insect attack is imminent. The oaks, as a result of the communication, are prepared to counter the attack by releasing a coding of tannins protecting their leaves. Of course, an attack of man-made machines or polluted rain would be too much for any tree to counter. Emily, like Shakespeare's "Forest of Arden," suspected that 'there were tongues in these trees.'

Standing against the silent evening sunset, the tall rich evergreens were respectful as the night approached. Shadows of the trees were noble in their own right. Emily was able to feel the envy of the early evening, as well as the honor of the night. Darkness began making its way through the towering beings with unusual lightings bringing out different forest sensations. She thought that anytime of the day in these ancient woods is special.

Looking deeply into the forest, as she searched the noble shadows of the giants, she found her answers still remained elusive. Although immersed in a nameless feeling, her intuition told her that she was close to an experience that the twilight could not hide much longer. Emily became relaxed as all seemed natural and close to unfolding. She thought the kind and enchanting beauty felt in the palpability was a preface to secrets that were to come. In the world of concrete cities there would be abusive street sounds and waves of anxiety often causing the inhabitants to run for artificially created tranquilizers to fight off the mental pain. The woodland's singularity was serene and layered deeply with wisdom which seemingly could be accessed somehow.

Emily turned to the Professor and shared some of her thoughts. "The intensity and immensity of this singularity of silence we are experiencing seems to have gotten stronger."

"Although this presence of woodland silence is indigenous to all forests it is not with the intensity of this power. Perhaps we are feeling a dormant power due to their over ninety million years of history. This history descended from their beginnings as redwood seeds and carried their secrets to their current power. The depth of the singularity's silence has never been over-shadowed by the sounds of the breezes, stirring leaves or bird songs. It did not matter what the season, a spring wildflower or a powerful snowstorm, the woodland's singularity remains; its power felt through all seasons."

Moonlight somehow found their campsite and easily complemented the forest's beauty. Tall moon shadows seemed alive within the night. The Professor turned to Emily and said after finding some stars, "There was a time when sailboats could navigate the oceans by the night's stars. At present, the night skies' dark seas are smothered by smog causing the ships to have difficulty accessing the information and the beauty of the stars. We must lift pollutions' veils and clear the night."

"The planet's lighting is actually dimming due to carbon clouds. Our weather satellites have verified less bright days across the entire United States. Earth's water supply has darkened as dams have affected our rivers with pollution."

"Even primitive societies respected certain trees and plants as sacred."

"Perhaps they weren't so primitive after all. Their respect is certainly deserved for many reasons. Our scientists have realized that each tree in the forest lifts hundreds of gallons of water with a simplicity that our species has still not been able to accomplish with its noisy pumps and so-called expertise."

Sitting deep in the redwoods, Emily continued to be aware of their majestic presence. The sound of the boughs in the wind was regal and told her of the power of these beings.

As the winds started to pick up, Emily mentioned to the Professor that the sound of the wind seemed haunting among these cathedrals. Emily then brought up the Aeolian Harp to the Professor saying, "Wind alone would pass over this musical instrument creating an unusually delicate sound."

"Yes, it is similar in principle to that of a wind chime, but more gracefully in tune."

"Perhaps the wind's essence is infused with the tones of nature's vibrations."

As the Professor's eyes started to close he thought, "Emily's mind always supported an unusual range of thoughts; her mind would stay nimble in accessing them all. Emily re-tained everything she heard, saw and read, but it never weighed her down. The opposite was true, as she learned more, the lighter her step became. The way new ideas rolled out and turned into important possibilities was an incredible part of Emily's thinking process. A better partner could not be found."

Stately giant shadows of the redwoods were powerful in the moonlight. Emily felt the night's presence growing stronger as the breezes of the ancient forest began to feel cooler. "Sweet dreams," said Emily to the Professor. Still looking out at the woods, the ferns, the brambles, the creeks and the violets, she sensed that they were all part of the secret. "In the empire of this woodland evening the answers seemed close," Emily intuitively felt as she dozed off to sleep.

An intelligence to the forest's presence connected to Emily immediately. The connection was deep and on an intuitive level and she wondered, "Am I experiencing a consciousness of nature? Is intuitive intelligence the most advanced part of being human? If my soul can connect with God, then why not my intuition with God's creations? Much exists that cannot be defined visually." She became more aware of the relationship between the tree trunks, the surrounding space and all the beauty around her. She looked down at the Professor and saw that he was sleeping soundly.

Emily began to walk, looking around at the massive forms and saw that they lacked solidity and were seemingly composed of a holographic haze. The massive red trunks were allowing moonlight through their essence, appearing ethereal and translucent. They seemed to be composed of a reddish rain with pine needles of green vapor.

"Professor, wake up!"

"Yes, yes, what is it?"

"Look around."

Looking around, the Professor responded, "What do you see?"

Emily looked around and now the colors and forms appeared solid and normal. A delicate dawn made its way between the giants. Seeing Emily's confused expression, the Professor said, "You must have been having a strange dream, child. Tell me about it."

"There was dissolution of the forms of the forest, yet the dissolution was individually contained within the outline of each tree. The forest seemed to become a molecular movement within each of its forms. The redwoods with its contained swirling colors, part of a translucent vapor of their forms, were actually drawing in the moonlight as part of their swirling energy."

"This dream you had came from our discussion of their presence and the singularity they created in these woodlands. The ancients became personally alive in their energy as you felt their presence in the silence of the woodland singularity. Aligning them with the moonlight emphasized the mystery and enchantment you felt. In your dream they revealed their power which was exactly the explanation for their energy you were looking for. They are magnificent beings, but to give them a will of sorts is clearly something that you wish were true. This would make them sentient beings, although combining imagination and science is not the worse path to take. Emily, you carried your thoughts into a world seen at the atomic levels of the forest."

"But, I don't think I was dreaming. There was an unusual stillness within the forest. There was a deep sound, a sort of music, as if there was an opening within the quiet." The Professor interrupted, and said looking thoughtful, "Let's say that I have an awareness of a structure to the stillness of silence."

Emily answered, "Now imagine that there are wells in this structure of stillness that allow a sort of music to flow to the surface."

"What does this indicate to you, Emily?"

The Professor was constantly amazed at the combination of intelligence and sensitivity within this elegant woman. The Professor continued, "Although I have been touched deeply by the energy of the woodlands, your connection seems transcendent."

"The singularity seemed sacred in its silence and completely true in its totality as an entity; a truth coexisting within the spiritual beauty of these magnificent beings."

"Truth's core is an existence too deep to be affected by time."

"Is it possible in this silence, this tangible stillness, this beautiful singularity, elegant with extraordinary power, that the spirit was revealed?"

Professor Kensington responded, "As a supreme sanctuary for life, perhaps the singularity in these ancient redwoods exists in all dimensions of the universe, perhaps you have felt logos. It's only natural with your science background and your awareness that all forms are really subatomic movement. The feelings of enchantment that you experienced since we have entered the ancient forest have been a strong catalyst for your mind."

"I guess you're right, but it felt so real and the brightness of their energy was disarming."

"It's not surprising to have had unusual dreams sleeping among the ancients. In this stillness we find a truth that is not present in the streams of jabber that are the noise of the outside world. Among these kings a connection to their wisdom and the wisdom within us is accessible to those that are sensitive to that which is beyond the obvious."

"I felt a beauty of eternal beginnings."

"This is perhaps a positive feeling that is persistent in the sustenance you meant to find. What could be more beautiful than a discovered "now" that holds the naissance of beauty? As more woodlands are cleared there will be fewer retreats from our so-called advanced civilization. It is ironic that we tear down what provides serenity and a retreat and replace it with more cities of stress. We must find a way to incorporate life in a balanced and healthy way. Our species, with the forests across the world, must live together in harmony." Emily's thoughts went to her recurring dream experienced during her Junior High School years. In these cities of her dreams there was a wonderful beauty and balance with nature.

Dawn's doors were beginning to open as the yawn of morning signaled a new day. Scents of wildflowers began to travel through the woodlands. The morning was emerging beneath the colossal beings cautiously as if in respect to their majesty.

The Professor said, "These skyscrapers do not pollute."

Emily, looking up to the tops of the redwoods thought that they appeared as proud pillars that supported the Earth's blue roof.

There came a point in their relationship where no words were necessary. The Professor and Emily knew their awareness and their connection to these ancients was a special experience that they both shared. Their eye contact lingered long enough to acknowledge their kindred spirits.

As they exited the edge of the forest they saw an eagle soaring above, seemingly honoring the majesty of the redwoods. The woodlands filled the air with fresh evergreen and an energy that invigorated the Professor and Emily with each breath.

Within the grand and noble power
There is a gentleness always felt;
Will they reach the heavens
With their poetic stretch?
There is much respect and kindness in
These nature's supreme towers.
Will they find celestial in
An advent new hour?

Chapter 28
Bookstore

Matthew promised to pick up a novel that his sister ordered from a bookstore near Columbus Circle. His arm was feeling strong again, but his mind kept going back to the woman he met a couple of months ago at Ogunquit. The dawn that they had shared for just moments would never be forgotten for him, and he dreaded the possibility of never seeing her again. Expressing his frustration to his sister, she would respond, "If it was meant to be, it will all work out." Matthew knew that it was only a matter of time before he would be taking the mound again and must have his concentration back on pitching. He thought back to his first time out on the mound wearing pinstripes. He remembered saying to himself, "Mister Batter, let me help you back to the dugout," as he threw a blazing fastball for strike three. He thought of an article he read saying how ironic it was that out of Canton, Ohio, which was home to the Football Hall of Fame, would come one of baseball's greatest pitchers. The hitters would say to the reporters that his fastball looks like an aspirin as it comes into the plate due to its speed.

Although his delivery appeared to be nonchalant, the batters knew better and remained at high alert. Their eyes had better be sharp to be ready for a ball that was turning and burning its way through to the strike zone. He recalled his chewing becoming faster as his gum represented his determination to strike out the last batter. He chewed hard and threw a bullet right down Broadway. Sixty thousand pairs of eyes, seeing strike three, stood up and cheered the Yankee win.

Arriving at the bookstore, he noticed that most of the books in the window seemed to be either romance novels or self-help. He entered the store and realized that some people had recognized him. Quickly he asked an employee for help and was told that he would have to wait five minutes while he sent someone to get the book. Avoiding eye contact with the surrounding customers, he picked up a non-fiction book from a nearby display containing various scientific commentaries on global warming.

Matthew heard the clerk's voice, "Your book has arrived, sir." Matthew put the book on global warming back down while noticing that there were several pictures of the contributing authors on the back cover.

"That will be twenty-five dollars, sir. Will that be cash or charge? I can ring you up at this register." Matthew turned around, looking back towards the display counter.

"Sir?" inquired the bookseller.

"I'll be right there."

Looking down at the back cover of the book that he had just replaced, he got chills. He could not believe what he saw; those eyes were unmistakable. It was Emily! His realization made his face flush and suddenly he felt light-headed.

Matthew closed his eyes, took a deep breath and was transported. He felt Emily's presence and could see her wild, rich auburn hair tossing with the sea breezes. He remembered the magical rhythms of that morning and how her beauty was part of the enchantment.

"Sir, are you okay?"

Matthew opened his eyes and was back in the bookstore. "Yes, I'll take this book as well; wait, I better take two copies."

"Are you a member?"

"It doesn't matter. Here, keep the change," said Matthew as he handed the clerk a one hundred dollar bill and turned to leave the store.

"But sir, it comes to one hundred and seven dollars." Matthew handed him a twenty dollar bill that he pulled out of his jean's pocket and headed once again for the exit.

"But, sir..."

"It's okay, keep the change."

"Why thank you sir, but I thought you might want to know that one of the authors will be doing a signing tomorrow at the New York Botanical Gardens."

Matthew knew he could have meant his sister's spy drama novel. Turning around with his fingers crossed, he made eye contact with the employee, who said, "I heard that you were close to ready, sir."

"What?"

"Good luck coming back, the arm is okay now, right?"

Matthew, gritting his teeth through a smile said, "Thanks, the arm is better," and asked, while trying not to appear anxious, "By the way, which author will be signing?"

"Which author, what?"

Matthew, barely able to contain himself, tried to remain calm as he said, "Which author will be signing at the Gardens?"

"Oh, let me think. I forgot the name."

Yelling to another employee at the information desk the clerk said, "Mabel, do you know which author will be doing the signing for the new book on global warming, Venus II?"

Matthew, now finding it more difficult to stay calm, heard Mabel say, "Sam, do you see that I'm with a customer?"

Mabel, snickering, slid out a panel from her desk and checked the listing. "There are two authors signing at the Botanical Gardens tomorrow."

Matthew, now beside himself, walked towards Mabel himself, "Who are they?"

Suddenly the customer with Mabel said sternly, "You were helping me first."

Matthew turned towards the cute elderly lady with curly gray hair and presented his best smile saying, "Please Mam, this is very important."

Smiling sheepishly, the elderly lady looked up at Matt's handsome face, and said, "Well okay." Taking Matthew by surprise, she added, "As long as you throw plenty of strikes when the playoffs arrive." Matthew smiled as he turned towards Mabel, waiting to hear the author's names.

Mabel said, "You do look familiar."

"Yes, yes, I'm with the Yankees."

"The Yankees, I thought you were from that soap opera, um..." Matthew, exasperated now said, "Please, the names of the authors."

Looking up from a sheet she said, "A Professor Kensington and an Emily Westwood."

"Yes!" Matthew exclaimed, while giving a fist pump. "Thank you, thank you."

Turning again for the exits, Mabel yelled out, "Don't you want to know what time?" Matt stopped, turned and saw Mabel, Sam and the customer all smiling, as he seemed to be even better looking when he glowed. Mabel yelled out, "At two o'clock."

Matthew could not stop smiling that evening as tomorrow he would see Emily. While lying in bed, he decided to acquaint himself with the book on global warming. Each of the five contributing authors was a scientist with an extremely impressive background. He learned that Emily was one of the youngest women considered for a Noble Prize. It was through her research that a drug to fight cancer was able to be synthesized. This drug previously needed the bark of twenty trees for only one dose of the medicine. Emily was helping to save people's lives as well as the lives of many trees. She was also making important medicinal discoveries involving various species of orchids in her research at the laboratories of the New York Botanical Gardens.

Matthew wondered why these scientists who collaborated on a book about global warming chose for their title, "Venus II," after all, there is only one Venus. Matthew thought the title would be more appropriate for a science fiction novel. He continued reading as tomorrow he would meet one of the book's most special contributors.

There is no brightness to be seen on unfolding events. Cloud clusters bring more fullness to dark days. These are Earth's warm coverings which are made with pollutants. Earth's beauty is less pleasing under a gray translucent. Satellites have shown in recent years that there is less brightness to our city's days.

There are no ambiguities hidden beneath the clouds of Venus. Although named for the Roman goddess of love and beauty, this is a planet of comfort only to fire or a demon. The merciless storms and fiery skies with blasts of red and white lightning penetrate the thick cloud cover of the planet. Orange fire scars are found on Venus due to the forked lightning cracking, as well as shocking the surface with its intense electric branches. Plains of lava under clouds of sulfuric acid stay angry and leave pastures of ashes. There is only one season on this planet and it is void of all life. No songs are heard, only the whirlwinds of fiery tornadoes and rushing rivers of lava. No one will climb Maxwell Mountes for the views of the farra. A few billion years ago, due to a runaway, rapid, out of control greenhouse effect, it is believed that the oceans of Venus' youth evaporated. Though similar in size and mass to Earth, and on occasions, known as our sister planet, you would not want to breathe in the atmosphere that consists of 96.5% carbon dioxide. There will not be a Manaus forest to clean the air.

Who will be left to say that we turned this garden called Earth into Venus II? If our planet is not respected, the fires in the sun will have no choice but to send flames bringing dances of violence by virulent winds. No barriers can be built to keep our oceans in place when angry storms arrive. Villages, states and countries will drown, and then the volcanoes and quakes of Earth will crack through the lands. Deadly heat waves have already affected many lives as millions of acres have been consumed by flames and whipping winds in America's West. Severe draught has fueled Brazil's brush fires as the dry winds swirl. There are rivers already being reduced to streams. The normally beautiful winds rebel and cause havoc. Confused winds bully each other with extreme temperature changes and harsh conditions. Sea ice disappears for the penguins and the polar bears, as glaciers appear where the salmon used to go. Dams cause ecological destruction. Building on a river's flood plains must stop. Cottonwood trees need wet soil for their seeds. Willow trees need islands in rivers just as the eagles need the trees and the islands as habitats. Building dams to divert water, while clearing forests will reshape our ecosystems.

Early signs of Venus II continue to appear. Should we purchase powerful blowers to part the heavy smoke so that we can again see the lights of the night? The shadowy light of pollution clouds has become increasingly common. More people are wearing masks to protect themselves from particle pollution. Will there be breathing shelters and a tune added to our cell phones to let us know that it's time for the oxygen tank? Preservation and reason must be the referee to stop this fight with our environment.

We do not want to see the planet's great green savannahs become burning sand. Continue to clear the world's green and who will be left to write the epitaph to photosynthesis? The lawless storms of Venus do not need to find a second home. The winds can sculpture the great canyons of Earth allowing the condors to soar. They also can bring a crimson season of fires leaving ash where there was pure clean snow. If the tyranny of the Greeds continues to steer the world, tearing our shared garden Earth and forming endless concrete factories, our Earth can be spoiled beyond salvation.

Polluting the Earth and disrespecting the sun will create a sibling for the planet Venus. Is it only when a large hole is detected in our ozone layer that we were able to have the awareness to ban chemicals from spray bottles and refrigerators that deplete our ozone layer with their carbon gases? Let's not bring solar radiation to melt the ice in the poles of our planet.

The warming of our planet also thaws permafrost, a soil that has been continuously frozen for years. As the permafrost thaws, it releases methane and carbon dioxide. This traps more heat and fuels the greenhouse effect. Much of the methane releasing permafrost is located in Siberia. Scientists must find a way to capture the methane that bubbles out from the permafrost and use it for clean energy. We must stop the heating of our planet which will stop the permafrost from thawing.

According to the Harvard Center for Health and The Global Environment, summer heat waves have become stronger causing higher ozone levels. Ticks and mosquitoes spreading Lyme, West Nile Virus and Rocky Mountain Spotted Fever are spreading to areas that were once too cold for their survival.

As Matthew read further into the book he noticed that it was Professor Kensington and Emily who focused more on the dangers of deforestation. The body of a tree, like a human's is an electromagnetic phenomenon. Our forests have a high electrical conductivity. Scientists have discovered that Earth's magnetic fields have been decreasing as our forests are being cleared and destroyed. Since 1838, scientists have measured a 10% decrease in our planet's magnetic field, paralleling global deforestation. Earth's magnetosphere and magnetic fields serve many important functions. They are an effective, protective shield against particle radiation coming from the sun.

Ronald Yates

Living in the rain forest, which covers only 2% of our planet, are an amazing amount of birds, insects, plants, animals and tree species. The clearing of these forests endangers all life on the planet. The Atlantic Forest of Brazil, which was once two times the size of Texas, is now approximately the size of Virginia. Drops of rain that were once welcomed in many of the world's forests now bring pain with their acid. Where are most of the chestnut and elm trees that were part of the Appalachians? Why are there declines in the songs of the wood thrush of our eastern US forests? Plants and animals living high in the cloud forest are being surrounded by acidic fog.

Let's find a solution for the world's smokestacks. The world does not want its buildings of stone to become gypsum. Many important plants with possible life saving medicinal properties are in trouble such as the orchid. The orchid needed the hawk moth for pollination, but with a loss of habitat, comes the loss of their population as well. The planet, fortunately, still remains fertile with forest gifts that are yet to be discovered. These forests absorb the heavy carbonic atmosphere that would choke and burn life if not for photosynthesis. Damaging the world's woodlands is actually destroying the lungs of the planet. The sun was made to bring life, not to take it away. A million Earths could fit inside of our sun. A more dangerous enemy could not be found. There is no species that can win a war with the sun. In certain cities, shoeprints could be seen on scorched pavement. On the tar of the gutters, tires have burst or glued cars in place. It's not only the forest burning but the towns and cities as well. The sun must forever remain a respected friend.

It is the sun that holds our solar system together with its gravity. Trees and plants produce food with the help of the sun's energy. The sun gives solar energy and creates wind energy in our atmosphere which could provide a clean fuel we could harness. The Aztecs, Babylonians, Egyptians, Iroquois and the Ancient Greeks are some of the civilizations that respected the sun, although at times it was to the point of a deity.

Powerful, angry derechos come with terrible thunderstorms and occur in the spring and summer. The windmills that can slow derechos to harness electricity would be colossus. The winds that helped sculptured the Grand Canyon over time and allow the condors to soar for hours can be an excellent energy source. Winds have the power to produce endless energy and electricity with no pollution left behind.

Hurricanes have become stronger and more frequent. The rains have become more unpredictable as well as draught locations. Polar ice is melting. Coral reef has been dying due to higher ocean temperatures. We are changing the chemistry of our atmosphere. Burning fossil fuels slows the escape of heat from our planet into space, thus the reason for the increase in the average temperatures of Earth's surfaces. Climate change is causing frogs to catch disease in the Latin American forests. We have lost many species of the Harlequin frog. The temperature changes have extinguished them with a fungus on the surface of their skin. Scientists have found that global warming causes more cloud cover from raised ocean temperatures allowing these fungi to grow.

The Kyoto Protocol went into effect in 2005 with the object of decreasing the Earth's greenhouse gases. This protocol must be taken seriously by all the countries of the world. The plants and trees were here on Earth long before humans. Conserving them is in our own self interest. There have actually been cases in cities where trees that beautified the streets and shaded homes were chopped down to make room for billboards. Environmental science has the facts that biological diversity is in trouble and could affect all of humanity. A simple insect, such as the bee, is responsible for pollinating one-third of our food supply and has somehow had its population decreased possibly due to toxic environment.

Ronald Yates

When the leaves fall and all the green turns brown and the air becomes poisonous to inhale then Venus II will have arrived. There will be no trumpets at the shores to give warning. The blast of sun storms will cause large wounds to our planet's cities. This could all be avoided if we stop ignoring the dark truths of a possible reality.

The issue is time and it's running out. Unfortunately, the most important timepiece in Earth's history may now be the thermometer. Should the rise in temperature continue to increase at a more rapid rate, eventually everyone's time will be up. Every moment is precious. These higher temperatures causing increased evaporation are fueling the intensity of Earth's storms. When winds collide, and their directions go wilder on the edge of super cells, destructive columns will be born. Greenhouse activities must stop. CO_2 and water vapor allow the warming radiation of the sun to come in while preventing the heat from escaping; enter a closed car that has been standing in the heat on a summer's day. The International Panel of Climate Change has reported that Earth's temperatures have been higher by one degree Fahrenheit in the last one hundred years. We have already seen more unpredictable floods and droughts on the planet.

Matthew continued through the book and read where the United Nations reported that if the planet's temperatures continue to rise, the Himalayan glaciers could disappear. Mountain glaciers nourish the Earth from above. Drinking water for millions in India is dependent on the Ganges River which receives its waters from these glaciers. In Tanzania, Africa, people just have to look up and see that the glacier of Mount Kilimanjaro has melted away. Glaciers receding in Iceland will affect hydro-electric power that their waterfalls provide, as well as their drinking water. Antarctica's importance as one of the cooling systems of our planet cannot be stressed enough.

Burning, blistering, a baker's sun,
Dry desert, all will be done.
Shades of soot clouds, slight relief,
Siestas of oblivion, lead to endless sleep.

According to NASA, the sliding ice sheets from glaciers cause glacial quakes. This causes larger amounts of water to drain into the ocean, which affects the sea levels and is a danger to coastal cities.

Oceans rise as ice caps die,
Levees lose as oceans power impossible to refuse.
How many people will the high ground hold?
Roofs will fold as the mountains are already sold.
Drowning fears, refugees' tears.

The ice melting combined with warmer ocean temperatures affects the ocean's circulation. Let us not change the beat of the ocean's rhythms. Erratic circulation is dangerous for the planet as the Earth's liquids are the blood of its circulatory system. The Inter-Governmental Panel on Climate Change working through the United Nations and the world's governments estimate that there will be many millions of environmental refugees created due to coastal flooding. We must stop the oceans from becoming more acidic as the warmer temperatures are unable to absorb CO_2 as well. Dolphins are hungry as food is difficult to find with coral disease and bleached reefs due to warmer water temperatures. The director of NASA's Goddard Institute says that changes must be made now or there will be extreme glacial dangers by the middle of the century. It is our species causing the carbon levels to rise and, therefore, the Earth's temperatures. Our people should not be choking on our planet's air. There will be no political or corporate spins that can change what is happening. According to the Inter-Governmental Panel on Climate Change, 20% of our greenhouse gases come from the burning and clearing of our forests.

There have already been earthquakes so powerful that they have altered the rotation of the Earth by changing the mass. An 8.8 magnitude earthquake in Chile has slightly affected Earth's rotation. Are these rumblings expressing Earth's unhappiness? Are we not part of nature's fate? Let us avoid the dark winds of Venus and clean our atmosphere. All nations must get along and work together for the health of the planet.

Matthew now realized the reason for the title of the book. As he continued reading, he found himself becoming increasingly uncomfortable and was happy to move toward the last part of the book which spoke about the solutions to a toxic environment and a decrease in global warming. He was happy to read that the Mayor of New York was using solar panels on the roofs of the city's buildings. The most electricity will be used on hot and sunny summer days. This plan will offset over 200 million tons of greenhouse gas emissions: Solar energy used perfectly.

The world must invest in creative energies and into harnessing the clean power of the sun, the sea and the wind. Development of alternative energies will create new jobs. There can be enormous prosperity in the world and at the same time a healthy environment. Incentives for clean energy must be a priority. Fast and clean rail systems could be put in place instead of the world's polluted parkways. We could bring back the electric trolley systems, as well as manufacturing electric cars. People could lower their thermostats when there is no one at home in need of heat. Much energy is required to purify water; as a result all measures should be taken not to waste water. Many countries, as well as the states of Texas and New Mexico, have a shortage of purified water. The world's deserts could easily provide an enormous amount of electricity by building large solar plants.

Matthew's eyelids were becoming heavy and starting to drop down. Before dozing off, he thought of how the importance of the health of our planet was brought to light by Venus II.

Chapter 29
New Morning

Brambleberries and floral essences filled the misty morning air. It had rained last night, awakening even the pine perfumes and the scents of different conifers. The white clouds were quiet in the softness of the light blue morning sky. Fresh breezes were circling every flower, hungry to capture their scent as they awoke from their night's sleep. At times, the flower petals seemed to be made of glow, channeling the sun. Dewy grass scents also filled the silent early morning air. There was still a light mist made green from the incense of the grass and gave an interesting allure to the surrounding trees. Butterflies, celebrating their new life, were gliding around flower tops adding to the atmosphere. The air was drying quickly under the sun and now a shiny morning presented itself. The flowers took notice, stretching their petals even farther while still holding dewy rainbows. There were more navigational glides as many butterflies appeared, dipping down to the flower tops for the energy of their nectars. The sunshine made the scents of the morning even more delicious.

Matthew walked into the Garden gift shop and there she was, sitting next to an older man at a large table. It was really her; and she was as wonderfully alluring as he remembered. He looked at the back cover of his book and saw that the man was Professor Kensington. Reading the bio, once again, which was next to his picture, he realized that this man was the head of the Botanical Gardens at Kew in London. He was pretty sure that this was the man in the distance that he had seen calling for Emily at Ogunquit. They smiled kindly as they conversed about their book while signing copies for interested readers. Matthew kept letting people ahead of him on line as he was nervous about meeting her.

"Who am I kidding?" Matthew thought. "She's brilliant and I'm way out of my league."

Suddenly his thoughts were interrupted, "Matthew Monroe," a man yelled, dressed in a Yankee cap and jacket, as he asked, "Can I get your autograph? My wife loves this place and who would have thought that I…"

"Sure, sure," Matthew interrupted while signing his baseball cap. All of a sudden, Matthew found himself next in line.

"I see we're not the only ones signing today," said Professor Kensington, while stroking his gray beard. Emily Westwood looked up and saw Matthew Monroe. Smiling, she said, "It's Matthew, right?"

"You remembered my name," he responded as he felt his face turning red.

"Of course," she said smiling, while standing up and extending her hand gracefully. Matthew squeezed her hand lightly while saying, "Emily Westwood."

It seemed for a moment that they were alone in the crowded gift shop. Professor Kensington, sensing something, suggested that Emily take a break and stretch her legs.

Matthew then added, "We could have a cup of coffee next door."

"I don't drink coffee, but I'd love a cup of tea."

Matthew looked towards Professor Kensington, smiling thankfully and extended his hand. The Professor winked and said, "Don't you want me to sign your book?" Embarrassed, Matthew fumbled, handing over the book while Emily was smiling at the Professor. Matthew quickly pulled back the cover to see what he wrote and smiled as he read, "Good Luck." Matthew smiled back at Professor Kensington as he and Emily walked toward the cafeteria.

Glowing, Emily returned from having her tea with Matthew. "Well," said Professor Kensington. "That young man was quite smitten with you."

Emily blushed and said that they were meeting for a walk in Central Park after the conference on pollution and the environment.

"Emily, are you saying that I will be joining you and this handsome young man at Central Park?" She giggled and Professor Kensington thought to himself, "Lucky man."

Chapter 30
Sphere of Life

Professor Kensington and Emily Westwood were happy to see that there was a broad coalition of groups, including important representatives from large industries that were in attendance at the conference on environmental health. More and more people had to be made aware of what must be done for a healthier planet. There were speakers from various universities, as well as laboratories for scientific investigation from botanical gardens worldwide. There were paleontologists present that studied the Earth's past through ancient plants as well as dinosaur fossils to determine climate patterns.

There were speakers that were concerned about the extinction of animals and plants, whether by climate change, greeds of industry or poachers. There was concern over the section of the Wilkins Ice Shelf, which is seven times the size of Manhattan, which broke off into the Antarctic Ocean. There is a sadness to the thought of a polar bear being sent adrift on a small piece of ice away from his habitat due to climate change. This is leading to a decline in their numbers. Whether the poacher is in Tanzania for the bull elephant's tusk or the black rhino, or a thief carrying away the valuable body parts of the red cedar trees of Washington State, the story is equally sad. Nature's valuables are being depleted and possibly made extinct.

There are many industries that dismiss climate change and the warming of the planet as total nonsense. They believe that tornadoes in California, as well as Georgia, are just a freak of nature. Pollution toxic to our environment was prevalent among certain industries that flew the flag of flagrant disregard. These certain leaders of industry somehow have convinced themselves to be abnegators of reality. They have no thoughts of the forest fruits and purity of air that they give. As they clear a living forest to build an unnecessary road for carbon cars, they are not witnesses of shame but are builders of convenience. There is no thought given to the countless arboreal creatures being left with no home. Any one of these tree inhabitants could be vital to the health of the Earth. Apathy is abundant in too many minds. How is it possible that the Greeds can be devoid of shame and not see the truth in the poisoning of our waters? They continue to build dams that destroy our rivers. We must stop disrupting the natural migration of creatures of the soil, sea and sky. Let's turn the gray rivers back to brilliant blue. Let's hear the song of the bird return to healthy forests. The pollution of industry across the world has the skies weeping tears of acid. The Greeds' satisfaction of material wealth will not only make our planet barren, but mankind's intellect as well. Knowledge to help, appreciate and improve our planet is for everybody's sake. These are the things that will profit the mind and health of all.

The importance of all species in the biodiversity is critical and any species lost is irreversible. We must appeal to the interest of the Greeds. When the large corporations realize that it is in their own interests to sustain the Earth, it is only then that they will invest in research and the preservation of the land and its species. Great plant biologists, such as L. Stebbins and A. Eastwood became heroes for Emily. All countries of the world must promote biodiversity, especially those developing industries in China and India.

Intelligent use of our resources must begin to keep our biodiversity safe and in turn save the lives of our children. The Greeds of industry have put the species of the world against time itself, for if the planet continues to degrade, what will become of the children? Earth's oxygen does not discriminate and all species have the right to breathe clean air. No life should choke on the dust of fossil fuels while filling their lungs. It is madness to taint the air which sustains life itself. We destroy the top soil with massive industrial farming; we clear large tracts of woodland forests; we drill for oil in the wilderness and the ocean; we dig up carbon that was stored safely underground in coal and oil and then spread it into our planet's atmosphere. These woodlands absorb and filter the air of pollutants, returning fresh oxygen for all. Approximately 80% of all medicinal cures come from trees and plants. They also provide food and shelter and we respond by attacking them, clearing them off the face of the Earth.

Solvents in refrigeration have already contributed to the depletion of Antarctica's ozone layer. A thinning ozone layer allows more ultraviolet rays to reach Earth which can harm all life including aquatic. The damage that chlorofluorocarbon has caused should have opened more eyes to the pollution of our stratosphere. It is well known to the world's scientists that the climbing atmospheric carbon levels need to be brought down to stop the poisoning of the air. Reality is fast. We can not allow humanity to be trapped by its own procrastination.

It is clear that earthquakes and tsunamis are dangerous enough without putting nuclear power plants in their path. The armies of war that bring the boom of bombs and the whine of bullets could be turned into armies of environmental accomplishment instead of environmental destruction. There are mountain valleys, waters and woodlands that are also bombed and drilled and torn and leveled in the name of progress and justice. Much of Earth's beauty is trampled by arrogant power hungry people. One speaker told of how arguments about preserving the world do not seem to have an effect on so-called advanced countries. There are rain forests still being destroyed by farmers for short-term gains.

Ronald Yates

We do not depend on oil and carbon fuels for survival. We do depend on clean water and fresh air. Rivers bring fresh water to nourish Earth's arteries of life. In the Southwest of the United States, droughts have already been taking their toll. Dry fires come with the western winds. There are many flood situations in the Midwest and West. Record breaking heat has resulted in droughts and floods in states such as Texas and Oklahoma, as well as across the country and the rest of the world. Australia, although surrounded by water, faces serious draught problems in many areas. Every drop of water, insect and leaf must all count. The same water travels to the other side of the world as well as through time. Intelligent nations should have worldwide consideration for the health of the planet's waters. Pillaging of the planet must stop. Water is still conceived to be an endless resource by many across the world, but the fact is that there could be a planetary water crisis.

Eutrophication is adding yet another component to a possible elegy of our ecosystem. Nitrogen compounds are affecting the water quality and our animal life. Blue-baby Syndrome is caused by decreased oxygen in a baby's blood due to toxic nitrogen pollution; this is courtesy of the contributors to the combustion of fossil fuels. The rivers and ground water are contaminated from nitrates which are found in fertilizers, waste dumps and pesticides. Environmental factors have been shown to contribute to autism and ninety percent of all cancers. Babies are now being born pre-polluted. There are droughts and water crises across the globe. Competition for scarce resources could bring violence and war; instead, the world needs to work together. A nineteenth century French economist, Frederic Bastial, stated: "Where goods do not cross frontiers, armies will."

In the Middle East, countries are experiencing a lack of fresh water and finally beginning to realize that water problems do not recognize borders. Countries must work together to keep shared regional water supplies fresh and clean. The journey of the planet's waters must remain pure, as should the rain that comes to our rivers and the rivers that flow to the seas. The hot water temperatures of the ocean are bleaching the coral and killing the algae. The coral reefs of our oceans are home to many species of fish and are an ecosystem in danger. Dynamite fishing hurts the coral as well. If modern day fishing practices continue along with environmental pollution, the world may have no fish at all. Climate change and pollution from coastal developments are often the cause of dangerous environmental pollution.

Trees help us with conserving energy. They block the winter winds to keep our homes warmer. They provide shade for homes in the summer. They protect from flood and storm damage. The storms that have assaulted the Gulf Coast met an unprotected coastline. There were many Cyprus trees protecting the Gulf Coast in the past from bad storms. An area that suffered much damage, St. Bernard Parish, had previously lost the majority of its Cyprus forest and was left the most vulnerable to the storms. Mudslides and sinking homes, from heavy rains, have even hit Minnesota and Oregon. There are still many trees brought down unnecessarily. Using the bark from downed mature conifers for mulch should be a crime when composted fall leaves are actually more effective as mulch. Certain trees around the world are so few in number that they are considered rare, such as the Ghost Tree of the mountains in China. Break not the boughs as lives will fall.

Londoners will be charged more for driving due to congestion pricing. The money raised will be invested in walking and bike paths, as well as public transportation leading to a healthier city and reducing CO_2 emissions. The Mayor of New York, being impressed with London's success and bold innovations will also encourage clean energy transportation.

Ronald Yates

Many solutions to pollution and climate change were brought across at the conference. It had been predicted that India's energy consumption could quadruple over the next twenty-five years. Traveling with train networks, using solar energy, wind energy and geothermal energy, could be used as clean electrical power sources. Bio fuels created from waste products don't destroy the forest which stores enormous amounts of carbon dioxide. Farmers should be paid to work around the trees; financial incentives of this kind can preserve habitats in poor countries. Bamboo is as dense as many trees. It is a very fast growing grass and is an excellent renewable resource. Its use could save many trees. Across the planet, all countries should stop participating in any activities that result in the extinction of species.

To over-consume the resources of the Earth is illogical. What of the future generations? Drip, drip, drip of the planet's melting ice at the poles should not be Earth's new time piece. The clock of the planet should not sound like an ice shelf melting. The capriciousness of our planet's weather system has been traced to pollution by too many scientists. This catalyst to our weather's moods of caprice must be addressed. Our planet and all its wonders have been a source of hope for all of life's children. When we set fire to hope, we set fire to all the children's futures.

Professor Kensington turned to Emily and said, "You are going to be late for your meeting with that nice young man Matthew, who I met at the Botanical Gardens. Don't worry; I'll fill you in on the rest of the conference." Emily smiled at Professor Kensington, wondering if there is anything he doesn't know. She discreetly left the conference room to make her way to Central Park.

Chapter 31
The Pond

Lovely white clouds wearing their power lightly were flowing within the bright blue currents of this beautiful sky. As their path led toward the Central Park pond, Emily put her hand in Matthew's. The touch of her hand seemed natural within the tranquility of the pond's environment. Emily felt a sense of protection as he lightly squeezed her slender fingers. Relaxed within their love, she turned to him, with her amazing eyes radiating happiness. Matthew's heart was wild with anticipation as he felt their connection and knew that soon he would feel her lips for the first time.

Standing under a windswept tree with graceful spreading branches, Matthew pulled her towards him thinking, "Where is the air?" as he was almost unable to breathe. Emily's eyes met his, sparkling from the light that was dispersed through the distending foliage, their turquoise color seemed even more incredible. Matthew's mouth met hers; her lips were sweeter and softer than he could have imagined. He fully understood how special she was as it felt like his first kiss many times over. Matthew had never felt more alive. He kissed her deeply, leaving past and future and only living in the moment. Part of the moment came from the love he felt since he first saw her that morning at Ogunquit. Everything that is good and beautiful in the world was Matthew; Emily now knew that love at first sight was true. They were folded in a passion and love of their own time and space; an intimate dimension that was theirs alone. Into the depths of loves well, deep into a world few really ever reach, an intoxicating light surrounded them, yet their eyes were closed. It was the same magical lighting Emily felt when she looked up through the elegant tree branches to the sky. Their beauty and grace seemed to merge with the azure lighting. Loves light, there for all to see, yet many people do not find the time to lift their heads and look up. Matthew felt dizzy as he was transported to a place he never thought possible.

Light shimmered from the moon and the lamps of Central Park which now highlighted parts of the pond. Reflecting off of the water it encouraged the trees' lower branches to extend farther over the pond. Moonbeams working with evening breezes brought an extra terrestrial glow to the small pond's shimmering surface. Its beauty had contributed to a kiss between Emily and Matthew that was also out of this world. Their souls lifted and they followed the path along the pond to the stairs that led to the Fifth Avenue exit. Feeling transported back in time because of the horse and carriages that lined Fifth Avenue and 59th Street, it would seem fitting if the people wore Victorian dresses and top hats; the atmosphere caused a feeling of quieter times to prevail around the park. It was one of Manhattan's special and beautiful moments. The streetlights on Fifth Avenue shimmered like an orderly line of stars as a light drizzle began.

Upon parting, Matthew thought, "This love must be what all the poets and songwriters are inspired by." The intensity and the thoughts of Emily were always present in his mind. "Will this special love really happen to everyone at least once in their lifetime, or has destiny smiled on just a fortunate few? Imagine the dizziness the world would experience if every couple were this immersed in a magical love."

He thought back to Ogunquit when he imagined what her lips would be like on his. He discovered that it was more wonderful than he thought possible. His heart felt like that of a hummingbird because of the excitement of its beat. He thought of the warmth that he felt in her lips and their two hearts' power as one igniting all of love's fires. Matthew wondered to himself if one lifetime would be enough to show her how much he loved her.

Walking through Central Park would become a favorite date for Emily and Matthew. There were times when they would meet very early in the morning, usually beginning their day at the pond. They enjoyed the privacy of their early morning rendezvous, usually finding the pond very still and serene, and yet to have woken up. Matthew was happy just to hold Emily's hand, which was so soft and gentle and he would often stop their walk for yet another kiss. He breathed in her fragrance and felt the sweetness of her lips and never knew love's heartbeat could always be fresh.

Emily saw him coming down the steps toward the pond. His posture was straight and his body quite beautifully balanced, and there was an athletic feel to his walk. Matthew's eyes were on her and were filled with the light of her sight. Emily felt his love even from the distance.

They walked on, moving slowly, the air was breezy with grassy scents. Passing the zoo, Emily looked to her left and spotted one of her favorite statues. She had thought Balto could be a wolf when first sighting him at Central Park years ago with her mother. The sled dog named Balto had led a team of Alaskan huskies through miles of rough terrain and blizzard conditions to successfully deliver medicine to the people of Nome, Alaska. The medicine was used to treat diphtheria. They sat on a bench across from Balto for awhile watching parents as they took pictures of their children posing with the sled dog. Emily and Matthew smiled as they saw many of the parents climb up the large rocks for photographs with the famous sled dog as well.

Emily knew the importance of exercise and the impact nature could have on children who grow up in cities. She knew well that it was mostly the concrete paths and playgrounds that made up their world. On several occasions, when Emily would return to her old neighborhood she would no longer hear someone calling out, "I have next game," at the area's basketball courts. A large majority of children all seemed to be captured by the technology of video games, developing quick thumbs and large bellies as they would stay at home in front of their televisions or computer screens. Emily hoped that humanity's path would not continue to lead away from the special beauty that is nature. She would wish the world would realize its importance and stop their attacks in the name of industrialization. She often thought, "If only I could do more." It made her especially happy to see school and orphanage outings that encouraged trips to the parks and the Botanical Gardens for the health of the children. It would give them the restorative power of green surroundings as well as new experiences.

Matthew cradled Emily's head into his chest saying, "You seem very thoughtful." Emily smiled and snuggled closer to him. She thought back to her reoccurring childhood dream. In this dream, there was a city divided by a soft flowing river lined with flowers and trees. Many of the city's buildings were crystal-like, reflecting the beautiful surroundings of the trees and gardens. Other buildings were warm soft pastel tones, seemingly part of the surrounding nature. She thought, "If only all cities were balanced in a harmony with nature; after all, aren't we all part of nature?"

Chapter 32
Lunch

As Emily walked down Crescent Street, she noticed the lawn that separated the two large brick apartment buildings. Seven large trees formed a circle in this section of grass and they always gave her the impression of being in some sort of conference. She was early for lunch with her mother and Matthew, so she decided to walk around the grounds of her old neighborhood. The paths through the housing projects had not changed. Though they were part of the here and now, at times Emily still found herself walking through memories. The connection of the past could be strong and she wondered how many others felt the power of the past when revisiting. There are those who do not want to let go of the past and actually try to recapture it and return through countless reunions. Others want to let the past go, but are unable to do so. Is the past really a time that has gone by? Cathy Westwood didn't want to move and insisted that the neighborhood had become part of who she was.

Looking across the children's playground, Emily saw the curtain of green that seemed even more full and powerful then she had remembered. There were strong winds blowing as there was a possibility of thunder storms occurring late in the afternoon. The apartment building to the right of the curtain was casting a dark shadow that gave the impression of mysterious canyons within the green. Powerful winds moved the trees' foliage within the green curtain, to and fro; but the trees held their form and nature's divide expressed its power. A strong white pigeon managed to navigate through the curtain by penetrating one of its dark portals.

Walking around the playground, Emily heard the familiar squeaky swings and saw a young boy soaring high. She noticed a few elderly women watching children from the benches in the interior of the playground. She thought how wonderful it was for families to have such helpful grandmothers; after all, they probably worked hard to bring up their own children. Emily thought of Grandma Grace and how important she was for her and her mother.

Emily walked down the path adjacent to the large lawn passing the beautiful magnolia trees and suddenly experienced an empty sinking feeling. Emily, looking past the magnolia trees should have been able to see her wonderful childhood dwelling. In this sanctuary she was able to avoid the neighborhood bullies and be led to special thoughts and studies concerning nature. This dwelling is where she learned the distinctive differences among the trees.

Emily's dwelling was gone. Her secret special place provided by the witch hazel tree that had meant so much to her growing up, was no longer there. She decided to stop a tall, slender ground's keeper that she remembered as being kind and giving special care as he planted flowers and tended to the grounds. She did not know his name, but she did remember him smiling as he would see her enter the witch hazel tree. The ground's keeper had sun lines around his eyes and his hair was now gray, but his face had not changed much. Emily had asked what happened to the witch hazel tree that was so lovely with its large umbrella-like foliage. She explained that she remembered seeing it just last month. The ground's keeper responded, "It was a beautiful tree. Unfortunately, management had ordered it removed as there had been muggings in the neighborhood. A few of the tenants complained that the criminals could hide there."

"I hope it was transplanted," Emily said in a concerned voice.

The ground's keeper suddenly recognized her. "I remember you as a little girl. You would enter this tree with books and a small blue blanket."

Emily smiled and said, "And I remember how well you always took care of the grounds. Where was the tree transplanted?"

The ground's keeper's expression became serious and he shook his head side to side. Emily's eyes watered up and the winds blew strongly through the thick foliage of the curtain and a thunder clap punctuated the storms in the distance. "Rain is coming," said the ground's keeper, acting as if he didn't notice the rain in her eyes. Emily thanked him and saw him walk across the lawn towards the tool shed.

She continued along the path outside of the lawn's rectangle and heard a familiar sentence among the foliage of the large trees that lined the lawn. In her bower she remembered hearing the wind speak within the foliage. Her mother would tell her that it was her imagination; that the wind and the leaves were not speaking. The words still called out to her and in her heart she felt that they had a meaning. In her sanctuary, where she would study the cycles of nature and learn all she could about the trees, it actually occurred to her how wonderful it would be if they really could speak. Emily thought that they would be wise and that their knowledge would be a wonderful accumulation through the centuries.

Tormented by bullies as a child, she would often be nervous and have trouble going to sleep when imagining what might be in store for her the next day. She found that if she imagined herself floating softly among the treetops, it would have a calming effect on her.

Emily's mother greeted her with one of her wonderful smiles which immediately perked her up. "Okay Emily, I can tell that you're upset. What is it?" Emily knew that she was considered extremely sensitive and her face with its different colors would always tell everything; especially to her mother.

"Remember that tree I told you about, with the beautiful umbrella foliage, the witch hazel tree?"

"Yes, the one you would say was the only one of its kind in the neighborhood. When you were young, you seemed very much attached to that tree."

Emily responded with an upset tone, "Would you believe that they removed it without transplanting it?"

"I'm sorry honey, would you like a cup of Irish tea?"

"No thanks, Mom."

Seeing how upset Emily was, her mother decided to change the subject. "Everyone at the diner is very excited about seeing you and Matthew, most especially John, Carolyn and Mary Ellen."

Emily thought that it was ironic that it was her mother that got Mary Ellen a job at the restaurant. As a child, Mary Ellen was the girl who most terrified her. Mary Ellen was now able to afford an apartment at an early age and become independent from her abusive parents. Bullies need not endure as long as they had someone to care about them.

The doorbell rang and Emily and her mother went down to the lobby to meet Matthew. Cathy Westwood loved Matthew from the moment she saw him and how he behaved with Emily. Their joy of being together was apparent as one look at the glow of their faces and the sparkle in their eyes told the story. These two had a special love. The first time they visited Cathy it was for dinner. Matthew was astonished that all the dishes and cups were light green.

"I see you like green also, Mrs. Westwood. I knew Emily loved green, but then it was always related to nature."

Cathy smiled and said, "It's called jadeite. John, the owner of the restaurant where I work gave me this entire set of glassware as a present. It's very strong."

"Yes, very thick and green."

Emily looked at Matthew and then her mother and knew it was coming. They all got hysterical laughing and any nervous tension that was once present dissipated. Matthew was charming and knew just the right way to flirt with her mother, Emily thought.

Cathy would chew Matthew's ear off about how wonderful Emily was growing up. "Emily was an excellent student and would always help me around the house."

"Mom, you're embarrassing me."

Matthew would interject, "It's okay Emily. I really do want to know everything about you."

Cathy went on, "Emily loved to learn. She had so many impossible questions. She would ask, 'Is there only one universe? What makes lightning?'" She turned towards Emily and asked smiling, "Oh, and by the way Emily, did you ever find out why snow is white?"

"Why yes, Mom."

"Oh no," Cathy Westwood thought, putting both hands on her cheeks as she smiled towards Matthew.

"Well since you asked, Mom; when a light proton enters snow it bounces light all around the ice crystals. The color of all the light frequencies in the visible spectrum combined makes the color white. Light energy will make the electrons vibrate around atoms."

Matthew said, "Emily, do you mind repeating that, I'm not sure that your mother got it all?"

"Well you see," Emily began. "Bouncing light protons in the ice crystals bring the visible..." Emily stopped as she saw them both smiling and trying to contain themselves. She looked at Matthew and knew that they were pushing her buttons.

Cathy continued, "Thank goodness Emily would finally have many of her questions answered in her continuing education. She would absorb lectures in college like a sponge."

Ronald Yates

Emily heard a certain Professor Kensington at a lecture and knew that this would be her field of study. The Professor spoke in detail about the field of dendrology. Every student attending his lecture became aware of the importance of the woodlands and the gifts of medicine, shelter, food and other supplies they would bring to the world. The Professor showed a certain sensitivity as he spoke, not only of the science of the forest, but he also addressed the spirituality that could be felt in the woodlands; an awareness that was a kind of interdependent kinship. Emily remembered the Professor stating that Earth's acme of grace is the tree, which is a being of an unsurpassed physicality in its form; its beauty a living poetry. He spoke of the connection with their presence as an instantaneously meditative experience; that to connect within a forest is to become part of a profound singularity composed of energy which is spiritual in nature. Emily felt the love of life and beauty in every tree and instantly related to the palatable power they brought. Even as a child, she would look through the tree tops and see the sky's beauty, then follow its branches down to the surrounding areas and finally follow its connection deep into the earth.

In the future, Emily the student would form a strong bond with Professor Kensington and investigate the field of dendrology as partners in science. They would experience together the beauty of the singularity that surrounds the spaces between the poetry that is the form of each forest tree. Working on important scientific data they both would not lose their acknowledgment of the spirituality of nature.

Cathy, Matthew and Emily all walked down Crescent Street towards Broadway and John's restaurant. There were some voices heard and finger pointing noticed on the way to the restaurant. "That guy looks like Matthew Monroe." "I think that's Matthew Monroe." "That guy could make it to the Hall of Fame." "Wow, is he gorgeous."

They were not in the restaurant for more than two minutes when a crowd started to form and linger outside with people pointing through the glass windows. John greeted them with a large smile.

Looking at Emily he said, "Did it get brighter in my restaurant? How did a ball of sunshine get in here?"

Emily hugged John and said, "You are not going to bring me a glass of milk and a cupcake, are you?" They laughed.

Looking at Matthew he said, "So, you're the lucky man."

Matthew extended his hand and said, "That's for sure."

The crowd was getting louder outside the restaurant and John remarked, "You seem to be a very popular Yankee. Come and sit at this booth. It is the most private and has a really good waitress."

Emily smiled as Carolyn was standing behind John with Mary Ellen. Emily introduced Matthew and everyone had a fine time.

During lunch, Carolyn said, "Emily, let me get you another napkin."

"No thank you," as she only used one napkin when eating out and when at home she only used recycled paper. She leaned over to her mother and asked her to see if John made sure that the restaurant used recycled paper. Emily knew full well that if every family used 100% recycled paper, the world could save millions of trees.

Mary Ellen looked kinder and happier than Emily ever remembered. Her face had grown soft and warm in its expression. She told Emily how excited she was for her and almost swooned as she shyly asked Matthew for an autograph. He gave autographs to the busboys, the kitchen staff as well as most everyone in the restaurant. Cathy was happy as she watched John pose with Matthew for a picture to hang up in the restaurant. Carolyn was thrilled for Cathy and told her what a great couple they were, not to mention gorgeous.

Ronald Yates

Matthew waved for a cab to get to Yankee Stadium. Emily and her mother smiled as he stopped to sign a few more autographs for the group of people that had been waiting outside of the restaurant.

Chapter 33
Botanical Laboratory

Emily inhaled the fresh air as the grassy dew of the beautiful spring morning also carried the scent of flowers. She decided to briefly walk through the Everett Gardens that were just in front of the Conservatory. She was working at least six days a week and would always find a new flower or tree to appreciate. Usually she would arrive early for work as she enjoyed her walks among nature's beauty with no distractions. The flowers in front of the Conservatory were happy to be waking to this morning's breezes. The breezes were frequent enough to cause small dances among the flowers. There was still plenty of morning dew drops resting on their petals. The sun's rays penetrated the dew drops refracting the colors of the petals. Each flower petal was now carrying dewy prisms adding to their glow. Baby water rainbows were formed on the trees' leaves as well as the grassy lawn nearby.

Emily enjoyed all of nature's rainbows, wondering what tree, leaf or flower would prove to be a deliverer of another gift of health to humanity. Walking back to the lab, down Lily Way, past the garden cafeteria, she breathed a sigh as she took in the wonderful scents and beauty of the evergreens. The pines, junipers and various conifers were now bright green and full with burgundy red cones being born on several of the species. Emily, looking at her watch, quickened her step through the majestic tulip trees lining the path to the library and finally the laboratory.

Plant researchers and other scientists explored lesser known forest areas for new plant specimens. The labs at the New York Botanical Gardens preserve and study new specimens. The scientists working within the communities of the Amazon Rain Forests or perhaps a forest in Vietnam may make important health and environmental differences around the world. For over a hundred years, promising minds have been provided access to the scientific facilities to train in plant research at the Gardens.

Emily's dedication to her work was selfless. She was saddened as she thought that many of these beautiful species of plants would no longer be on the planet. We keep building gene banks and seed banks to protect the world's diversity; ironic that many have been destroyed by wars and poor environmental conditions. The seed bank of Spitsbergen Island showed how the Norwegian government was affecting more security and intelligent construction as well as location. The height above sea level would keep the vault dry even if the ice caps melted. This global seed vault could preserve seeds of important foods, as well as grains, for possibly thousands of years. The death of a species such as birds or insects, due to the destruction of various habitats leads to the loss of many plant species as they lose their pollinators. Emily felt helpless as the beauty of the flowers and plants with their endless medicinal possibilities could be lost.

She would somehow find ways to confound the assassins of the particular disease she would be presently at battle with inside the walls of the garden laboratories. Emily's goal was always to improve the health of all living things. It was only in the middle of this century that an effective cure for malaria was synthesized. The bark of the Cinchona Tree would yield quinine to treat malaria. Who knows which forests will give us more answers for cures?

Emily had developed synthetic substitutes for promising anticancer drugs that only came from stripping down the bark of certain trees. These synthetic drugs would now save the lives of many people as well as trees. Her formula could possibly be applied to countless other cures derived from various species of trees. There was still much to learn.

Saving the trees was also saving the planet's biological system, which affected all life. Emily was acutely aware of the importance of her work and was relentless in her focus. Everybody and everything could be an important contributor to the world's health.

At the laboratory, Emily's observations of a test had a laser scrutiny. There were few people that had this focus and there were few who cared this much about the world having a healthier future. Her constant sacrifice was seraphic, pushing herself to the limit to find new cures for the ill as soon as possible. She was currently studying an unusual species of orchid. It was unusual in the fact that only the moonlight could bring out its silver flower. When she encounters a mysterious area in her microscope slide, at times a door would open revealing a new cure for the ill. She had discovered that this orchid's leaves have a special anti-inflammatory property. She sighed and thought that fortunately it was discovered before its home forest was cleared. She wondered when the world would realize every life form, plant, insect, and microbe or otherwise is important to the Earth's balance and possibly even the universal balance. Surely we are not even close to comprehending the important information nature has to offer the world.

How deep the beauty of the Supreme Intelligence must extend. Everything is in a perfect balance: Planets' orbits and rotations balanced with gravity and extending through and around the entire universe and its stars. How can we not be pantheistic when considering the incredible tranches of the universe?

"How does the money that countries spend on war compare to the money that they spend on curing cancer?" she wonders. "The research that is necessary to help humanity is endless. Monies could be put toward healthier ends. Why were the people of Cash County, Utah, living ten years longer than the people anywhere else in the United

States?" Emily's mind was always working to try to find new ways to help humanity.

Emily's assistant, Maria Torrez, was five feet tall with loads of jet black hair cascading over her full figure. She was a very positive and perky assistant who was a delight to work with and very intelligent. Maria loved her work and particularly enjoyed the flowers surrounding the different parts of the Gardens. Emily was contemplating her experiments while listening to the "Symphonic Dance, Opus 45," by Rachmaninoff which was very magical sounding. She often found new inspirational directions in her research while listening to certain classical pieces. At times she would think back to her mother and their trips to Lincoln Center. Somehow, she always knew that most of these classical composers felt like she did about the beauty of the world. Maria's voice interrupted her concentration reminding her that it was time to leave. Emily smiled and thanked Maria as she would often get lost while focusing on her studies.

Emily, looking up at the lovely blue sky as she prepared to leave for home, saw a bolt of lightning. "It was odd to see lightning against the blue sky," she thought. She knew rebel bolts from outside of a storm could be seen. "The weather did say afternoon thunderstorms; they must be getting closer. Knowing lightning bolts could be hotter than the sun and five miles long, why not harness their energy? Lightning rods could channel the energy through a conduit for a type of storage cell."

While on Metro North heading home, Emily was reading an article on the use of mushroom fungi to decompose organic pollutants from the soil. Ridding the soil of these pollutants would benefit plant life enormously. Her concentration was interrupted as her stop was announced. Exiting the train, she looked up at the still blue pastel sky with vivid glorious gold beams of sun penetrating the clouds. There was a purity of white exhibited against the blue. The wind, respecting the depth of beauty presented at this time of day, halted all of its movement.

Chapter 34

Pub

Emily was on edge while walking to the sports pub to meet Matthew. Concrete drills, clangs of heavy machinery; this must be the third construction site she passed. An enormous truck trying to negotiate a turn on Third Avenue and 60th Street sent all the car horns blasting. Another truck driver started pounding his horn which seemed louder than the sound of a ship's horn while docking. A traffic cop began yelling at the truck driver as well as some of the passenger cars. While Emily was at the intersection, she heard people on their cell phones with their criss-crossing complaints about being late; piercing what free space was left within the noise of the city. They cannot break away from the televisions, computers and cell phones. Emily recalled one of Wordsworth's quotes, "The world is too much with us; late and soon getting and spending, we lay waste our powers: Little we see in nature that is ours."

She decided to walk several blocks out of the way just to avoid the bludgeoning noises. Street sounds had become more alarming as the ringing of cell phones were everywhere. Suddenly, Emily felt an industrialized William Tell Overture attacking her relentlessly. She thought, "I love Matthew, but I think this will be my last Friday rush hour rendezvous with him. How do these people focus under the continuing confusing sounds which must add to their stress levels? Everyone seems in a rush yet always accessible due to technology. Is it any wonder that we hear more and more cases of ADD and memory decline? At times the city itself seems like one anxiety attack after another. Everyone is interested in speed; everyone is waiting impatiently for the light to change; the cars honk and the people scream. Manhattan seemed like a world of orderly disorder. Shoppers, tourists, workers—all bodies in a moving mass which was scary and exciting at the same time."

The first time in Manhattan during rush hour Emily actually momentarily froze in her tracks and remembered her mother reassuring her. The huge buildings were powerful and remarkable, but they were intimidating as well. Emily thought of Central Park, a large sanctuary within a restless metropolis. It was a beautiful refuge where people could find nature and breathe easier.

Showing her pass at the door and entering the pub, Emily was taken aback. The people were so close to one another and all seemed to be talking at the same time. There were sports updates on five large TV screens which were mounted on the surrounding walls. They were loud, overwhelming, relentless and impossible.

"Be strong; I must find Matt," she thought as she tried to make her way through the crowd. She had a sinking feeling. "I'll manage. This is part of Matt's press obligations as a Yankee. Matthew warned me that these functions could be loud."

Her senses seemed to magnify in the pub's surroundings. Glasses clanking at the bar sounded like cymbals and the conversations were so loud as if the people were all competing for their own stage. It was odd that although they were in a social setting many of the patrons were yelling into cell phones. Emily wondered about the possible dangers of second-hand exposure to their magnetic fields as cell phones were now everywhere. In close quarters, actually pressed up against one another, the people seemed to be in a swirl, blurred within the pub's spotlight lighting. The crowd's noise became quiet as several people said, "Look, it's Matthew Monroe."

Matthew, upon sighting Emily, knew something was wrong. This pub was packed like a subway at rush hour.

Strange women with an overabundance of ornaments and makeup started to head in Matthew's direction. A couple of men carrying unfounded illusions and quick intentions started walking towards Emily. Matthew broke through a resistant pack of people and made his way towards her. Emily focused and spotted Matthew's blond curly hair and began to squeeze between the patrons moving towards him. Her legs and arms felt like heavy oars trying to navigate through thick air and could hear her breathing pick up speed as she pushed forward. The swirl of people began to circle with the entire room as she tried to yell out for Matthew, but she found only a soft voice.

Emily's elegant fragility at times was so ethereal that Matthew worried she would be cloaked by invisibility and lost to him in these surroundings. Matthew once again spotted Emily in the crowded club. She appeared blanched; something was wrong. Emily was a super sensitive person; this type of environment could trigger fear and confusion. Matthew knew that she came here to be with him and support him. His eyes only saw Emily; she appeared unsteady and frightened and then he saw her starting to fall. Heading straight to her, he pushed aside three men surrounding her. Matthew lifted Emily into his arms to take her outside of the pub. "Is she okay?" several of his teammates asked. "Is there anything we can do to help?"

"It's okay guys, I'll handle things."

Matthew gently sat down on the long bench that was situated in front of the pub with Emily still in his arms. She opened her eyes and saw the silhouettes of the people walking against the red brick wall of the pub. They seemed to be strangely tinted blue moving briskly with erect posture. Matthew put his hand on Emily's shoulder and let it slip down to her hand.

"Emily, you have goose bumps, are you cold?"

"A little bit, but I'm mostly nervous."

To Matthew, even Emily's insecurity had a certain charm. Matthew squeezed her hand and whispered, "I love you," in her ear. She looked up at him seeing his magnetic smile. He was so handsome and debonair that he gave her the energy to smile back.

"There is a large bruise on your arm. I didn't realize that you had fallen so hard."

"I'll be okay, Matthew. It's just that the room was starting to swirl and my knees kind of gave way."

She was thinking that she should tell him that one of the symptoms of her blood disorder was dizziness and weakness. Looking up at the night sky from Matt's cradled arm, she seemed to have a unique connection with all of God's creations. A bright blue moon had given titanium tones to a lone night cloud as it softly sailed by. The moon reflected romance in its light, but Emily knew it could only be with the help of the sun.

Manhattan had rarely been clearer with stars everywhere. It was as if the whole Milky Way was revealed within the fresh radiant lunar blue of the night. Surely from these special skies, star-ignited dreams would have to follow. Looking into Emily's eyes, Matthew found star shine, twinkling in the turquoise. He thought to himself, "Am I bewitched by love, or is this woman holding starlight in her eyes?"

FUTURE

Chapter 35
Blood Test

As Westchester's Metro North train was riding through the rain, Emily thought that Matthew's concern for her health had grown. He knew that lately she wasn't quite as strong as usual.

Matthew was waiting at home impatiently for her train to arrive from work. He would not meet her at the station as she would accuse him of being over protective. Emily could sense the feelings Matthew had. There was no chance of keeping his constant fear for her health hidden inside, yet still he would try. A large smile and a big kiss at the door and perhaps he could fool himself that all would be well. The very thought of Emily not being alive filled him with a dark gloom. He must try to be more positive. Ironic that it was Emily that gave him the strength and hope that this enemy of her body could be defeated. Emily would reassure Matthew that they would research and discover a cure. The doctors say it's a matter of how long before her body succumbs to the disease. Matthew would pay any price to keep her well and said so in his prayers.

"Where is she tonight? Why is she running late?" Rain rapped on the windows with a strong sweep of the wind. "That's it; I'm going to the station."

It was then that he heard the car pull in. His heart took over and at the door he pulled her to him. His arms were drenched with rain from hugging her raincoat. He kissed her and ran his hand through her hair. Emily smiled and said, "Matthew, I was only gone for the day."

"I missed you," he said as his lips touched her ear. Emily realized that her illness was taking its toll on him.

"Matthew, I feel excited today. The doctor called and was hopeful about a new medicine they are developing."

Matthew felt one of despair's demons leave his heart on this ray of hope. With an anxious voice, Matthew said, "Tell me!"

"A different ratio involving a combination of immune enhancers had shown promising results. Actually, I read that only recently researchers at the University of Aberdeen, Scotland, and the Laboratoire de Biologie Moleculaire du Cancer discovered compounds in kava that inhibited the growth in cancer cells. Test tube research showing kava extracts killed leukemia and ovarian cancer cells without harming healthy cells. This research is also very promising."

Emily continued to wonder to herself, "How many plant cures are being lost by the deforestation of the planet?"

Emily arrived early for her tests and decided that she had time to stop at Starbucks for a cup of tea. One of these tests would be a blood test that would determine how effective this new medicine would be on her blood cancer. As she walked inside, she looked up at the sky and thought that it looked like it could rain. She took a quiet table in the back of the coffee shop to contemplate all the events.

Deciding to research the recent occurrences that took place around the world she opened her laptop and began to chart the events relative to the time of day, locations and conditions. Space anomalies would have to be considered. Her concentration was broken by a group of very loud women. At the table on the other side of her were a group of loud suits. One of the suits crunching loudly on chips was discussing negotiation tactics as some of the chips fell out of his mouth. The other wolves at the table remained attentive and eager animals. One responded, "Fucking great plan," while laughing crudely. Another suit added to the conversation, "We are dealing with douche heads." Attacked on both sides by loud and vulgar voices, Emily decided to take a seat outside. "Amazing, in this huge Starbucks with every table available, these two groups decide to surround me." She smiled to herself, "I'm testy from concern. This is not a library after all." Looking out the window there were clouds but not rain. She could study under the awning outdoors while drinking her tea.

Large shadows were crossing the skyscrapers from quickly moving clouds. The wind chased shadows to the ground from the overhead pigeons that were trying to negotiate the increasing turbulence. With the clouds becoming a deeper shade of gray Emily's thoughts went to Matthew. "I wish I could be everything to him." She dreamt of being more, but deep down in her heart, she knew the strength needed for children was not hers at this time. She preferred that he didn't keep her company, even for a blood test, as the worry and stress in his face was upsetting to her. Matthew, a fighter, and a strong competitor refused to believe a battle could possibly be lost. Emily knew her immune system was in a battle usually lost to this type of blood sickness and was feeling more fatigued lately.

Clouds were becoming grayer with a dim blue aura surrounding their dampness. Increasing scents of rain suggested that the coming clouds would soon surrender their liquid load. Ratter-tat-tat, a light symphony began. Emily sipped the tea with more quickness and suddenly a rushing wind brought allegros in various crescendos to the rain in sweeping proportions. The awning shook simultaneously with a slap of thunder causing her to shiver. She thought of recent nightmares that she had experienced. There were frightening dark storms, with lawless winds, which would wake her up shaking. Emily had seen the signs and they've come to be a great fear. Temperatures were rising and the storms and tornadoes were becoming larger and more intense. Matthew would feel her tremble and wake her saying, "Was it the storms again?" The awning shook more severely and she knew the winds were announcing that she better start for her doctor's appointment.

Shadows of fear were a constant strain in her mind lately as she was not optimistic about this appointment. Past medicines had only been able to provide temporary positive effects on her blood disorder. Doctor Fisher told Emily that it is important to stay positive and that even if the new medicine turns out to be ineffective, he had learned about another possible treatment. "There is a promising new genetic research involving RNA interference that could lead to new cancer treatments." Emily knew these discoveries took time to implement but was appreciative and thanked the doctor.

Emily always tried to shop at a farmer's market knowing this avoids shipping foods which uses fossil fuels. The skies had become a pale gray, but it was calm now and there would be no wind or rain in her face. She thought she would stop at Union Square for some fresh basil and organic carrot raison cookies.

Recently, she had read a frightening article in the newspaper about a mystery concerning bees. Many scientists were worried about their disappearance and the collapse of their bee hives. There were many empty hives and large bee populations missing. One theory was that the cause was pesticides, and another theory implicated that global warming was subjecting beehives to unusual temperatures; yet another theory that was being investigated as a cause was cell phone waves. Emily thought that these scientists had better move fast as one third of the world's food supply depends on bees for pollination.

Once at home, her phone rang and they both knew it would be the doctor with the test results. Emily picked up the phone and listened as Dr. Fisher updated her. Matthew looked at her face; her expression spoke volumes. Hanging up the phone, she turned to Matthew and said that the tests showed little improvement although there was a slight stabilization indicating that the disease's attack may be slowing down. Matt tried to be reassuring saying, "Well, at least that's something," and he took her in his arms and held her softly.

"At least I can continue working."

Matthew thought, "So frail, yet with unrelenting determination to solve the unusual mysteries involving the world's recent events."

"I love you, Emily," he said as he kissed her. She looked up smiling with some color returning to her face and with a sigh said, "Oh Matt, I'm such a problem."

"You're not a problem, you are a gift."

" You are really something." Then they kissed.

Chapter 36
Space Station

The International Space Station is more than just a vehicle for space exploration. It was also built to improve conditions on our own planet. Studies in its laboratories can be beneficial to the people's health and well being. Advancements in science and medicine are sure to result from the six state-of-the-art laboratory modules. Space environment in itself will improve studies on disease by offering unique controls for protein crystals. Special innovative research projects will concentrate on studying the environment of our planet.

Looking out at the endless beacons of space, Sue Lee wonders how many travelers have had the need for the guidance of the stars.

Vladamir Dar interrupted her thoughts saying, "I know we have taken the right route with our foods being from crops grown hydroponically in space. The plants won't compete for oxygen in the space station as animals will. The contrary is true, as they would release oxygen and clean carbon dioxide from the air. Considering all of that, I must admit that I really could go for a good steak."

"Sorry Vlad, no cows on our space station; and I for one like the food here. I particularly enjoyed the quinoa and tomato salad yesterday; of course I am a vegetarian."

"Since we need more calcium and vitamin D, due to weightlessness, I am happy to see your kale and soybean salads."

"Personally, I think the scientists at Cornell have come up with some healthy and tasty dishes."

"Remind me not to apply for a stay on a Mars colony in the future."

Walking over to Vladamir, Sue lightly put her head on his chest and nuzzled closer. Vlad even drew her closer with soft kisses on her neck, as joyful sensations of passion began to fill them. Sharing in a trance of love as they stared out of the porthole into outer space, an eternal feeling came over them. There was supposed to be a constant musical tone to the universe, but Vlad only found the silence of space. He did find a light in space. Whenever Sue Lee was in the same area as him it seemed to make the space station brighter. His hand gliding over her every curve, he thought of how warm and soft she felt.

The next morning, Vlad found Sue checking out her bonsai and said, "The pot seems special for your ficus tree."

"Yes, my friend loves little trees and gave me this Shuho bonsai vessel because he felt it would relax me in the space station as it is a lovely blue container with a soft circular shape."

"The ficus does really seem to be happy within its vessel; it seems to be quite healthy."

"Did you know that there were districts in Thailand that were named after the ficus tree species?"

"And all this time I thought your specialties were in the fields involving physics," Vlad said smiling.

"You forget that I am now acquainted with Professor Kensington, a leading world dendrologist who is currently working at the Royal Botanical Gardens. Professor Kensington is a strong advocate for preserving biodiversity as are the Botanical Gardens. The scientific research at these botanical gardens around the world can lead to enormous discoveries that can preserve the plant kingdom and future life on Earth. It was Doctor Peters who introduced us as they have known each other for years."

Vlad turned towards the small willow leaf ficus tree on the table thinking that it was good that NASA approved this ficus bonsai for the space station; it will filter indoor toxins from the atmosphere and it has also made Sue happy.

"Sensors are showing minute impacts on the hull of the space station," said Gene Fieder, astronaut and engineer.

"Kessler Syndrome?" asks Doctor Dar.

Sue Lee added, "This space junk is a real problem; two space satellites have already left a cloud of debris. One of them crashed over Siberia and their debris could threaten future space flights."

"No, our orbit is too high to be attacked by metal debris. Space junk is found in a low orbit, but I will strengthen the station's shields just to be safe."

Sue Lee said, "We should probably notify NASA."

"Wait, that's odd, I have Cecilia Washington calling from NASA for Dr. Peters on a priority channel," said Gene Fieder.

Cecilia Washington gave Dr. Peters a detailed briefing of the recent occurrences on Earth's surface.

Dr. Peters said, "This has to be some sort of a geomagnetic phenomenon."

"Yes, I agree, but an event of terrestrial magnetism occurring within certain boundaries globally?"

"It seems unlikely as natural phenomenon, yet we must consider it. These events appear as controlled geometric eddies; currents of gravity forming a series of whirlpools creating hyperspace within normal gravity."

"What or who could have the advance technology or ability to manipulate gravity as well as electromagnetic fields? It is inconceivable to my mind that this is a result of a sophisticated attack based on science."

"That is what we must find out. An electromagnetic field inhibiting normal gravity even in a limited area is an incredible feat."

"The President does not like to take any chances based on your initial analysis; as impossible as it may seem, we must consider a planned attack as well as natural phenomenon."

"Cecilia, you realize that if it is a country that has this advanced knowledge of gravity manipulation, they have clearly conquered areas in quantum physics that we have only touched upon."

"NASA has considered using super colliders creating tiny black holes to have a better understanding of gravity and its curvatures; this kind of gravitational control is extraordinary. The seventeen-mile long Hadron collider will eventually answer some important questions that may help, such as: What is the reason that the mass of the universe is mostly hidden? Is it true that there are more than three dimensions?"

"I understand that the power of this particle acceleration may create tiny black holes for a nanosecond."

"Let's hope they stay tiny, but the process with the colliders will take time for these answers; time which we may not have."

"We need a link to the NASA computers at all locations to analyze these unusual readings."

"The ATU should arrive there in nine hours. It will be carrying a new, multi-quantum current analyzer, developed in the European Space Agency."

"I read the research. This new European high-tech laboratory device has a built-in intelligence link to the space station's computer. This will save valuable time."

"I know that you have already been on duty for five months and your international crew of seven scientists must be feeling fatigued."

"Working off planet can be claustrophobic which is ironic with the views we have from up here. This is an international crew, after all, and I'm sure they will find the strength for a global problem."

"We really need you now."

"Cecilia, don't forget that in our little village in space we don't have to sleep as much due to the microgravity."

Cecilia broke off communications with a "Thank you," to Dr. Peters and thought that it was fortunate to have such dedicated people in the space station.

Any person that would have the privilege of viewing the beautiful azure orb that is Earth from the space station surely would agree that Earth is love's dwelling. Sue continued viewing the beauty of the planet. Pointing out the hole in the ozone, she said to Vlad, "If the people continue on this destructive path, the present will not have a future and all that will be left is what was."

"You are right; time does not stop to give out second chances."

"I was recently thinking of a trip I took to Greece and the beauty of the green gorges of Mt. Chelmos."

"Now that sounds very nice."

"If the free running rivers of crystal waters continue to be polluted and then dammed, like the River Styk, no life will be able to ever drink from it. The Institute of Space Studies said that the year 2005 was the warmest for our planet on record. The continuing rise of temperatures combined with the pollution will in time cause all the rivers to bubble with fire and begin the birth of Venus II. Have you read Venus II?"

"Yes, I downloaded it as soon as it was available. Hopefully, it will shake people into acting positively toward making Earth a healthier planet. I for one do not want to see fire replace water. The sun is a wonderful gift and will allow us to become wiser and learn how to explore the universe for at least another five billion years. Uncaring polluters can turn the sun from a gift to a weapon that can destroy Earth. The red hell of Venus would then come to our planet. Crimson collisions crashing through clouds of carbon would crease the darkness with fireballs. The entire Earth would gasp for air as carbon nooses would squeeze out life's last breath. Our green forests would cook and crackle with endless fire storms and only soot to breathe. Bake the wheat fields before the breads and there is no food. Continue to destroy the gifts given to all by the Supreme Intelligence and our garden planet would be a victim of the sun's violence brought on by our disrespect. Boulders would burst beneath the blazing sun, becoming scalding swirling sand storms suffocating any left over life, as the breath of the biosphere becomes totally black with soot. The terror of low black clouds pushing more heat down would raise our street temperatures. There would be no people picnicking in parks or conversing in courtyards, much less daring to walk on the angry asphalt. Yes, I read Venus II. Venus may be closer to the sun, but it is a very dark place and it's not because of the clouds surrounding it. I certainly do not want to see Earth turn into a planet of fire shadows."

"How can we possibly consider slowing climate change in order to allow for nature to adapt? The forests are cleared and pollution continues to destroy; there is no luxury for adaptation time. There is no winner when warring against nature. Nature is what the people and all of the species of the world are part of within our planet. Nature is our home, destroy it and Earth will become Venus II. The Magellan Satellite data shows Venus was once thought to be like Earth. Four billion years ago, the information from the satellite shows that the planet's atoms were similar. It is now a planet with nightmare conditions, lava flows in arachnoids' craters pushed by Venusians' winds. An atmosphere of CO_2 clouds acid rain and a rocky furnace landscape. Temperatures reached 900 degrees Fahrenheit. Most scientists agree a greenhouse effect is most likely the cause of Venus' hell-like conditions. The carbon dioxide on Venus prevents the heat and infrared radiation from escaping into the atmosphere, just like the glass of a greenhouse."

Sue Lee continued, "What if the energy arriving from the sun could be radiated away from Venus?"

Vlad looked at Sue with amazement thinking, "How could she be worried about our planet in crises and at the same time find ways to save the planet Venus so it could be available for colonization? He couldn't help but admire her brilliant mind as well as her beauty; it was no wonder that he fell in love with her.

Sue continued, "How many of life's tomorrows will the Greeds of the world tear away with their concrete cities supplied with chemically made food? How much of the Earth's energy will we allow them to continue to drain?"

Vlad answered, "We certainly should be able to figure out how to waste less energy. After all, the human brain, the most magnificent computer there is, functions with the operational power needed to energize a ten-watt light bulb." Knowing Sue well, he thought he should try to change the subject as he knew how upset she could become.

"Have you heard any news on the tiny moon discovery around Saturn by the Cassini Space Craft?" Sue responded, "No," and decided to keep the conversation on the environment.

"If we can bring fifteen-thousand pounds of equipment to this international space station that will purify sweat and urine into drinking water, then we certainly should be able to address the water shortages on Earth with green technologies."

As they were viewing the Antarctica, Vlad added, "There is no reason that zero-emission homes and offices should not be a reality. Worldwide wind turbines and solar panels would be able to generate electric grids for energy and a pure, healthy planet. Water waste could be purified and reused in the homes and the factories. The Belgium government successfully commissioned a science station in Antarctica that has a zero emissions research facility."

"Lofty and sturdy sales in the subspace currents could bring energy from the planet's winds. We can feed the ocean's iron that would enable the phytoplankton to capture CO_2."

"The ice is melting now and the solution for global warming must be initiated immediately. Procrastinate and invite peril to our planet."

"I think I'll go for a walk outside the space station."

"No space walks now, as there are strong plasma storms on the sun that cause the Aurora Borealis which can be dangerous to satellites as well as space walkers."

"Did you know that if we could harness the energy of the Aurora Borealis then we could supply one year's worth of light for the world?"

"Another solution could be species DNA banks as well as seed banks to safeguard our plant and animal life. Establishment of a repository on the moon could represent Earth for future colonization as it is possible that society may have need for a future option."

"Our space probes that are sent to investigate other planets probably will be too late. Our species will not have the luxury of a new globe in which to relocate. We better move fast in colonizing Mars because of the rate of human consumption of our planet's resources. Our billions of inhabitants would need six more Earths to continue to live."

Trying to be positive, he responded, "If we have rapid technological improvement we could make Gliese 581C possible. The Harp's telescope has discovered this so-called new Earth as capable of harboring life. The importance of these discovered exo-planets increases as we continue to damage our planet."

"I understand that at least two hundred exo-planets have been discovered so far, but to reach these planets that circle other suns seems to be an extraordinary difficult undertaking."

"If we could conquer traveling with worm holes we could make this possible."

"I suggest we concentrate on saving our own Earth, or the exploratory research won't have time to count. If there are other Earths in other galaxies with life, let's hope that they've avoided polluting their planets. Venus II is an alert that the pollution of our planet by our species must stop now."

Once again, trying to change the subject, as he saw Sue, becoming increasingly upset, said, "Did you hear of the unusual energy readings that Gene reported to Dr. Peters? I'm surprised we haven't heard more about it."

"There was that priority call from NASA, but I'm sure if it related to the energy readings, Dr. Peters would have found the answers. Who is more likely to understand unusual magnetic readings that would be coming from outer space? I would feel better if you would look into it as well, in case it affects Earth."

"Of course I'll look into it, but you need to relax as you constantly worry about our home planet."

"Dr. Peters, Cecilia is on the line for an update," said Gene Frieder. Dr. Peters told Cecilia that his research showed that these events were affected by gravity's ability to bend space and time.

Cecilia said, "I thought that was the case as people's wristwatches at the event locations showed different times."

"Cecilia, we have a long way to go and a lot we still have to understand."

"Our scientists at Kennedy Space Center are trying to bring into consonance the four forces of nature. Our scientists have had some success with weak and strong nuclear and electromagnetic forces, but the assimilation of gravity still causes road blocks, not to mention the complexity of how the sun shines."

"Yes, the sun is still complicated. In physics, quarks, electrons and neutrinos are the main constituents of all matter. Still, neutrinos' ghostly particles coded with elusive disguise are still frustrating our great physicists. Exotic particles, some reclusive, are surrounded in a sterile phantom zone."

"Mr. President, we have the space station link and the link to NASA established," said an aide. The President took the call. An advisor interrupted, "Mr. President, all communications have suddenly been affected."

"I heard that," Dr. Peters said, as the link with the space station was still solid. Dr. Peters said, "Our instruments show solar wind penetrating Earth's atmosphere and the ozone layer is unstable as are the Van Allen belts."

The President responded, "These effects must be coming from outer space."

The President recalled meeting Dr. Peters at NASA. The President was known for his excellent memory and remembered Dr. Peters as being a short, balding man with thick-framed glasses who spit saliva when he spoke and wore suspenders. He also recalled his age to be approximately sixty-four and he also remembered that he loved coconut macaroons. This gift of recall helped the President's diplomatic abilities enormously.

With Dr. Peters and Cecilia still linked to the White House's connection, the President asked, "Could these occurrences be coming from outer space?"

Dr. Peters replied, "Definitely not. There are no asteroids or gravitational changes. The sun, the moon, the planets, everything is right. It is only the Earth that is showing these unusual changes."

President Hansen said, "There are members of my Cabinet who insist that the events that have taken place are a result of a coordinated attack. Is this possible, Dr. Peters?"

"Think of our gravity surrounding the planet as fluid and moving. An advance knowledge involving the science of quantum gravity could coordinate gravitational events. The ability to integrate time into the gravitational equation would involve incredible intelligence. We cannot explain it, but we are working on it. Due to the circular area that was affected, as in Central Park, we are considering the Einstein Ring Theory."

Cecilia responded from NASA, "Of course, the bright refracting light staying within a circle and indicating control would support the ring theory."

Dr. Peters continued, "Gravitational warping of space has been known to create a circle of light."

Cecilia said, "This ring of light would require great distance. It would need a galaxy acting as a lens warping space."

Dr. Peters responded, "Not necessarily. A glass lens and a beam of light in alignment might cause this effect. My associate, Dr. Dar, notes that gravitational warping of space that creates weightlessness, such as a floatation that occurred at the events would involve more than light; yet who among us truly understands all the effects of relativity?"

Dr. Dar turned from the space computer and signaled to Dr. Peters with his hand, saying, "We may have found something; I'm putting Dr. Lee on the speakerphone."

Sue Lee said, "We have located energy power points that do not match past planetary charts. Thanks to the new computer system, just installed from Canada, we can see that there is a definite new web of electrical power showing globally. The large magnetometer is showing variations in Earth's magnetic fields at one part per million correlating with this electrical web."

"Dr. Peters, can you get longitude and latitude for these points from the space station?" asked the President.

"Yes, if we tie our technology into NASA's network with Marshall's Space Center's newly developed communications equipment coordinating from Alabama."

"Mr. President we're on it; Marshall's research and spacecraft instruments have enabled much of our space discovery. The logistic modules will provide assured and accurate results," said Cecilia Washington from NASA.

Sue Lee turned to Vlad and said, "We better fine-tune all of our readings."

"Have Robonaut 2 interface with the system for the power point analysis. The Bot could link and bridge all systems."

Sue Lee responded, "R2 has plotted and coordinated."

Dr. Peters thought it odd that the space station had picked up signatures of gravitational waves radiating outward and connecting to many locations across the globe. The majority of the locations that have experienced similar events to Central Park were tied into a global energy web. The White House soon received a second call from the International Space Center. Dr. Peters wanted to speak to the President, and Cecilia Washington was tied in once again from NASA.

Dr. Peters spoke, "A sort of vector field has been created in which time and space have been coordinated. This electromagnetic field is a three dimensional continuous wave-like, yet smooth field of photons. A net composed of charge distribution is creating this electromagnetic field to somehow counter or negate an area of charge distribution temporarily from gravity in the affected areas. Through a special relativity of these magnetic and electric fields is how this event was produced."

"In English, please," said the President.

Cecilia interpreted, "Someone or something has the ability to affect the force in a gravitational field which is no small feat."

Dr. Peters added, "Mobile machines measuring the spectrums of light at each location should show the gravitational influence."

The President responded, "It appears that General Rudd was correct. These occurrences were a planned attack and not due to space phenomenon, weather phenomenon or related to global warming."

Dr. Peters replied, "It seems that way, although the computers are showing continual hard particle penetration

238

in the atmosphere. This could be a separate event that is actually due to global warming."

Cecilia came back on the line, "We have been able to trace the points of origin for the events by tracking the energy waves. Kennedy Center has pinpointed those power points. It forms a web that encompasses the entire globe. The most powerful energy points of the web seem to emanate from Broome, Australia; John's Island, South Carolina; Knill, Sweden; Gloucester, England; Perth Shire, Scotland and the White Mountains of California."

Cecilia asked an aide to identify the three most powerful locations. Dr. Peters, upon thinking, could not imagine what possibly could be emanating such strong electrical pulses.

Vlad turned to Dr. Peters and explained, "There are patterns changing fast in the currents of power. The electrical field being created from the power points is intensifying. The CO_2 increase in the atmosphere is definitely related to the gravitational fields within the web surrounding the planet."

Sue pointed out to Dr. Peters that the planetary charts are showing more power points appearing across the globe.

Chapter 37
That Night

Emily and Matthew's bond could not be stronger, as it was based on love. Matthew was thankful that his wandering days of being surrounded by women at various Manhattan bars and his forming of meaningless relationships were over. There was no glamour in being single, much less being hounded at 7:00AM while leaving his apartment for breakfast by intense fans or the press.

Matthew smiled as he went to the large garden chair, adjusting its position so he would be able to see Emily at the window. Emily's focus was incredible. There were answers out there and she would be relentless at her desk computer until she came up with some. Matthew decided to go into the kitchen for a root beer. Sitting at the white kitchen table, surrounded by the happy, yellow walls, he drank his root beer while munching on some veggie chips and became aware of the clock. People would only wait so long for answers to the unusual events that occurred at the park. His eyes went to the kitchen window and fell upon the miniature cloud forest orchids. There was a beauty to their tiny scale and there were hundreds of these small treasures in the various orchid tribes.

Emily emerged through the kitchen door, her auburn mane loosely cascading everywhere. Her eyes were intense and alive. Matthew recognized this expression; she had an idea. He couldn't help but notice that she was a vision, even in her simple white sun dress.

She made a cup of hot cocoa and they headed into the living room. As Matthew sat down on their richly colored burgundy sofa, he moved some pumpkin colored throw pillows making room for Emily to sit near him. He turned towards Emily smiling and noticed that her face blanched as the mug of hot cocoa slipped from her hand. She appeared wobbly as he quickly got up, caught her in his arms and helped her onto the sofa.

"Oh Matthew, I've stained the carpet. I'm sorry. It's just that I feel weak all of a sudden."

Knowing that Emily's concentration was incredible and that she could be relentless when working towards answers, Matthew suggested that she take a break occasionally and rest.

That night Emily, having difficulty sleeping, gazed out the bedroom window. Midnight breezes swayed the tree tops in a hypnotic motion within the moon's light. She continued going over the progression of the day's events and could not help feeling that the cause was not a natural phenomenon. Restless, she gently got out of bed, deciding to go to the den and listen to some classical music. She found that when her mind would race, listening to music would give her mental clarity. Turning the dial to her favorite classical station, she lifted her feet up, while laying back on the love seat. Recognizing the piece as a Mendelssohn string quartet, soon the beauty and the excitement of the violin filled her.

Matthew heard her leave the bed and knew where she would be when needing time to contemplate complex problems. Emily would play classical music which would enable her to relax and think clearly. One night, when he walked down to the den, he found her listening to one of her favorite pieces, a very thoughtful piano concerto by Shostakovich. Emily explained that she felt connected to the composer and was sure that he was celebrating nature's beauty. She heard light exciting dances and could easily imagine hummingbirds zipping along colorful flower tops during this Opus 35. There were butterflies celebrating life within the Opus. Matthew knew her sensitivity brought her richness to each moment.

At times her awareness of the emotions involved with the relationship of all things would be a burden to her. Unkindness at any type of gathering would be difficult for her to manage. Matthew often thought to himself, "If only she would not feel so overwhelmed at times."

The next morning they woke up to find that everything was working properly. All electronic communications and computers were functioning as they should. It just seemed like a normal spring morning in his backyard as Matthew relaxed in his lounge chair. He spotted Emily through the large glass partition which separated the den from the backyard. Once again she was hard at work at her desk.

"Did yesterday morning really happen? It was all so strange," he thought. After leaving Central Park and while waiting at Grand Central Station for the Harlem line, there were no strange incidents. They asked a few questions at the ticket window and to some of the conductors, but they all said that the day passed normally at the station.

Happy to be at home this Sunday morning, Matthew took a sip of his orange juice and leaned back in his lounge chair. Perhaps it was all a dream, as sometimes he thought his entire life was a dream.

Growing up in Canton, Ohio, his father always made sure that there was a football available to be tossed around. He remembered his Uncle Al telling his father how Matthew had a natural talent to be a great football player. He was built big, he was fast and football was what it was all about. When his Uncle wasn't tossing a football his way, his father was.

"Let's take a break and discuss some strategies. A great football player is always aware of the playbook," said his father. Matthew, being a very good looking young man, would often have girls stopping by the house. His father would say, "You're fifteen years old now, tell these girls to stop coming by; time to get serious and run some pass plays." Matthew could still hear his father's voice from his teenage years as he would round third base for the Yankees, "Run faster, Matthew."

The sound of a squirrel gnawing on a branch, high above him, brought him back to the present. He turned slightly to the side as his back started to feel stiff. He knew that he would miss much of the Yankee season this year; as a starting pitcher for the Yankees, the irony of his childhood did not elude him. Though coming out of a football town, he always secretly dreamed of one day being a pitcher for the New York Yankees. Amazingly, something even more fantastic occurred: He met Emily.

Turning his head he saw her still sitting at her desk, hard at work. The majority of people relaxing in their lounge chairs would be facing away from the house, especially considering Matthew's garden view. It was a beautiful spring morning. Bluebirds tested their liberty as they played gliding games through the trees. The sunbeams would often highlight the color of their wings as they would push up toward the sky. Matthew's view deeply affected him more than the beauty of the flowers and trees in his garden; a view that gave him more light than the sparkling spring sun of the morning. His view gave him Emily. At times his heart was so full with love that he would find it difficult to consider any other thoughts besides her. What pleased Emily gave him life. If she was unhappy, he would feel dark clouds around him.

He had found his life's journey's true beginning when he had found her. In Emily's silence he would look at her and feel all the beauty that there is to life. Matthew never thought it was possible that a person could affect him to that level. It did not matter how many eternities existed in all the dimensions, in all of the worlds of the universe, he knew that he wanted to be with her through all of them. He thought it funny that at times he felt he was in a different time zone; each moment seemed so slow until he would see her again. On sighting her, he would often stand motionless and it would seem so long until he heard her voice, soft and smiling. He would lose his concentration on what she was saying as her eyes, unlike any that he had ever seen, would momentarily hold him captive. The combination of her soul's depth of purity merged with her intelligence could be spellbinding. He wondered how rare this love was; he could not imagine anyone else having this feeling. Emily's existence enhanced every moment of his life. He would think to himself, when experiencing new things that he wished Emily could see and taste these things so they would be able to share everything.

"I wish I could be everything for her at all times, but I know that this would not be fair to the rest of the world," thought Matthew. Emily, as his wife, was an unbelievable dream; the eternal love that poets talk about had found a place in his heart.

Emily looked back at him through the window and smiled knowingly. She was totally aware of the elegant quintessential special connection that was theirs. He thanked God for her every day and would wonder, "What on Earth was she doing with him?"

Her intellect was huge and enhanced her beauty with a feeling that could only be described as endless. The intelligence that radiated from her eyes could not be more alluring. She was lovely to hold, slender and exquisite; the most graceful of all flowers. He would hold her carefully and tenderly in his muscular arms and she would look back up at him and say, "Matthew, I promise that I won't break."

Their home in Westchester was quiet. There was a soft blue tablecloth with a white orchid at its center that added warmth to their dining room. Indirect sun light would find the flower, highlighting the purity of its petals. Their winding driveway was lined with small, beautiful colored stones. At times a rabbit might pop out from the bordering conifers.

Ronald Yates

Their windows were very large and brought a lot of light into their home which gave panoramic views of the garden and trees. The house itself was a caramel color that fit well amongst the trees that surrounded it. Once inside their home, everything felt kind. The furniture was simple and had a comfortable feeling. Emily's views from the windows of the house suited her love for nature; she would not miss appreciating a fern, flower or tree.

One spring morning, Emily stood in front of her garden smiling and admiring the party that was in full swing. Huge Pink Bey Peonies would bump heads with Le Jour Peonies with their full white petals and their yellow centers which were bright in May's sunshine. Across the way, facing the Peonies, were the Oriental Poppies. The Prince of Orange with deep purple centers was guarded by interior rows of the Black Corridors of Mystery. All was surrounded by the tiny soldiers of the Camelot Mix in their pink and lavender uniforms. Invited as well were different garden Pansies, as well as the Nemesia of the Blue Lagoon. Serving the drinks to all were the Iceland Poppies, of course being of the Champagne Bubbles group, they were being quite careful not to mix with the Sorbet Orange. They were being served at the garden edges by other Violas. Emily, with her hair tied back in a French knot, would begin to tend to her flowers.

Emily received her degree in biophysics at the Massachusetts Institute of Technology at Cambridge. She was brilliant. Honors accompanied her degrees in botany and evolutionary biology when she attended the University of California at Irvine and Harvard. Most importantly, she spent two years directly assisting and studying with Professor Kensington, without question considered the foremost dendrologist in the world. Matthew's admiration for Emily was endless. Her knowledge of the sciences would coalesce in her mind in ways that would lead to paths of new healing drugs. Emily was able to view one flower and see the beauty of the universe in its components; it was not at all surprising that she found beauty in mathematics as well. She was always able to find hopeful and undiscovered roads in her studies, and somehow knew how to get to the stars. Many people would talk about saving the world, Emily would really do it.

Matthew did not mind missing the parties and the weekends that would have been filled with celebrities and fans. At times while sitting near her on the garden lounge chairs, she would extend her arm towards him with a smile. He would put her hand in his and squeeze ever so gently. He knew that this love was wonderful and these moments more special than any celebrity party. Emily was a super sensitive person that actually would feel pain at loud, crowded bars, restaurants and parties. It would become too overwhelming and raw as she would feel all the insecurities as well as all the hostilities that emanated from the people that made up these gatherings.

"Why does she love me, all I do is throw a baseball," Matthew often thought to himself. She was very relaxed when she would attend the Little League games at an orphanage or charity event. At times hundreds of children would surround Matthew for an autograph and Emily would giggle. She loved children and loved that Matthew brought them joy, and seeing their faces light up as they arrived. She could feel the children's happiness and knew that Matthew was responsible. His love had no bounds and she hoped that one day he would not only be a great husband, but a father as well.

Emily was now a scientist doing research work at the laboratories at the New York Botanical Gardens, Their home being in Westchester was convenient although Emily was not comfortable driving; the Gardens were just a few train stops from their home. One day Matthew had heard the phone ring at five in the afternoon and he had a bad feeling. Emily should have been home. The phone call was from the library building at the Gardens. Emily had fainted.

Their magnificent love had one horrible uninvited attacker. Emily's health was being stalked by a serious disease that was becoming more destructive each day. She had a rare form of blood cancer. Matthew could not make the worry leave his mind. There was no cure for her illness. His heartache was as deep as his love's passion. Matthew looked up towards her from his lounge chair and saw that she was still busy working in the den and he started to cry. "How could I possibly lose her?" At night worry tossed him like a salad and he would wonder if she would have all her strength in the morning. If only he could be free of this vise of reality that was her illness. If only a cure could be found.

He saw her getting up, probably to come out to the garden. He thought, "She has my whole heart and some say that there is a risk to this, but how could their love be what it is otherwise. If I lose her I would rather carry my heartbreak because it would still make me part of her." There were intruders that now became part of Matthew's heart. Good health for Emily could lift these intruders named "fear" and "sadness" from him.

Matthew heard the screen door squeak. "I'm sorry Matt; I'm just not strong enough." The screen door was not correctly aligned. Matthew easily lifted it slightly and opened it. Emily looked upset.

Matthew gathered himself thinking, "I must be strong for her."

"What's wrong?" Matthew asked.

"It's starting again," Emily's voice sounded concerned, as she continued, "Nothing is working properly. My computer is blinking in and out and I checked the television and we're only receiving two channels. These signal interruptions are really quite bizarre."

"You could use a break in your work anyway." She agreed and decided to go upstairs and shower.

Emily heard the steps and knew that Matthew was coming upstairs. "Amazing how my heart still races," she thought. She stepped out of the shower and looked at the fogged mirror noticing that her image was not clear but present. The mirror contained a concealed image, yet an image seen. Of course Emily knew it to be her and then thoughts of David from the orphanage came to her mind. The mirror was David's sanctuary. David took shelter in reality's reflection. She realized that this boy's fear of the world around him was severe. The music she was listening to suddenly captured her full attention. She recognized that the beautiful classical piece which was now playing on the radio was Grieg's "Peer Gynt Suite No. 1 Opus 46."

Looking at her naked body as she dried off, Matthew gently took the towel from her and let it drop to the floor. Lifting her gently in his arms he carried her to the bed. He put his hands on her waist and softly kissed her neck. His tenderness intensified her passions as she began to tremble. He gently pulled her closer, feeling her still wet hair against his check as he kissed her shoulders. She put her hands on his powerful arms as she felt her breathing pick up. "Oh, Matthew," she said softly. Matthew, during their kiss, felt that nothing in his life was more special, as he had found what every man hopes to find—the woman of his dreams.

Endless waves of love were lifting him to pleasures that were almost too incredible to believe. This kiss would lead them to the special door that was passions naissance. Emily knew that she had found her home as she melted in Matthew's arms. The combined love and passion of their kiss began to overwhelm them as tears rolled down their cheeks. The intensity of their emotions brought them to touch the very heart of love. The heat from their love was suspended in the air around them; a vapor so thick that their surrounding environment seemed barely visible. There were only the two of them and the fires of their passion. The strength of their feelings filled each second with an intensity that fueled their love and allowed it to engulf them and become totally in charge. The touch of her delicate fingers swept over his powerfully sculptured shoulders tenderly; a caress as sensual as silk. Every moment with Emily became a part of him. The steel of his shoulders was softened by her delicacy as he felt an excitement and the quiver of his body's surrender. The energy of their passions ignited the kinetic kiss that instantly connected their hearts. They became one and an ocean's release took them to a wonderful place unique to themselves. Folded in completeness they looked into each other's eyes as they had merged. Matthew found a sweetness that only existed in his beautiful wife. There was no past, no tomorrow, only the enchantment of their love as their moments together transcended time. He heard his name in her voice, softly swooning through their shared passions.

"I love you," Matthew heard while drowning in love's sensations. He found his voice and said, "I love you, Emily."

Their union was almost unbearable in its electricity. Though Matthew's eyes were closed, he was sure he saw brilliant sparks emanating from their ardency. He opened his eyes to meet her eyes; their glow was amazing. She smiled as they were one basking in each other's warmth. Is eternity where the seas meet the sky? Does eternity lie in the sunlit horizon? Matthew and Emily had opened the door to horizon's house and saw a love that was forever. Matthew heard her soft sobs as he caressed her smoothness. It was like being intertwined in a shared dream fueled by love's magic as they had left the world as most people know it. Pressed against each other, while moment upon moment came, they just pondered the feelings behind their smiles. She felt his warm, passionate breath as he kissed her neck and inhaled her skin's fragrance. He traced her breasts with soft kisses and felt her strawberry nipples respond. She felt a swelling against her as Matthew continued to find her loveliness incredible. Emily brought another cavernous reaction from his body that was now so quick and powerful, he once more began to tremble. Her continued light touches along his body dazed him as he continued to caress her softness with his lips. There was now composure to the rhythm of their intimacy as it became effortless and celestial.

Emily lightly let her head rest on his chest and nestled her body sweetly against him. Matthew pressed her even closer, but gently and preciously. He softly kissed her temple, her breasts, and then his lips moved back to her neck, then to her ear saying softly that he would always love her. Matthew knew that they would always be together in this world and the next. He came to understand the beauty of what she felt around her, he then was able to feel even closer to her. Their love would transverse the entire universe if necessary. Emily's lips lingered on Matthew's chest softly as she fell asleep. He noticed the sweetness of the beauty on her face as she slept. The classical station was playing "Prelude to the Afternoon of a Faun," by Debussy.

Emily's garden always flourished. When September's hurricane rains came and the flowers and plants surrounding most of the neighborhood homes would become weather beaten, her garden would find new energy. All of her garden residents, the ferns, the mums, the begonias, even a dianthus would continue flourishing. When their friends and neighbors would visit, they would look at the garden in amazement. "Our garden is so scraggly and dry and yours still seems to be doing so well," they would remark. They all assumed it was her background, being the Director of the Gardens. Matthew knew that there was more involved than her enormous knowledge of fauna. There was something special about Emily's connection to nature and he could feel it.

Within Emily's limitless self, nothing would fall outside the scope of her mind. Even the autumn leaves were more vibrant around their house. They would cascade down upon the smaller conifers and would be briefly mistaken for flowers. Emily tried canceling catalogues and phone books from being sent to the house knowing many trees would be saved if other people would follow suit. The companies clearly did not get the message. Sadly, saving a tree is not tops on their agenda. She would be frustrated as they still continued to arrive on their doorstep unsolicited.

She would use crushed pecan shells and peanut hulls as mulch for the garden knowing this method would not harm a leaf of a cypress forest or any forest habitat. She would only shop at markets that represented local farmers as their produce would not be traveling thousands of miles which would cause the emission of greenhouse gases. The only pesticide she would use would be natural and Neem based. The twigs of the Neem tree are chewed by many people of India. Studies have found that the twigs have inhibited the formation of plaque on their teeth and gums.

Emily had already considered the possibility of using the Neem tree's properties for cardiovascular benefits. She made her garden's compost from dead leaves and vegetable peels which would enrich the soil. She knew that when certain plants were grown together it would deter pests. By planting basil next to tomatoes, she improved their growth and helped them to overcome disease. If she noticed any bug attacks in her garden she would simply make a mixture of water with a little bit of liquid soap and spray the plants.

Emily would use trains and buses to avoid pollution from cars as she was too weak to ride a bike. She would take a lunch box to work to avoid paper bags. At home, she would try to remember to unplug all of her appliances when not in use. It was important to save energy and at the same time not contribute to pollution in any way.

Chapter 38
Realization

Vladimir turned to Dr. Peters saying, "Earth's magnetic field has definitely been affected in specific areas by an advanced intelligence that is able to fully understand the quantum and structure components comprising gravity and electromagnetic phenomenon."

"This kind of understanding would have to encompass knowledge of space, time loop, as well as, vortex intricacies in various field laws."

Sue remarked, "How could this be possible? The most knowledgeable physicists on gravity phenomenon are currently with us on the space station."

Vlad interrupted by informing Dr. Peters that the White House was calling. Dr. Peters activated the phone link and found himself talking to the Secretary of Defense.

General Rudd, with a stern voice said, "Dr. Peters, our men are currently at the locations of the strongest power points you indicated. Our field agents have called in from all three locations and discovered that there was nothing going on at those coordinates."

"Were you able to actually check the pinpoint locations, sir?"

"Yes, Dr. Peters. We just get an area of land with a few large trees. I suggest that you check your computer systems against NASA's center for errors and be quick about it."

As Dr. Peters ended communications with General Rudd, he asked Vladimir to cross check the three locations with NASA and the Kennedy Center. Upon quickly doing so, Vlad exclaimed, "The most intense power points still match exactly for those locations, Dr. Peters." Dr. Peters was silent as he stared at Sue Lee's ficus tree on the table across the room. Suddenly he exclaimed, "It's the trees!"

"What do you mean, Sue's ficus tree?" asked Vlad.

"Everything has its own electromagnetic signature as all atoms contain electrons. Trees can conduct extremely large electrical currents. The ability to control these currents and form electromagnetic pillows caused the floatation effect found in the event locations. Trees working in conjunction could create an extreme electromagnetic levitation effect. Now that I'm aware of these beings as the cause of these events, their sophistication is easily understandable. I need to be connected to Cecilia and President Hansen immediately."

Vlad, looking at Dr. Peters said, "You're saying that the mysterious cause of these worldwide events with electromagnetic fields being manipulated is due to trees? Have you gone crazy?"

"I'm sure you will not be the only one surprised. It was always right in front of our eyes. Through the years, our perception of them as immobile closed our minds to other possibilities. Their abilities encompass the mobility of thought and energy."

Sue Lee exclaimed, "It's amazing what these computer read-outs are revealing as we're picking up a resounding shock wave in the upper biosphere. Somehow, something is harnessing an unknown form of energy which is acting as a repulsive force to counter- act the pull of gravity. Our scientists believe the missing energy in the universe has yet to be detected. This all could be related somehow to dark matter which for us has been undetected particles that we believe could be everywhere."

Dr. Peters looked at Sue Lee and said, "I agree that this has to relate," and then looked at Vlad and said, "No I'm not crazy. I am sure it's the trees. I have a close friend, a dendrologist named Professor Kensington. He once told me that trees, like human beings, exist as electromagnetic phenomenon. An electrical charge is incorporated in atoms everywhere."

The Secretary of Defense put his agents on the assignment of locating Professor Kensington. General Rudd thought to himself, "The President said I should do whatever Dr. Peters requests, so, okay, I'll find this tree expert. Perhaps Dr. Peters has been in space too long as he is coming up with some strange and curious thoughts. I should introduce him to the Secretary of Energy, Ed Thomas. Yet, the President asked me to investigate it and never to dismiss any requests from Dr. Peters."

The General's thoughts were interrupted by one of his aides, "Mr. Secretary, we've located the Professor. He's in the South of France, not far from the city of Toulouse. I have spoken to their Chief of Police and have notified him to connect Professor Kensington to our direct line as soon as he's located. General, we have also been informed of new and large energy readings."

The General responded with an inquisitive tone, "Yes?"

"We've determined their source to be from the Island of Borneo as well as the forests of Southeast Asia."

General Rudd thought to himself, "Could this actually be possible; is it really true?"

Professor Kensington, with Danielle at his side, turned towards the gendarme who was yelling his name frantically. "We have an emergency call for you, Professor."

"This is incredible, I'm actually speaking to you while you are orbiting the planet on the International Space Station," said Professor Kensington.

Dr. Peters gave his friend a quick evaluation of what has occurred and ended by telling him about several of the most powerful points of energy and explained that they indicated that it was the trees. He told the Professor of the lime tree near Gloucester at Westernbirt Arboretum, the Fortingall Yew Tree in Perthshire, Scotland and the Angel Oak at John's Island, South Carolina. It was also noted that there were several powerful readings from the state of California, although for some unknown reason they were more difficult to pinpoint.

Professor Kensington responded, "I know these trees, and they are especially old. The lime tree is at least six thousand years old and the yew tree is at least nine thousand years old and continues to renew itself. After considering the entire situation, do you know what this means?"

"Yes. There is a coordination involving instant communication to cause these events."

"Although separate sources, these physical beings across the globe must have an instant awareness, a global brain so to speak, a separate but shared intelligent consciousness. Branches of each tree would be comparable to the neurons of the brain. The diversity of each of these tree beings, located everywhere on the planet, and witnesses to everything, would have enormous intelligence within their collective. We know that there are some trees that have a proven chemical communication when there is a threat indicated by an invasive organism. In response to the communication, increased tannins are released by the trees, deterring the invasion without harm to itself or the invading organism. This is an intelligence of a high order which incorporates mercy to organisms which do not know better. If there was a total destruction of caterpillars, for example, the world would lose the beauty and freedom of the butterfly. In a world composed of a plurality of entities, their communication has to be telepathic and go beyond the metaphors of language. The brain is the command center of the body, processing information as an electrical impulse travels along a sending branch or axon. In the neurotransmitter, a chemical crosses synapses to other branches called dendrites. The brain's countless neurons, with all its branches, passes messages from neurons to neurons."

Dr. Peters responded, "It had crossed my mind that the tree branches are interacting in the same way. Their communications are worldwide and are somehow involved through their branches and communicate for all their functions. That's why I called you immediately. We do the same, but their communications are more sophisticated, as we must rely on carrier devices, such as cell phones. Their species must be communicating with an evolved telepathic means. These trees, although individual beings, are operating as a large worldwide family; with their longevity and centuries of knowledge, it's no wonder that they would have developed superior communications."

"They certainly have the world's attention."

"If all this is true, then for what reason?"

"Apparently to send a message."

"What message?"

"I'm sure this will be revealed very soon."

Professor Kensington, after speaking with Dr. Peters turned to Danielle. Danielle was frightened after witnessing the severe storms which had sent dangerous lightning to the forest and destroying parts of the woodland. Professor Kensington decided to inform her of the situation when she was calmer. Thinking of Dr. Peters, Professor Kensington remembered that a great scientist once said, "To see beyond the known and dare to believe in what seems to be unbelievable makes him special." The Professor thought to himself, "Of course this is all possible." Deep down inside he always felt that this could be true, and felt that trees were capable of affecting the atmosphere.

Professor Kensington continued with his thoughts, "They are the lungs of the Earth and have shown electromagnetic abilities. There have been explanations by great scientists that have been overlooked. The trees can discharge electrical voltage between the Earth and the atmosphere due to sap flow. Trees have the ability to defy physics. The giant Sequoia, as with all trees, has an intricate circulation system. The water collected by the Sequoia's roots must travel four hundred and fifty feet to get to its highest leaves.

A man-made suction pump can raise water only a mere thirty-three feet. These trees are not only outperforming our species' mechanical pumps, but they're defying gravity with ease. The intensity of the Earth's magnetic field is affected by the trees' electrical conducting abilities due to sap flow; thus forests are large magnetic fields. When our species clears a forest, the Earth's magnetic fields decline as does our own protection from hard particle radiation from the sun. One scientist has proven that plants can auto-regulate their electrical currents and the source is the living being that is themselves."

Professor Kensington reviewed all of this by phone to Dr. Peters and Sue Lee on the way to Gloucester, England. He asked them to call Emily Westwood at the New York Botanical Gardens and have her proceed to the power point at the California White Mountain location. The Professor had told Emily the entire story and added, "It's all quite logical."

Emily responded, "I agree, if you picture a tree's branches after losing all its leaves in late autumn it appears much like a brain cell. Like the branches of a tree, the dendrites are the branches of the brain cells which project and carry impulses transmitting signals to each cell. It is easy to picture each tree as part of a whole intelligence. As you well know, the word dendrite derives from the Greek word for 'of a tree.' The strong power points could be the directing forces."

Professor Kensington had forgotten how incredibly cerebral Emily was. He remembered her illness as he said, "I know that The White House is sending Air Force One to pick you up. Do you feel strong enough to handle this situation?"

"I'll speak to you when I get to the White Mountains."

The President was informed that according to all scientific institutions, the radiation levels on Earth were getting worse. Oxygen levels were also shown to be lowering across the globe.

Sue Lee spoke to Danielle from the space station as Professor Kensington sent Danielle to Scotland to the Fortingall Yew in Pershire. The tree which continually generates from its trunk is basically immortal and over nine-thousand years old.

Sue said, "This is crazy, what are you going to do there?"

Danielle was in front of the tree and sensed its presence. Speaking out loud she repeated, "Please stop what you are doing! Please explain!"

At the space station, Sue thought she saw a down swing in the energy signal, or was it her imagination; then suddenly it looked as strong as before. Sue turned to Vlad and said, "These beings hidden for centuries right before our eyes have superior access to the power sources of the Earth, but why reveal themselves now?"

"Unfortunately, their purpose is still hidden, but it must be difficult to arborize if you're under constant attack."

Professor Kensington arrived at the arboretum at Gloucester. NASA had provided him with a unique phone computer that sent electrical signals which were coded to a numerical language. He set the electrical currents directly in line with the lime tree and spoke into the power unit. "Please help us understand." He pressed receive, hoping for anything, a beep, an impulse, yet he received nothing. Suddenly, an electrical pattern appeared on the device's monitor that kept repeating. "I don't understand," the Professor said. Speaking to one of the assistants assigned to him, he asked that the computer be tied into Langley as well as NASA. The agent replied, "This will take a couple of moments." The agent returned from communicating with NASA and Langley. "It's coded to ancient hieroglyphics. We have deciphered it. 'The arrogance of humans.'"

Professor Kensington thought to himself, "It is true, it is the trees. Naturally, we have always considered ourselves the most intelligent life force on the planet and the universe. Now right here on Earth we discover our sophistication pales to what these intelligent beings are controlling. Yet, why now? They have always been around us; peaceful, beautiful and beneficial to the world."

The codeologist spoke again, "We have just received a second translation: 'Seek the Old Man; we will only communicate with the sentient one.' I hope that means something to you, Professor."

Professor Kensington knew at once that he was right to trust his instincts and had guessed correctly: "Methuselah Walk." This was the grove containing the bristle cones in the White Mountains, which were on the Sierra Nevada and five-thousand years older than the pyramids. Emily would have to be there soon.

The White House connected the Professor to Emily. The Professor told her to think back to their experience in the ancient forest. "We both knew that we were not alone." Emily thought back to the energy of the ancient forest: The multi-leveled power of the singularity that existed within the presence of the woodland's silence. The presence felt everywhere was filling the space between the giants. It was seemingly a source of the forest power, like energy of a universe contained within a larger universe.

The Professor continued, "Our connections to these tree beings were not only theory. We both sensed the deep intelligence, especially when we were in the redwoods. Emily, you and I always sought the answers for the deep intelligence and mysteries we felt the ancient woodlands held. Their first communication is a type of intervention of the highest order. These beings interceding are unprecedented in Earth's history as far as we know. They communicated to me in code, but I am sure that they will speak in a more personal manner to you."

Emily responded, "Telepathy."

The Professor's mind went to the Brain Gate in London. This sensor had allowed a paralyzed victim to control a device simply with his thoughts. This was done by implanting electrodes in his brain.

The Professor said, "They have already shown their ability for psycho-kinesis. I understand that NASA had already been collecting objects from the event locations for psychometry testing."

"Telepathy is the purest form of communication as it involves instant imaging and transcends any one language."

"We all know the saying, 'A picture is worth a thousand words.' The speed of thought will convey in seconds what it would take language much more time to do because of its physicality."

"The use of metaphors should be a common ground since we both share the planet. It should not be difficult for our scientists to comprehend that beings with more history than ours would be able to communicate instantaneously around the globe through electrical bridges."

"Where our language can describe a situation, their telepathic abilities could probably put you there. If their communication involves the experience of a past event, it is more readily understood by placing the receiver into the experience. It is more than the language we are used to, but somehow I'm sure the beauty of our language has not been lost to them."

Professor Kensington and Dr. Peters coordinated their calls to the White House and then Air Force One.

Chapter 39
White Mountains

Matthew knew full well that he could not say "No." Mankind's future was at stake, yet it was very uncomfortable being trapped in sacrifices' stockade. He felt helpless and found himself immersing deeper in the worry and concern he had for Emily's extraordinary unprecedented mission. She had been showing more signs of weakness and had a recurring fever. He knew that although she was fragile physically, she would not hesitate to accept this mission. She would be holding the weight of humanity's hope for the future in this encounter. It was ironic that it was Emily who had a confidence, seemingly coming from within, telling Matthew not to worry in order to ease his fear. He tried to smile as he said, "When the path ends, and the encounter begins, you will be on your own. If only I could go with you." One of the President's agents opened the door to the limousine and Emily was on her way to Kennedy Airport. Matthew could not help but feel that part of his heart was leaving with her.

Emily's frail beauty was not lost to the President. Emily thought the President's face was warmer in person.

"Ms. Westwood, you seem pale. Are you okay? Can I get you anything?"

"A glass of water, thank you."

Professor Kensington reviewed all the messages and Dr. Peters reviewed all the information he had from the space station regarding the world events as she listened on her communication tie-in with the President on speaker phone. As her mentor spoke directly to the President in a steadfast voice, the Professor's integrity was not lost on the President's ears. The President, ending the communication, turned to Emily and said, after a tangible hesitation, "We've been killing these beings; how did you know that they were intelligent?"

"Mr. President," Emily responded, "I am not the first to suspect that there was more to their presence. The Cherokee Indians called the trees "standing people."

"Our world is in your hands. My agents will escort you to the path."

The President watched the slender woman walk down from the helicopter towards the path in the midst of strong breezes and random dark storm clouds.

Professor Kensington wished that he could be with her. He knew how weakened her condition was and how fragile she was. The Professor hoped that the Baiser Tree would be able to help her; yet his last look back at the Baiser grove saw only flames from the repeated lightning attacks. As Emily thought back to her home in Westchester, she thought of Matt asking who all the men were who were walking towards them. Matt was so strong and so kind that Emily explained that it would be all right and that he should trust her, knowing that he would understand. Matthew just looked into her eyes and knew that his trust was important. He also knew that the door that let this woman into his life could be even more important to all of humanity.

President Hansen, looking back at Emily thought that she gave him the impression of a secret princess: Fragile and pale, yet unknown to him. As the President sat in his helicopter he thought to himself how unprecedented these circumstances were; a lone traveler to a destination that may lead to what may be the most important and fantastic communications of all time. As the agents escorted Emily down the stairs of the helicopter, the President thought what a special combination of courage and grace this woman had.

Music of the Winds

The President assigned two of his best agents, Williams and O'Neill, to escort Emily to the path. These were the President's personal security guards and they were both rugged and savvy. Standing at about six feet tall, Williams could crush a walnut with two fingers and O'Neill at a lean six foot two inches had reflexes that were fast enough to catch the hull of the nut before it hit the ground. They both rarely spoke, but were extremely alert. Arriving at the foot of the path to the grove, Emily asked the agents to wait. "I don't know," said Williams. "It's okay," O'Neill responded. "The President said that it was up to her." O'Neill thought to himself, "She seems so frail. I wish I was able to accompany her."

Emily, after just walking a few feet, turned around and looked at O'Neill with a smile and kind expression that seemingly sensed his concern. A thought of a flower turning towards him in a breeze came to O'Neill's mind.

The air was alive with life's vibration as Emily felt part of nature's surrounding energy. This connection seemed more powerful than her past connections with nature. She thought of the area of her sanctuary of her childhood. She also thought of her trips to Central Park, the power of the Redwoods and Ogunquit, all energizing her, but not with such a unique power. She continued on her upward path encountering light, whirly white snowflakes. Some were gliding in the air, some were landing while tracing the branches, and some were highlighting the forest floor as well as adorning her auburn hair. Mossy decorations were along the trail on the rocks and branches and somehow gave her the feeling of ancient times. Within a split second, everything around her flashed brilliant white as lightning cracked and thunder boomed right at its heels. She looked up and noticed dark clouds were surrendering to a suddenly sweeping wind. As quickly as the wind arrived, it decided to pause and the lightly falling snowflakes began to float gently once again through the air. As Emily continued onward, the path began to feel separate from the rest of the world; mystical and seemingly just for her. Feelings that were not unfamiliar touched her senses and once again she was reminded of the feelings she had while contemplating in her witch hazel tree sanctuary. There was a feeling of comfort and safety that made her more confident as she continued making her way slowly up the path. The path was now decorated with snowflakes and the white seemed to add to the freshness and beauty.

The President continued to watch Emily walk towards her unprecedented meeting; her body appearing even more tiny and thin against the darkening mountains. Sweeping cloud shadows were darkening the rest of the terrain as well. Emily turned back for a moment and saw the presidential helicopter, thinking that it seemed very tiny.

Emily continued walking up the path; she felt a harmony and a familiarity even though she hadn't been there before. The remote breezes carried pine scents and wild flowers as she became more excited with each step. Hearing a sound to the right, alongside a small creek, she saw a tiny finch playing on a city of moss in between some vines that held deep purple berries. The trees on both sides of the path displayed the unnamable quality that fills your heart with beauty at first sight. Each tree was mystical with their dark leaves contrasted by the snowflakes.

Walking uphill and feeling somewhat tired as the path steepened, Emily thought she heard a voice from a distant moment in her past; clearer sounding than the windy voice of her childhood enclave, yet the same. "Let us help you the rest of the way." Familiar with temporal physics, the voice's sound felt incarnate. This was the sound of the presence with the sound of the past always next in line. Approaching the top of her climb, a procumbent of several trees directed her towards the right of the summit. She thought to herself that she felt weak from walking. Kind words entered her mind, "Let us help," as she was lifted and lightly floated up the incline. She thought that their gravitational manipulation must somehow tie with psychokinetic abilities.

Emily, now standing on Methuselah's Walk, needed no one to point out the elder. Her super-sensitivity and intuition would know who the "Old Man" was. She could see a light rainbow behind the grove of trees. She walked towards it; the power she felt was enormous. One of the bristle cone pines seemed to have a flame of energy; it was a small Pinus Longavea. There seemed to be more bark than pine. She walked closer seeing what appeared to be transparent steam all around her. She knew that it was the power of the "Old Man." A kind voice entered her mind. The voice supported a sound of extreme wisdom that can only come from history. Though Emily was receiving these thoughts telepathically, all the experience of their centuries of existence resonated in their regal tones in her mind. There was no question that each word was worthy of a genuine and unquestionable acceptance. The ancients' intelligence, superior due to centuries of knowledge, did not have a trace of condescendence.

"The singularity within our ancient beings has affected you deeply. Emily, you heard the music in the silence and connected to the depth of experience and substance that makes our species."

Emily recalled the beauty and poetry of the ancient woodland and thought, "The high level of living poetry that is what composes the being of these species is what I felt."

Emily spoke, "What can I do?" Hearing a voice in her mind she was not at all surprised by the telepathic communication; she realized after all, that there are synapses everywhere.

"Emily, you have always been aware that all life forms are to be respected, as well as knowing every action causes a ripple in the universe and our living planet. You have always been aware that all is linked and all is precious. The music of the universe comes from its harmony. The understanding of the universe by your species of beings stays nascent. Humans have destroyed much life. Many of our own family lives have been taken. This must be stopped. The effrontery of the Greeds of your species toward the planet will no longer be tolerated. They are beyond elucidation; they simply do not care. We all share this great planet and it must be healed now. The land must be freed so that the great forests may return and then the waters will again become pure and plentiful and the atmosphere clean. Unfortunately, the march of ignorance still grows in large numbers among your species. It is still not too late for change.

"We are ancient beings to your species, as the diamonds of the night make us seem young. The longevity of our species has given us enormous knowledge of past events. We have been everywhere; witnesses throughout time. The memories of all the trees of yesteryear stay within our total consciousness; all time periods are accessible. Our life form has been tied together throughout time. Our beings and yours share the time on this garden Earth."

Experience itself shaped the words Emily received telepathically. In her mind she saw the beauty of Earth as well as the storms that could be turning the beauty to Venus II.

The "Old Man" continued, "Our garden Earth, benevolent, bountiful and fertile, sustains us all, not only physically, but in its beauty, spiritually. There is a harmony, a gravity that balances the moon, the sun, oceans, and land. Disrupt these things, schismatize our planet and we all lose. Let us not make a breach in the union of our planet's energies. Your species considers itself the most intelligent, yet you clear forest beings, pollute the planet's waters and drop bombs on all of its lands. We have studied what has been that which your species call 'history.' Unfortunately, your species still wars and shares much greed. This violence to the Earth, and one another, goes back throughout your species' history. Clearly, your species has learned nothing from your poets who wrote of their love and respect of nature. They knew that Earth as a gift from the great intelligence, the creator of all things, as something to hold dear. They are the great minds and to be studied and heard: 'Cherish the wild rose.' The Greeds of your species continue to litter the roads of your history with destruction. As you have been known to us since your youth as a being who has a unique comprehension and appreciation for the importance of all life, our Elder Council has agreed that you are the best choice for our listener."

The ancient being continued to communicate by using telepathy. "What you are about to hear must be relayed to the leaders of your species. Our planet can no longer tolerate being beset with the destruction your species continues to put upon it. We have stood by many centuries, and still most of your species place greed ahead of generosity. Our world and all the worlds of the universe are connected through the Supreme Intelligence. Humans, by disrespecting our planet, disrespect themselves and all life."

The elder's voice resonated deep with contained knowledge. "To take for granted the gift of our shared garden planet will bring penalties to our species as well, which we are not willing to suffer. Earth is a shared home that we will not allow to be exploited. Destruction of all our fellow beings haunts us as we have an awareness of one another. We stand over the globe feeling emptiness in our collective presence, as the ancient, as well as the young are being taken from our population. Many of our family members were lost in what you call the Umpqua Forest of Oregon. We reach to the sky for consoling warmth, yet we know we can be stripped no more.

"Strident strife attacks Earth which stems from the arrogant and inconsiderate actions of your species. Terrestrial conflicts throughout your species' history continue adding more tolls to the planet. The sun's life giving sources are being disrespected, as your pollution distorts its purpose. In the ocean that is the universe our shared planet is a gift; a living, breathing poem among the stars."

Emily thought to herself, "The sonority of their words had a depth of sincerity that elevated the pureness of truth. Telepathy was indeed a voice that could be a vanguard for the expression of validity."

The Methuselah tree continued, "The Supreme Intelligence holds constant the edges of time's river keeping an order and balance to all things. We are all guests of time and must make the moments of our lives count. Humans are destroying the very cycles of life which enables their species to exist as well as endangering all others. The perpetual ecosystem cooperates with all species. The continual burning of fossil fuels must now stop as the harmony of terra is being endangered. All of life forms, from the smallest microbe, to ourselves, whom are the largest beings on the planet, are important to the biosphere. The power of the luminous one reaches to other worlds, but it is our Earth that has been given the garden spot. Although your scientists have advanced from the movable printing press, which was used to share ideas, and evolved to electronic and radio devices, there has really been little advancement.

The information shared around the Earth, although slowly, should have set off alarms to all of your species. The damage to the life of various species, and the planet itself, has reached a point of crises. Copernicus showed the members of his species the existence of the star which was the center of our solar system. This fact alone called for a respect for what your species labels the sun. In your history, the power of this star brought names such as Apollo, Helios and Phoebus. Use the power of the sun intelligently and you will find all the energy you need. As many of your scientists know, they need just to mimic photosynthesis with photovoltaic panels. Feed your excess carbon dioxide to the phytoplankton in the ocean. The pollution of this planet must stop now. We have the power to act upon these things and change them now. We have shown you that we will not allow a further dissolution of terra. In an instant, the entire intelligence of all my fellow beings is made aware of all happenings. With our sap flow, any and all gravitational and magnetic fields on the planet can be manipulated.

"We do not believe in war or violence as we are beings who believe in kindness and generosity; but our way should not be mistaken for weakness. The paleobotanists of your species would confirm that it is since our Gilboa Forest of four hundred million years ago that our species has kept Earth's air clean and cool while absorbing carbon dioxide. The human clock of history shows repeated roads leading to ruin. Born at the same time as our family member that you have named 'The Big Tree' which resides in the ancient forest of what you call British Columbia, your Roman medieval times were an example of the violence of your species. Forest, villages and cities, crumbled throughout time as a result of bombs, lethal poisons and machines that level the life of the woodlands. Your species still has not solved their problems of respecting one another, much less have found solutions for world peace. These answers will not be found in particle accelerators investigating structure balances for anti-matter at subatomic levels. This type of research could be dangerous. In the future, we will teach you about the use of magnetic fields without the necessity for huge colliders. Invest your billions of monies in helping remove contaminants in the soil, water and air, instead of smashing atoms."

The centuries of wisdom in these words was easily heard in Emily's mind.

"Our global families' planetary surveillance has determined that even the life of the ocean is littered with skeletons of creatures that burn and melting ice continues to feed the oceans. If our planet continues to heat, your species will be endangering all of the children's tomorrows. Disrespecting our Earth can affect the lives on other worlds in alternate realities as well as other dimensions. Let us show you."

Emily found herself at the Botanical Gardens in her mind. "I am at the Botanical Gardens," Emily said.

"Look closely, Emily," said the elder being. Emily looked closer and saw the tram was traveling counter-clockwise, the opposite direction that it usually traveled. There were large blue flowers lining the paths, yet they were not a species she had ever seen before. A woman with long blond hair, who was walking toward the library, looked somewhat familiar. It was her assistant, Maria Torrez, or was it? Emily thought, "Maria Torrez never wore high heels." Emily realized that this was not the Botanical Gardens she knew.

The elder said, "There are many different realities and worlds within our multi- universe. There are worlds with no shadows. There are worlds with blue suns. There are those that exist at the same moment we do, but in other dimensions. All is connected. Each dimension will provide a new host of beauty and wonders which will always be accompanied by new questions and new mysteries.

"As the oldest beings on the planet, and having the advantage of time, we have never used our superior knowledge to harm any living thing. No longer will we have woodlands thirsty from droughts. Winds' electric power has carried history's wisdom into our beings. All is connected. There is knowledge in every breeze. In time, you will understand. It is not unlike our water we drink that comes from the beginning of time. We have seen the past and we know. As ancient beings, our life span goes back centuries. Wars among humans continue throughout your history for power's sake. Destruction of your own kind and much of the planet, whether collateral or deliberate will no longer be tolerated. We have witnessed the courageous few who speak of peace and new ways to preserve life and land and have seen them struck down.

"Emily, we know you touched the spiritual part of our reality when visiting our ancient forests. It is your sensitivity and kindness, as well as great intelligence that made you best suited to be the listener. We dislike establishing rules, yet at times teachers need attentive students. The magnetic occurrences we caused across the planet will not only make us known to your species, but will awaken the importance of respecting the sun and the Earth. We could not continue to allow Earth, with all its innocent lives, to be destroyed in the name of greed, instant gratification and madness."

The Elder continued, "The six billion of your species with their machines clear landscapes to satisfy their needs. The reality that your species will double in population within a century is frightening as we see our forests continue to suffer extinction of life. Humans foolishly endanger their children while disrupting the connection of all living things. The assault on biodiversity must come to an end. We are pacifists, yet we are pledged and bound to protect the garden Earth and its entire species from any violence that destroys its balance. Our species will die, and have died, for our principles of non-violence and non-interference on our shared planet. It is unfortunate that our centuries of patience cannot continue due to the scope of your species' destructive ways and arrogance. In front of your species' eyes, yet mostly taken for granted, we are now revealed.

"Emily, you have often wondered if the city of your childhood dreams could exist. It is a geographical reality and is over eleven thousand years old. We had communicated this dream to you and had communicated its location with the shadow symbols you recorded seen on our bodies. There is only one person that you should share this location with."

Emily answered, "I know."

"The dream from your youth was our message of what the future can be. The Methuselah tree then gave Emily additional details of the city they called "Unitas."

"I know that you have leaders that must be respected and communicated with, just as I have a group of elders that I respect and communicate with. Your species refers to the elders of my species as Yews and Limes. These elders are even older than me. I will now communicate information for your President and all your world leaders that represent all the families of trees."

The Elder ended the communication with these thoughts: "Emily, since you have been known to us as a child, you have been a source of hope for our planet. The music of the winds cannot follow indifference. You were the best choice we knew of for an ambassador representing our species to the world." Emily with tears in her eyes thought that it was her honor.

She looked at her watch as she started back down the path, and noticed that only five minutes had passed, yet an abundance of information had been exchanged. She became aware of the changing sky. Clouds were being pierced by bright sun rays as pastel started to appear under the now silver and white clouds. The beams of light formed different sized cylinders of beauty. They had a grace that was all their own as they angled in the same direction through the silver. The enchantment of the celestial show was irresistible as Emily thought that everyone had seen these supernatural skies at some time in their life and felt the spell of their divine beauty. Even the surrounding mountains seemed to give pause as part of the backdrop for what was now a pastel sky with golden sunshine splashing through and parting the remaining white clouds. She thought that there was a responsibility to these skies that depended on a healthy biosphere. She stopped momentarily, taking in the beauty of the synchronized nature. Birds that were originally battling unpredictable winds with trembling wings were now flying through these graceful skies with ease. She noticed a rainbow that seemed to sparkle around the remaining snow, thinking that it was another one of nature's lovely surprises. The incredibly distinct rainbow was filtering the light, bringing a colorful prism to patches of snow in the surrounding area.

One of the President's security team members, waiting at the bottom of the path for Emily's return, spotted what he thought was a person floating several feet above the path. Rubbing his eyes, he refocused and saw Emily walking towards them from the bottom of the path. As she drew closer, the security member saw that her face was flushed and asked if she was okay. Emily responded, "I'm fine and I must speak to the President."

As she was being escorted back to the helicopter, Emily, although feeling somewhat weak, was excited about briefing the President.

Chapter 40
Briefing

The President asked everyone to clear out of the conference room on Air Force One, as he wanted to receive Emily's briefing in private. Emily explained to the President that the tree beings' actions on the planet were based on science and that they could be repeated at any time, as the quantum and electromagnetic physicists of the world would confirm. President Hansen expressed his surprise on how quickly her encounter transpired on the White Mountains. She explained to the President that these tree beings were telepathic.

"As standing beings, they were revealed to our eyes, yet not truly seen. They and all their fellow beings live to help all species in as many ways as possible. Their species are totally non-violent and concentrate on intellectual growth. Their synaptic branches regenerate and grow over countless years, networking their accumulated worldwide knowledge instantaneously. They have no need for communication aids, such as cell phones, as they communicate telepathically. They are individual beings within a large inter-connected consciousness that spans most of the Earth. Their ideology is based on giving and helping to keep all life healthy. Together, their species possesses the power of cohesiveness."

Emily continued, "Telepathy among their beings allows for an instantaneous as well as a naturally advanced communication. Complete ideas are conveyed in a flash of thought. They have explained that in the future our species' minds may develop and become telepathic and we can all throw away our cell phones. The minds of all living things have fields of mental energy that are both chemical and electrical extending well past the body. Cell phone fields extend well past the phone itself, and soon our brains will be able to do the same. They are aware of the fact that several of our scientists are knowledgeable about these facts. All living things have an energy field around their core, a morphic field which the tree beings can access. The Earth itself, as a living garden, is tied to the universe through its gravitational field. Their collective conscious has a clear link to a collective unconscious in certain species. They will save this discussion for a future time.

"Eventually the future will bring our species to this universal communication. Like them, our thoughts will ride electrons and evolve to this language of energy and become closer to the universe. During my communication with the tree beings, I was not only able to hear, but see, feel and smell all the images in their language. Pictures appeared in my mind with all the accompanying sensations in an instant. The amount of knowledge that I was able to receive was incredible in such a short period of time.

"They explained that our footprints of violence continued to strain the circle of life. Our living globe is for all life. The war among our species and nature must stop. They have decided to intervene as they felt that this garden Earth is being disrespected and they could not let our ignorance destroy the planet. Life had always been grateful for the sun's warmth, but now from our pollution the sun's energy has become dangerous. It is clear to the tree beings that all that comprises the universe is concatenate. Most of our species across the planet are simply insensitive or unaware of the tragedies that are occurring in nature. Our pollution and wars are poisoning the planet. There have been parts of nature that have adapted to the confusion our species has brought to the planet, but many have ceased to exist and countless others are in danger.

"They feel that environmental consciousness has yet to enter the majority of our minds. For the sake of all life on Earth and Earth itself, they have sent this motivating message. Every species has been given the gift of life on this beautiful garden Earth by the Supreme One; respect for this gift must now be a priority. It is essential that a collective understanding is brought to human societies of the importance of all life. Many see technology as the answer, yet many of these technologies travel through seas, mountains and woods threatening the health of many species; everything is connected. The bees, the plants, the waters, and even the frogs all impact on our planet's food and ecosystems. It is a mistake to marginalize the importance of any of them.

"Earth's biological diversity has been balanced by the Great Intelligence. Who are the fools who disrespect the Creator? Even with their ability to control certain gravitational forces, the tree beings are not powerful enough to turn back history. They will not allow a toxic environment caused by us to destroy this garden planet that we were all given the privilege to share. If the toxic environment that we are causing continues, the universal balance in our dimension, as well as other dimensions, could be warped. They can continue to help humanity with the medicines, food and shelter that they have provided through time.

"Time does not give second chances. To be put as simply as possible: Past, present and future are all located in the continual wave of time. Our species has made the mistake of assuming that time's course could always be circumnavigated; this is a dangerous mistake. Time manipulation, even if possible, would be a danger to all living things, in our reality as well as alternate realities. Many of our species have made the dangerous mistake of assuming that time's course can be circumnavigated. Time's triangle is truly eternal. The past is tied to tomorrow's coattail. The present, in its pure existence, composes the threads that hold the past and future forever together. Disrupt the threads of time, and all eternity is affected."

Emily continued, "They said that the Earth itself, as a living garden is tied to the universe through all its many electrical and gravitational fields. The tree beings can access the memories of their ancestors from yesteryear as they stay within their consciousness and are a life form that is eternally linked together throughout time. Each individual being of their species contributes to the knowledge of their entire species. Their intelligence is a collective of memory and facts accumulated over thousands of years. They share all their collective intelligence to help the planet, with all its life forms, as their most important directive in life. Their collective consciousness has access to any and all experiences that members of their family have learned throughout time. All knowledge is imprinted in their shared consciousness and any species member can access that information."

Emily continued, "They explained that what we do on Earth can possibly affect alternate realities. There are dimensions full of new wonders, unique to their own space and all is accompanied with new mysteries. Worlds with crystal mountains reflecting soft blue suns eventually can be explored and shared by humans when they become more evolved. They can show us how to open the doors to dimensional tunnels, but first an evolvement of our appreciation for our space in the universe must be seen to take place.

They will not allow the violence of our species to destroy this garden planet that we were all given the privilege to share. They do not conquer: they simply need our attention."

President Hansen interrupted, "They certainly have gotten it."

Emily continued, "These ancient beings will continue to help humanity with the food, medicines and shelter they provide as long as we respect all life and the environment.

Every life form on Earth is important and the destruction of any one of them could affect the health of the planet. They feel that mankind has not yet evolved to the point of understanding the importance of all life. The gifts of the creator of all that exists must be cherished and respected by all beings. It is only then that the profound beauty of the poetry of the universe will be totally known. Incredible new windows will then open to delightfully, delicious and amazingly new adventures."

The President turned to Emily with watery eyes. "We have been murdering what is perhaps the most benevolent and kind species to all life on our planet without a caring thought."

Emily, hearing the sincerity in the President's voice knew that he was going to do whatever was possible for the health of all life on Earth.

Chapter 41
Conversation

Professor Kensington listened in amazement as Emily spoke to him of her communications on the White Mountains as soon as she was finished briefing President Hansen. Emily told the Professor of the tree beings telepathic communications in detail. They spoke of how they became the planet's largest beings when the last Sauropod no longer walked the Earth. They spoke of how their branches interconnect through electro-chemical corridors within their species to communicate and process information, just as the branches of the human brain's neurons do. They spoke of how their species across terra are aware of events instantly through their network. Traveling at synaptic speeds, their thoughts were able to synchronize the gravitational events that occurred across the planet.

Their mental coordination makes their worldly presence akin to ubiquity. Through the longevity of their species, they have for centuries gathered data, organizing them into their thoughts, each time reaching higher levels of ideas. Needless to say, their communication and organizational skills continue to gain in sophistication with time. They explained how their use of spin and vortical motion combined with their quantum studies enabled them to affect magnetization. The polarity of particles within magnetic fields relative to controlled vortices contributed to their ability to manipulate electromagnetic fields.

Emily communicated much information to the Professor and ended with an interesting statement about the tree beings. "Their entity ramifies from both ends of their physique; their abilities to access knowledge and energies within the interior and the exterior of the planet are greatly enhanced."

"It makes perfect sense that they would be in greater touch with Earth's interior and exterior than our race was capable of."

The Professor was excited about calling Dr. Peters at the Space Station to discuss some of the amazing results of Emily's communication with the Ancient Being at the White Mountains. Excitedly, the Professor told Dr. Peters that much of what he expected about their advanced knowledge turned out to be true. Listening with very attentive ears to what was learned, Dr. Peters seemed to focus mostly on the tree beings' advanced knowledge of gravitational manipulation.

Dr. Peters said, "Newton brought us the knowledge of gravitational forces to consider, yet we have learned little. This is an advanced knowledge and we can learn from them. Perhaps they could answer the questions, 'Will gravity be the breaks to our universe's expansion? Is universal gravity keeping the speed of expansion in check? Perhaps gravity itself can not hold back the expansion of the universe.' Magnetism plays a role in everything and everywhere. The big bang theory states that it is gravity's balance that is instrumental in holding everything perfectly together as the universe reached outward. Gravitational pull, as you know, is linked to everything."

"Of course."

"Through gravitational manipulation they must have discovered signatures that would help us to understand the universe. We know of the enormous pull of gravity in black holes that could vacuum all that exists; nothing can escape the power of the gravity of a black hole, not even light. These beings could be wise enough to have an understanding of the wind relative to different gravitational forces. I hope they will share their knowledge, which must include light and worm holes that travel through time and space."

The Professor responded, "Their brilliance was no surprise to me. We are all surrounded by an electromagnetic field, as is our brain. Their electromagnetic control seems to be superior. Anyone who has seen the branches of trees have seen the similarity to the neurons of the brain cells. The waves of knowledge that they accumulate are able to be shared instantly. According to Emily, theirs is a telepathic network with their knowledge shared on a planetary basis, with a higher sophistication than ever before for well over six thousand years. They have always been there through all the years of history helping our species and other species in countless ways."

Dr. Peters said, "There are many unanswered questions in the science of the universe. They may know where certain space time tunnels lead. Their science may understand dark matter and the extraordinary invisible indivisible force within all things."

The Professor responded, "They spoke to Emily of the superior intelligence of the Creator of all things that holds the multi-universes together within eternity. They also referred to our knowledge of the universe as being at the very beginning of understanding. It is my belief that certain answers for all scientists, from all species, and all worlds can only be answered by accepting the divine intelligence that is God. They will answer our questions and they will continue helping the Earth and all our species as long as our race respects the planet and its other members."

"Humans have been arrogant and selfish for many years; plundering the Earth as well as each other. It is surprising that they have not interceded earlier."

"Our global climate change due to our heat trapping gasses can react very quickly. Their patience and non-interference policy was put aside for the safety and the health of our planet."

Ronald Yates

"Fortunately for us, these beings do not look to be kings and conquer as it is clear that they always have had the power to do so."

The Professor responded, "They are already kings; nobility is their crown. Who among us could be grander or possess more outstanding qualities? Their benevolence is the heart of their species."

Chapter 42
Storm Damage

Moody dark clouds had come and gone, but only after opening up with plenty of rain. The fire, unfortunately, had taken much of the forest. The adjacent vineyard would survive the heavy rain of the severe storm. The forest had more to survive than the attack of heavy water. It had to survive lightning. Deep shades of green were covered with fallen and burnt trees. The lightning had lashed out repeatedly as the storm was severe and the fires that rumbled under the thunder were difficult to extinguish.

The Professor and Danielle had rendezvoused at Castres and had made their way back to the forest of the newly discovered Baiser tree. Two officers were to guide them through the emergency equipment and the rubble of the scarred forest back to the area where the unusual growth of trees was found. The last time the Professor and Danielle had walked through this forest there were special scents of green and flowers. The abundance of the sweet smelling berries of the briar was gone. The once deep green and plentifully ramose forest held many pockets of openly sad space. Much of the forest life lost their special bowers. The damage to the forest was harsh. The cacophony of the thunder had shaken the forest and the ears of the villagers. There were never storms of this intensity experienced here before. The lightning attacks left a ménage of burnt offerings. The forest floor had turned from lush green to shades of charred brown and cinder-laden mud. Lightning bolts, with temperatures hotter than the sun's surface had ripped apart much of the forest's trees.

Danielle turned to the Professor and said, "This forest was so beautiful."

The senior officer, overhearing Danielle said, "It is sad to see all this damage to the woods. The emergency crews were not granted immediate access to the forest as they were ordered to stay back for safety reasons. They had to wait until the radar showed that the storm was at least ten miles away. The rain waters forming pools on the forest floors could have carried dangerous electrical charges. I have lived in this area for many years, and have never seen such a storm."

The Professor looked at Danielle with a sad expression saying, "This doesn't sound good for the Baiser tree."

The lighting was strange. Cloud shadows were dark and of a different type. They were haunting and comfortable with their convert presence. The officers helped the Professor and Danielle around the cluster of boulders, lifting branches from their path. Danielle recognized this group of boulders as those that preceded the special grove of trees. Amazingly, the small crooked creek with the large smooth stones that curved through the Baiser grove stayed recognizable. Unfortunately, there were ashes to the outside of the forest creek, charred branches and shredded stumps of trees.

"Shall we escort you back to your car?" asked the senior officer.

Danielle responded, "I would like to continue a bit deeper into the forest, if you don't mind."

The officer threw up his arms saying, "I don't see why, but okay."

Walking further down the stricken area, Danielle noticed a group of green briar under a large fallen oak. Quickening her step, she wanted to investigate the area ahead. Stepping over some fallen branches and into some mud and continuing deeper into the ravaged forest, the Professor recognized a lavender color within the briar.

Danielle turned to the Professor upon sighting the briar, and said with hope in her voice, "There are some survivors." Danielle loved the Professor and often thought that she was born too late. She recalled a trip to Russia with the Professor where she saw white deer running through the woods like romantic spirits of the wind. It was so romantic a sight that she thought of telling him how she felt. Danielle was surprised to learn that the Professor had once seen white deer before. The Professor saw her parting the briar that was pressed under the large trunk.

"Professor, come and see," exclaimed Danielle.

The Professor had hoped that the lavender he spotted was not a hallucination as he bent down and looked at the tiny tree. There were deep emerald branches and after lifting overlapping compressed leaves, small lavender, oddly shaped flat berry-like fruits were seen.

Professor Kensington looked up at Danielle with a broad smile saying, "Who says there are no miracles?"

Chapter 43
United Nations

There was energy to the silence in the great hall as President Hansen stepped to the podium to address the United Nations. Standing tall, the President said that he knew that everybody in attendance had been aware of the worldwide gravitational events.

"There has been great fear and even some of you thought the world may be coming to an end. I felt that I lived a lifetime in these past few days and it really has been enlightening."

He continued, "In the past, thoughts that there could be the possibility of wiser and more powerful beings than us had most of the world's scientists looking to outer space. The truth of an intelligent life form sharing the Earth in plain view will become an exciting reality. We have discovered that we are not necessarily the most intelligent species to inhabit this planet. Fortunately for the world, the tree beings that have made themselves known to our planet have probably assured healthy tomorrows for us all. Indeed, there are tongues in the woodlands, perhaps heard before by Shakespeare and others.

"Clearly, the excitement that comes with the knowledge that our world is more inclusive than we ever realized is incredible. The beings and life that we share the world with will offer countless new learning experiences that can only extend our thought processes. Right before our eyes there stood beings that have always been there for us, and all species of life. Our arrogance must never again cloud our awareness and judgment. The tree being society and harmony is based on benevolence. The power of the many facets of their individualities, when shared, creates an extraordinary capable whole. No longer of the unacknowledged, these tree beings' beauty of mind joins the poets of our species as the appreciated seers of the Earth's magnificent gifts. Let us all admit that it is time to change our ways and there is much to learn and appreciate. The universe has magnificent wonders including our planet and we must not lose our opportunity to appreciate its beauty. Let us all feel the quickening, a birth of a wonderful new way. Let us all respect the gifts and beauty of our planet.

"Internationally, actions are being put in effect as I speak. These actions are against dangerous climate change and toxins to our environment. This is necessary to heal our planet's pain and as a result, improve the life of not only humans, but all species. Only in helping one another can the world's beauty find total freedom. Every nation must work together and sit at round tables of peace to end all wrongful ways. The participants at these tables will all be of equal stature. We must treat each other with respect and allow the Table of Winchester to host communications with true laws exhibiting a clear fairness: A table that is based on virtue.

"What beings could be more benevolent than those who compose the forests of the world? Year upon year, their beauty, food, shelter and even oxygen were some of the ways the various tree families have given to many different species inhabiting the Earth. We are fortunate to now know beings that care so deeply about our planet and all life. They will continue to ally with our species by providing support in many ways as long as we do one simple thing: Respect our shared planet and all its life. The parents of the world are on the front of life's line in time's scheme. They represent the past. They hold the keys for success for their children, who are the future, and are presently last on time's line. The children will look to your legacy. Let it be a legacy of knowledge and respect for our planet and all of its life.

Let the interests of the unborn always be protected. This cycle in time will determine all for our children's children. Let us no longer do harm to our own species or any species on our planet with violence. As the President of the United States, I will see to the safety of our planet and with joint cooperation will set up international committees that will monitor these implementations.

"From this point on, I will encourage all architectural designs across the planet to complement nature so that harmony and beauty will rule the Earth. Ethnobotany will be a top priority for all student curriculums. The respect and value of all plant life and our interactions with them will be emphasized. We will know the importance of protecting all species of plant and forest beings. This will enable us to learn new cures and foods for the health of world species. Botanical gardens, their libraries and science networks will be expanded across the globe as per international agreements.

"The ultimate fate of this planet will not be controlled by the indifferent. Total respect for the biosphere, for the sake of all living things, must begin right now. Ignorance coupled with arrogance is a lethal combination. There are military attacks that have taken place in parts of this world that have harmed men, women, children, the land and its entire species. There are industrial attacks that have harmed wild life and woodlands in the name of progress. Let us bring a future that melts the world's tanks and artilleries and turns them into strong homes for the needy. We cannot consider ourselves an enlightened species until we stop all violence against our home planet. The only just war is the war against war. In the future, all industries will be prosecuted for any destruction to life and for not following healthy practices in all their aspects of production. The magnitude of the knowledge of the tree beings will take time for all people to comprehend. Their knowledge has been accumulated over thousands of years, so our species has no reason to be embarrassed. Their venerableness is without question. One thing is certain, they are worthy of respect, not only due to their age, but especially for their benevolence. A magnificent future has been patiently waiting for the planet Earth. A general consensus among all, with a visualization so powerful of a world of peace that it will bring to reality all of the kind hopes of the world. This road will also bring to all new, beautiful and surprising wonders: A road well worth taking. The sun will illuminate the splendors of our garden planet. This garden will renew our air as well as our lives. In closing, I recall something written by Shelley, one of my favorite poets:

> 'What if Earth could clothe and feed
> Amplest millions at their need,
> And the power and thought be as the tree within the seed?'"

The President left the podium to a heartfelt standing ovation with many of the members of the UN holding hope for the future.

Chapter 44
Woodwinds

If love could shine, it surely would be the light of this day. Hope comes with this new morning. Enjoying a pretty spring calm, basking in the blue, most of the children were buoyant and at play. Cathy, Matthew and the Professor quietly exchanged eye contact as the breeze began a noticeable stir. David and the other children continued playing unaware of any changes as Valentina tugged at Matthew's hand. Unusually aware of all things related to nature, Valentina seemed to sense something. "Matthew, I think I hear the flowers singing in the breeze."

"You mean you smell the flowers in the breeze."

The Professor, while smiling, lifted Valentina and said, "Perhaps there is a little music in their scent, eh, little one?"

Cathy said, "Wait, I do hear music."

A momentary hum clearly heard by everyone in Central Park, was responded to by a very deep silence by all. The winds suddenly became very still. There was a silence with a presence of a prelude arriving. Returning winds were lighter; a soft sound like that of a violin was noticed by everyone.

Valentina looked up at Matthew, "This rainbow sounds so pretty like smiling music. Where is it coming from?"

Matthew turned to Cathy and the Professor asking, "Do you hear that light, sweet sound?"

Suddenly, a crescendo of sound of unsurpassed beauty, well beyond any known symphony, filled the spring air. There was a poetry felt in the gracefulness of the music. Sublimely subtracted, then adoringly added, gentle levels of loveliness was heard in every chord. An amazing Legno harmony reaching unheard of heights would have all maestros looking to the skies. It was as if one could hear the enchantment that was the azure ceiling of Central Park. It was as if notes of ethereal azurite were seasoning the park. The world's ears were euphoric with unknown chords, merging with vibrations of beauty that only spring's naissance would be able to present. Winds were flowing through all of the planet's forests. Every leaf, every pine needle and every branch of every tree on Earth, bended and moved while vibrating. The planet's winds touched them all, as does the bow to the violin, made from the same woods as the tree beings. Winds drawn by the entire world's trees bringing the beauty of the Earth's forests to all ears.

The tree beings brought the music of the winds. The harmony of sound, found in the deepest beauty of an ineffable seemingly inconceivable symphony was carrying the essence of the forest's spiritual singularities. Sunbeams, within unheard harmonics were radiating and intensifying the beauty of the day. Children leaving their shoes and socks behind were dancing on the sweet grass, as only children can. City streets that were no longer filled with nervous people were alive with hopeful smiles. The world's woodlands were bringing forth a music never imagined by mankind. Tranches within tranches of harmony were expressed within the music creating an inexpressible depth of beauty. This magically, complex symphony was lifting and soaring and ramifying upwards towards our blue roof. Each chord was a Kestrel in the sky hovering then soaring within the symphony's sea.

The Professor turned to Matthew and said, "This is incredible. It is like listening to Mozart to the twentieth power."

The future will make note of this morning's occurrence, yet this turning point in mankind's history will never be mythologized. The music continued circling the planet and in its flight of beauty, bursting everywhere, was making all its inhabitants quiver with joy.

The Professor said to Matthew, "These ancient beings are brilliant, music is a language that is universal and
through the sharing of this symphony all are connected in
the experience. They are musical masters; they have perfect tone and pitch which they are controlling with gravitational manipulations of vibrations. The different wood
compositions of the branches have become extraordinary
violins teaming perfectly with the different speeds of the
winds. We are hearing the sounds of countless strings synchronized ethereal violins soaring skyward. The trees with
their multi-sized branches are able to use gravity and wind
to form these violin-like sounds. Violins, of course, are made
from wood, as is the piano. The sound of the violin is affected by the pressure the player exerts on the bow. The
player must also take into account the speed at which he
bows the violin. The vibrations that are transmitted throughout the forest created this magnificent sound. To conceive
of the complexity involved when considering the different
resonance frequencies of all the woods is an amazing accomplishment. Each vibration must arrive earlier than the
others; otherwise the sound would not be heard and would
be canceled out. The volume of air that must be manipulated within the world's woodlands is incredible."

There was now a new and wonderful timbre being
heard for the first time.

The Professor continued, "The bodies of the trees themselves are transmitting vibrations through the atmosphere.
The different woods that make up the various families within the tree species have somehow coordinated their resonance frequencies. Never had anyone heard such sus-
tained tones and distinctions of variations. I am sure that
Antonio Stradivari would have loved to speak to the maples
involved in this symphony, not to mention Nicola Amati."

Ever-changing winds coursed over the planet's woodland population and the Earth's symphony began. The
world's woodlands with the benefit of instant telepathic

communication manipulated different densities of branch and wood to form an alliance with the winds.

The various woods of some of the world's most beautiful beings were collaborating perfectly to express these sounds. This symphony's notes were oscillating between the forest families throughout the world. Drawing from the winds, these forest violins played with telepathic batons conducting the Earth's forests. The joyous trees continued playing symphonies within symphonies.

Professor Kensington said, "Is it possible that at one time trees could have used sound waves for their communication? What species would be better positioned to communicate with music? There have been interesting comments by several ethno musicologists when hearing the songs of certain ancient tribes while on expeditions for the Smithsonian. They likened the music to the sound of wind whistling through the trees. There have been stories passed down from these tribes across the globe speaking of the songs of trees. I have a feeling that in our history there have been a few privileged who have heard some symphonies before from these beings. The names of some of our great composers have crossed my mind."

As the music continued soaring on the wings of the winds, Cathy noticed that the children were dancing around a tree as their laughter was soaring with the symphony. She thought of her daughter Emily and her love for all the trees. As she continued to listen to the symphony, she actually felt the connection of love expressed even in the distance between notes. The melodic patterns of romantically sublime came again and again, weaving new chords, each time bringing new levels of ecstasy never before experienced. Music of moonlit mountains, crystal rivers and the ocean's waves were vibrating through the air only made possible by these ancients forming the harp of the planet. Spiritus coursed through the Earth's forests bringing sensitive strumming as the world's woods continued vibrating. The music was alive and breathing. It was an apollonian symphony for the appreciation of the hope for a healthy Earth bathed in only beneficial sunshine: An Earth experiencing a renaissance.

The most magnificent collective of living poetry, nature's breathtaking forces of beauty, tree beings continued to bring the winds and gravitational fluxes over themselves. They were creating such a spectacular symphony that all instruments, from Aeolian harps to violins would be proud. It was impossible not to succumb to the combinations of affection that attached each note that formed. Flowing from love's core, compounds of tones reached levels that even beauty gave deference. The only thing that was possible for the entire planet's inhabitants to do was to absorb each symphonic breath as it passed through their bodies penetrating all their hearts with a once unknown delirium of beauty. It was as if the music was filling the sky with chromatic rainbows. Riders of the winds, ethereally enchanting, wave upon wave of music's unrealized beauty soared freely from the symphony's sea of sound.

Sometimes the winds would feel like a dream. Scents of the sea were carrying beach memories for some reminiscent of their younger days on the ocean shores; to others, the scents carried mountain memories and brought to them the cedar and the pine of the forest. Wondrous rainbows sprung from the sea as the arcs of Iris reached for the sky. Within the symphony, the mountains and the oceans seem to be calling. There was a consciousness to the music of the winds talking of the world's nature: Past reminders for the world's future awareness; winds in tune to time itself; powerful, soft, elusive, here and then gone, as it chooses within the music.

Valentina told Matthew that she felt she was breathing in the happiness of the air.

Ronald Yates

The Professor said to Matthew, "It does seem that the whole of our atmosphere is occupied by enchanted harmonies."

The symphony story was clear; a new morning and a new hope for all that shared this planet was now a reality. The world could come together and create a higher form of human behavior with constructive cooperation and the end of destruction and violence. The world's music felt fresh and free announcing that nature would be back with its waterfalls of joy again splashing excitement as they traveled along the mountains from their glacial peaks.

The beautiful trees were releasing their poetry in a language and a breath all life could understand: Music. The beauty of life's love was translated into sound so that all could understand. The amazing beauty of the music celebrating the creator's garden Earth was brought to the world by the most ancient conduits of Earth's life: Trees. If ever there was a sound for love, it was in the music of this symphony. These musical artists continued to splash the atmosphere with notes of every color combining power and beauty into the living poem that was this symphony. Spring with ephemeral episodes spoke to the symphony. Its varying transitory white puffs were sweetened by its pastel blue. The symphony seemed to know boundlessness as it was reaching out through to the infinity of the universe.

Professor Kensington said, "Perhaps it is through music that we will learn to travel even through time itself. Time has no need for boundaries, but must have respect."

Matthew responded, "Only the Creator of all things knows true boundlessness."

The Professor smiled, "That sounds like something Emily would say. What better symphonist could ever be found than the trees? Their very being is a living poem, and the gifts of kindness make up much of their essence. Surely even Aeolus would be happy to relinquish the rule of the winds to them: Earth's living harps. Who better to control the tuned unison of their branches than themselves? It is only fitting that the music they compose be a symphonic poem, unrivaled, as they themselves are the instruments alive with the music of the winds."

Cathy turned to the Professor, "I remember Emily saying that she repeatedly heard the words 'Music of the Winds,' when she was twelve years old in her tree sanctuary. Not only did she hear the sentence that they wait for the music of the winds, but they also said they waited for the sentient one. I always thought that she just had an active imagination."

Still holding Matthew's hand, Valentina tugged on his pants with her free hand. Matthew looked down at Valentina's face feeling the sensitivity and the innocence of her questioning eyes.

"Where's Emily?" she asked.

Matthew's own eyes began to fill with water, as he turned to answer her, but his voice was constricted. Emily's mother, Cathy, kneeled down and hugged Valentina as she said, "She's with God."

Hopes sweet kiss was felt around the world with the music of the winds. A curtain of music's magnificence was really an overture to the opening of a new age. This symphonic curtain's beauty was lifting from the Earth's grasses and becoming one with the azure sky. The children were still dancing in the musical steps of hope's happiness.

Of New York City's forty-million yearly visitors, many of them found their way to Central Park. Watching the children dancing in the grass and circling a large maple, one could almost touch the purity of their play; a type of joyful abandonment that was only found in happy children. Suddenly, as the children were dancing around the tree, the air seemed to lift them at least a foot off the ground. The children laughed and held each other's hands, knowing inside that this fun was coming from the kindness of the tree.

Ronald Yates

Golden lights penetrated the clouds of the arriving sunset. A powerful light will rise with the new morning's hope and shine as never before.

Chapter 45
London

Taking a break from his studies in his office, Professor Kensington's eyes fell upon the antique planter that he had purchased in a London shop. The planter was named, "A Woman of Keswick." Antiques were true time travelers. Once part of the present, then acquired for their belonging to the past and finally, they become part of a person's collection. Collecting antiques represented a small bit of control over time. "A Woman of Keswick" reminded him of Emily. He thought of the Baiser fruit: If only he could go back in time.

Chapter 46
Valentina

Matthew knew that a part of him left with Emily. He also felt the importance in her parting words, "Please be there for the children."

Matthew's sister fell in love with Valentina upon meeting her. Married to a wonderful man, they agreed happily to adopt Valentina as soon as possible. A year later, they were approved to adopt David, the oldest orphan that resided at the Westchester Orphanage.

Being only twenty minutes from his home in Westchester, Matthew would visit his sister's house often. This day was special as it was Valentina's twelfth birthday and he had promised Emily that he would give Valentina a book that she had written about trees when she was the same age. Emily had it wrapped up in pink paper with a blue bow shortly after she had returned from the White Mountains.

Matthew, after having picked up Cathy Westwood from Astoria, pointed his car towards the Throgs Neck Bridge and on to White Plains. Arriving at his sister's house, he and Cathy gave everybody a hug. Everyone received plenty of kisses, including licks from Valentina's new puppy, a six-week old White Highland Terrier she named Frosty. After enjoying a wonderful dinner and chocolate cake, Valentina and David went to the den to play with their new video games.

While in her room with Frosty, Valentina heard a knock at her door. It was Matthew who said that he wanted to drop off a present from Emily explaining that he had held it till her twelfth birthday. Valentina thanked him and moist pearls appeared on her face as she realized that this gift must be very special as she never forgot her strong bond with Emily. Love filled Matthew's tears when feeling Valentina's emotions. He explained that it was a special book, a sort of diary, of a summer Emily spent when she was twelve years old.

Matthew turned back from leaving the room and said, "I almost forgot, Emily had told me to tell you that within the book there was a special mystery."

It seemed that during one summer, as Emily walked a cement path along the large rectangular lawn in her neighborhood, she had noticed something strange. The morning light shining through the foliage of the trees would appear to form some sort of shadow symbols on the trunks of each successive tree. The shapes almost looked like letters of the alphabet. Emily decided to take out her pad and draw them. At times there would be up to three odd shapes on a tree trunk. Emily walked up and down all the sides of the large tree lined rectangular lawn and eventually had a full page of these shapes. At the time, Emily thought to herself that this looks like a very strange alphabet indeed.

The book told of a wonderful city that Emily dreamt of often and even included a map she had drawn. The city seemed to be located adjacent to a deep green elevated savannah on one side with rolling hills on the other. There appeared to be a river running in an "S" pattern through the center of the city. Valentina knew that the map was showing a part of the Earth she had not seen before. Emily had called the city by a name, "Unitas." According to Emily, this city did actually exist and it was not just a dream. Valentina could locate it if she put together the clues within the book. Valentina had never heard of this city and decided to involve David with her special present.

David remembered Emily well and looked through the book, absorbed with an amazing curiosity. The symbols on the trees had really intrigued him. Valentina drew his attention to the name Emily had given to the city. "Have you ever heard of this place?"

David smiled as he took Valentina's hand and brought her in front of her bedroom mirror. "I have never heard of this city but we now have a guide." He then held up the book to the mirror which contained the page that displayed the unusually shaped shadow symbols.